HAUNTED
LAS VEGAS

SECOND EDITION

HAUNTED LAS VEGAS

FAMOUS PHANTOMS, CREEPY CASINOS, AND GAMBLING GHOSTS

PAUL W. PAPA

Globe
Pequot

ESSEX, CONNECTICUT

Globe
Pequot

An imprint of Globe Pequot, the trade division of
The Rowman & Littlefield Publishing Group, Inc.
4501 Forbes Blvd., Ste. 200
Lanham, MD 20706
www.rowman.com

Distributed by NATIONAL BOOK NETWORK

British Library Cataloguing in Publication Information available

Library of Congress Cataloging-in-Publication Data Available
ISBN 978-1-4930-7032-9 (pbk. : alk. paper)
ISBN 978-1-4930-7033-6 (electronic)

∞™ The paper used in this publication meets the minimum requirements of American National Standard for Information Sciences—Permanence of Paper for Printed Library Materials, ANSI/NISO Z39.48-1992.

*This book is dedicated to all those spirits
who came to Las Vegas and found it a city
far too intriguing to ever leave.*

CONTENTS

ACKNOWLEDGMENTS

I would first and foremost like to thank all those people who sat with me and retold their spooky—and often creepy—stories. Thanks also go out to Mark P. Hall-Patton at the Clark County Museum, for both his assistance and his understanding of a writer's needs; Laura Hutton at the Boulder City/Hoover Dam Museum, for letting me rummage through so many records and stories in a not-so-haunted basement; Cowboy Joe at Bonnie Springs, for taking me on my own private tour; and Branden Powers for taking the time to speak with me at his wonderfully fun Tiki bar.

Special thanks go out to Kerry Giese for all his help, Ray Jones for his guidance throughout the writing of this book, and Melissa Parsons, who kept my grammar on track (not an easy task), and let me use the word "*and*" every once in a while, when I wasn't supposed to. Finally, I'd also like to thank my wonderful editors, Tracee Williams and Greta Schmitz, for their insight, guidance, and obvious desire to make this the best book it could possibly be—thanks!

INTRODUCTION

Ghosts in Las Vegas? How couldn't there be? After all, it's a town that was controlled by the Mob for close to thirty years. Who knows how many people were "persuaded" to cross over to the other side at the hands of a crooked-nose gangster with a nickname like "The Ant"? Not only that, but anyone who is anyone has played or performed in Las Vegas at one time or another. Opulence is king in this unique town, which was home for many years to the king of opulence himself, Liberace. When you arrive in Las Vegas, you are treated like you're the only person in the world who matters. Is it any wonder that many of those who came here decided never to leave?

Las Vegas is a one-of-a-kind place. Where else can you find a town haunted by both Elvis and an elephant (that's right, an elephant)? It even has its own ghost town and haunted museum. Las Vegas is known for discarding its past like most people discard clothing, imploding buildings with little care for their historical value. Yet it is also a city rich in history—even though it's only a little more than a hundred years old. The Rat Pack made Las Vegas its home, and the town is still closely associated with the glitz and glamour known only to the likes of Hollywood.

Strange is another word often associated with this town, and what can be stranger than stories of ghosts? Haunted houses and schools, bathrooms with faucets that turn on by themselves, a showroom where the audience has never left, a gangster who remains at the resort he never got to see succeed, a museum with a box so evil it must be guarded by a sacred prayer, and a restaurant where the deceased owner still commands respect are just some of the strange and ghostly occurrences Las Vegas has to offer. And whether you believe these eerie tales or not, one thing is true: They are all very Vegas.

One of the best things about writing a book like *Haunted Las Vegas* is that you get to see your town through a different set of eyes. In choosing which stories to tell, I have tried to give you a slice of Las Vegas that combines a little of the old with a taste of the new. Because so much of this town is lost to the present, only viewable in photos or secret videos found on the Internet, I have chosen stories that help link Las Vegas to its past.

According to the History Channel, Las Vegas is a "hot zone of cold spots, unsettled spirits, and well-documented anomalous experiences." The question, therefore, begs to be asked: Are these stories true? Do ghosts really haunt Las Vegas? I'll leave that up to you to determine for yourself. So whether you read this book before your next trip to Las Vegas or wait until the "dead" of night during your stay, I hope these stories appease your creepy side, while at the same time giving you a taste of just how great this little town really is. Just a word of caution, however: After you have read these stories, you may want to follow a time-honored Las Vegas tradition and leave the "ghost light" on. Enjoy!

FAMOUS
PHANTOMS OF
LAS VEGAS

WHILE LAS VEGAS IS KNOWN AS "SIN CITY," it's also known as the entertainment capital of the world. Many of the greatest entertainers in the industry have come to Las Vegas and made it their home, and when some of them died, they refused to leave. So many singers, dancers, and musicians found fame and fortune in Las Vegas—whether they were discovered here, or became a success the second time around—that even though they died somewhere else, it didn't stop them from returning to the city they loved. Some returned to homes they once occupied in Las Vegas, while others chose places that meant something to them, like a restaurant, or the stage where the roar of the crowds greeted them every night.

Las Vegas is known for entertainment, and what better place to start than with the people who made Las Vegas famous. In this first section we'll visit the restaurant Liberace opened and frequently entertained friends in, cooking for them himself. We'll travel to the suite in the Las Vegas Hilton where Elvis stayed during his record-breaking years of performing. We'll also visit some spots where the pressures of entertainment proved too much and the results were . . . well, ghostly.

So tip the maître d' and get ready for the best seat in the house.

"I'LL BE SEEING YOU"

In a restaurant that once served Hollywood's elite, side by side with Las Vegas's most notorious crime element, the flamboyant previous owner still roams the halls. Diners and employees alike have all experienced the playfulness—or wrath—of Liberace.

What did she say?

It couldn't have been what he thought he'd heard—could it? Could that bartender have just said that, about Liberace, in his own restaurant?

Jacob Harding had walked into Carluccio's Tivoli Gardens Restaurant only a few minutes ago, thinking he would have a drink to honor the famous musician on this, the anniversary of his death. After all, Liberace had opened the restaurant, which was then only called Tivoli Gardens, and what better way to honor the man who helped make Las Vegas famous?

The bar where Jacob sat was over one hundred years old. Liberace had imported it from England, and frankly, it was gorgeous! It was gorgeous because it was ornate and it was made of wood. Not that fake wood they make things out of nowadays, but real hardwood, harvested from real trees. The wood was reddish-brown and it seemed to fill the space perfectly. Decorative panels made up the bottom section of the bar, the top of which was covered in granite.

Twisted columns opened to flaring flowers that supported the top portion. It too was adorned with decorative panels. Wine glasses hung upside down at positions strategically placed to allow the bartender easy access as needed. Wine bottles sat in racks on the upper shelves. Small ledges allowed the wine to sit at an angle without the danger of falling. Bottles of hard liquor decorated glass shelves that were attached to a mirrored back. Liquor glasses rested on other shelves atop another granite counter.

Jacob gave a quick thought to what Liberace would drink, but opted instead for a rum and Coke when the bartender looked his way; he was sure Liberace wouldn't mind. "To you," he said, more to himself than anyone, and raised his glass.

The bartender was in her forties, and he could tell she was no stranger to the back of a bar. She washed glasses, poured drinks, and removed plates, all while attending each of her customers. The bar was full. Three men and two women all looked over when she spoke.

"Who're you toasting?" she asked him.

"The late owner," Jacob responded, "the man who made this all possible. Liberace. May he rest in peace," he said, and took another sip.

"On the anniversary of his death. Nice gesture."

"Did you know him?" Jacob asked.

"Not really."

"Didn't he die from AIDS?" one of the bar patrons asked.

"Complications of AIDS," the bartender confirmed, sitting back on a chair behind the bar. She continued talking about Las Vegas's most flamboyant musician, explaining the rumors she had heard about his lifestyle, and his sexual preferences. She had the attention of the entire bar and took advantage of it to tell an off-color joke about those sexual preferences.

While most of the bar patrons laughed, Jacob was shocked. He sat there, mouth agape. He *had* heard it right. That bartender had just slurred Liberace's good name—in his own restaurant. Apparently, Jacob wasn't the only one who hadn't been impressed by the joke. As the bartender stood there, three wine bottles seemed to jump off the top shelf, hitting the chair where the bartender had just been sitting. She leapt backward and two of the patrons quickly scrambled off their stools. Someone screamed, but Jacob couldn't tell who. How had those bottles fallen from the wine rack? How could they have fallen when the ledges had always kept them secure? And, more importantly, if they *had* fallen on their own, what were the chances they would have hit the chair the bartender had just been sitting in?

Liberace was born Wladziu Valentino Liberace on May 16, 1919, to a Polish mother and an Italian father who immigrated to America. He was born in West Allis, a suburb of Milwaukee, Wisconsin. He was known as Walter to his family and Lee to his friends, but he was most widely known simply as Liberace.

Like Elvis, Liberace was the sole survivor of a twin birth, weighing thirteen pounds, and, also like Elvis, he was born with an amazing musical gift. By the time Liberace was seven, he was already a talented musician, the piano his instrument of choice. He was able to play intricate pieces by age seven, and by age eight was studying with the famous Polish pianist and composer, Ignacy Jan Paderewski. However, most of his talent was developed under the tutelage of Florence Bettray Kelly, his music teacher for close to ten years. Kelly was the only music teacher who was able to stay with the young musician, who was so talented that he often surpassed his instructors, who would then have to be replaced.

Liberace was a gifted pianist who received no less than seventeen scholarships, the first of which was to the Wisconsin Conservatory of Music, received through the help of Paderewski. Liberace loved to play and he was a quick study. He could play classical music in the style of many different composers, and by the time he was twenty years old, he had played as a soloist with the Chicago Symphony Orchestra.

He obtained his musical talent from his father, Salvadore, who had played the French horn in John Philip Sousa's marching band, and his mother, Frances, who played the piano. Salvadore Liberace had always dreamed of making it big as a musician, and while he did manage to achieve some small success, he often found himself working in factories. Still, he kept the dream alive through his children. Musical talent was a family trait, one which Liberace shared with his brother, George, and his sister, Angelina. Liberace and George played in trios, Liberace on the piano and George on the violin. In 1940 Liberace signed his first performing contract at the Plankinton Arcade (the Red Room) in Milwaukee. That same year he worked as an intermission pianist in the Persian Room of the Plaza Hotel in New York City.

While he received much acclaim for his playing, Liberace knew that he would never achieve complete success until he expanded his repertoire to include more popular music, mixed, of course, with the classics. It was not uncommon for him to play "The Beer Barrel Polka" one minute and "Clair de Lune" the next. Having no publicist, Liberace promoted himself by mailing postcards to places where he wanted to work. The scheme worked, and in 1944 he was noticed by the Last Frontier in Las Vegas, where he was offered a contract to play in its showroom. He received $750 a week at a time when the average person made $30 a week.

Liberace wasn't only talented, he was a showman. He was flamboyant and knew how to please the crowd. He played on oversized pianos and added props, such as the candelabra that he would eventually become famous for. He would talk to the audience, taking requests and cracking jokes. He didn't just play the piano; he made sure that attending his show was an experience, one that his fans would want to repeat again and again. To promote himself, Liberace took the advice of Paderewski's stage manager and dropped his first two names, using only the name "Liberace" exclusively. He added a phonetic spelling of his name

"Libb-er-ah-chee" to promotional materials to help cement it into the minds of his fans. It worked, and in one year the Last Frontier had doubled his salary. In 1945 he also returned to the Persian Room at the Plaza Hotel and was noticed by *Variety* magazine, which proclaimed him a cross between "Cary Grant and Robert Alda."

In 1952 Liberace sat in as a summer replacement for Dinah Shore on *The Dinah Shore Show.* He was a natural and received his own television show on NBC that same year. *The Liberace Show* ran on television from 1952 to 1969. He also appeared on many other television shows, including *The Ed Sullivan Show, The Jack Benny Show, The Red Skelton Show, The Monkees,* and *The Tonight Show* with Johnny Carson. In 1966 the twin theme emerged when Liberace played the dual roles of the villain Chandell, aka "Fingers," and his evil twin Harry on the television series *Batman.* During lunch breaks, according to Adam West, Liberace entertained the cast and crew, playing the piano and taking requests.

During the time Liberace had his television show, he worked extra hard to create the persona of "Liberace." He began to wear elaborate costumes covered in sequins, jewels, and rhinestones. One of these costumes—the King Neptune—weighed more than two hundred pounds. He also sported feathered capes and furs, such as his full-length black diamond mink cape. Rhinestone-studded pianos and piano-shaped rings became standard. He even had a platinum candlestick with diamond flames. One of the cars in his elaborate collection was a Rolls-Royce he had specially covered in thousands of mirrored tiles.

Liberace achieved huge success. His paycheck for the first two years of his popular television show was reportedly $7 million. He had a home in Las Vegas and one in Palm Springs. He was also named the "Pop Keyboard Artist of the Year" by *Contemporary Keyboard Magazine.* Yet throughout it all, he never forgot his family. His mother and sister Angelina were often in the front row of his TV show, and his brother George appeared frequently as the guest violinist and orchestra director. It was the television show that gave him his signature sign-off, the song "I'll Be Seeing You," which he softly sang at the close of every show.

While Liberace's passion for the piano and being "Mr. Showmanship" was well known, his passion for cooking was lesser known. In 1970 Liberace published his first book, *Liberace Cooks,* featuring a photo of the author in his piano-themed kitchen. The book would go on to have seven printings. Liberace was a great cook and he took to the kitchen just as he took to the piano. He loved to cook for his guests, so much so that in 1983 he decided to open his own restaurant in the plaza he had purchased back in 1970 to house his museum on Tropicana Boulevard in Las Vegas.

He named the restaurant Tivoli Gardens, reportedly because it spelled "i-lov-iT" backward. "Garden" was the theme in almost every room. Each room had its own twist on that main theme, each designed to make the diner feel as if he or she was sitting in Liberace's own garden area. Outdoor fountains, statues, and elaborate shrubbery adorned almost every room of the restaurant. Liberace himself chose the location of every piece of furniture and decoration included in the restaurant.

The bar, imported from an English pub Liberace frequented, was next to a room designed to look like a performance showroom. Called the Piano Lounge, mirrors covered each wall of the small room, giving it the illusion of being much bigger than it actually was. The words to the song "I'll Be Seeing You" were etched at the top of the mirrors, all around the room. Thousands of tiny lights decorated the ceiling, making it appear to twinkle. But the focus piece was a gigantic, mirrored, grand piano-shaped bar, complete with piano lid, nestled in the corner of the room.

Liberace had an apartment built off the restaurant that had a separate entrance to the kitchen. He often stayed there when he cooked for his guests, holding private dinner parties. Of course, the restaurant also had a piano and many entertainers would perform there with Liberace. The restaurant soon became a Las Vegas staple and you never knew just who you might see there on any given night.

The restaurant almost immediately became a hot spot for the Mob, often frequented by Anthony Spilotro and his brother Michael. One of the rooms was positioned toward the front of the restaurant. The room was covered with scalloped wallpaper and had only one stained-glass window. It could also be closed off from the rest of the restaurant. This made it the perfect meeting place for the Las Vegas branch of "The Chicago Outfit."

Liberace's last stage performance took place on November 2, 1986, at the Radio City Music Hall. As with almost all of his performances, this too was a huge success. He performed eighteen shows in twenty-one days and was paid over $2 million. On December 25, 1986, he appeared on *The Oprah Winfrey Show*. It would be his final appearance. Wladziu Valentino Liberace died on February 4, 1987, at the age of sixty-seven, from cardiac arrest due to congestive heart failure, brought on by subacute encephalopathy, although Herman "Hank" Milton Greenspun, publisher of the *Las Vegas Sun* newspaper, reported that he died of complications from AIDS.

The restaurant sat vacant for more than a year before the Carluccio family bought it and reopened it in 1988 as Carluccio's Tivoli Gardens. While Liberace's body was entombed at the Forest Lawn-Hollywood Hills Cemetery, it appears he may not have stayed there. From the moment the restaurant reopened, strange things began to occur. Waiters reported leaving tables set up for the next day, only to have the candles all grouped together on one table when they showed up to work the next day. On one occasion those candles were all hidden behind the bar. One night John Hosier, the general manager, was standing at the bar. He set his drink down while talking to a guest. When he turned back to get his drink, it had been moved to the other side of the bar—there was no one in sight. Another night a woman excused herself from her party to go to the restroom. When she didn't come back for more than thirty minutes, the people at her table began to get worried and asked their waitress to check on her. The waitress went over to the women's restroom and turned the knob on the door. The woman rushed out, running past the waitress, screaming that someone had locked her in the restroom. She had been trying to get out for more than half an hour, but had been unable to get the door open. None of the entrance doors to the bathrooms have locks.

The restrooms seem to be a frequent location for hauntings. People and staff alike have seen the faucets suddenly turn on and the toilets flush on their own. Moaning has been heard at night, as has stomping that gets louder as it comes closer and then suddenly disappears. Knocks occur at the back door of the restaurant, but when checked, nobody is there.

In the room frequented by the Spilotro gang, now called "The Mafia Room," pictures cannot be hung on the walls. "They would just slide off the wall and sit there," says manager Hosier. Renowned psychic Sylvia Browne stated on *The Montel Williams Show* that she believed two people died in the restaurant; that story has often been expanded to two people being killed by the Mob in the restaurant.

Besides the women's restroom, the Piano Lounge is the most frequent source of paranormal activity. Employees have reported seeing Liberace standing behind them as they cleaned. The fake trees in the room have been known to shake, and people have been sighted walking in after hours, yet when the room was checked, no one was there.

Many paranormal investigators have visited Carluccio's Tivoli Gardens and reported the same thing as the restaurant's employees—that there is just something about the place. Longtime waiter Alfredo Rangel summed it up best when he said, "I think the place is haunted. Definitely, there is something there." Every year on the anniversary of his death, a place is set at the bar for Liberace . . . just in case. Who knows—one day you may enter the restaurant and see Liberace "in all the old familiar places."

ELVIS HAS NOT LEFT THE BUILDING

When the King first came to Las Vegas, he was less than stellar. When he returned, he would set records that to this day have never been broken. When he left, Vegas never forgot him—that is, assuming he has left.

He had to admit, he was a little nervous. It was just another bright, sunny day in Las Vegas as he watched the crowd making their way into the little show-room inside the Greek Isles Hotel and Casino. He had chosen the place specifically because it was once owned by the deceased's friend Debbie Reynolds. Now here it was the twenty-seventh anniversary of the man's death and he, Dixie Dooley, was about to conduct a séance to get in touch with this dead spirit. And not just any spirit; Dooley was about to contact Elvis Presley.

Dixie Dooley was an illusionist and escape artist who specialized in re-creating the tricks of Harry Houdini. He was no stranger to performing on the Las Vegas Strip, nor was he a stranger to holding séances. In fact, they were often part of his show.

It was almost 2:00 p.m. on August 16, 2004, when the crowd, many of whom were new to the whole séance scene, walked into the packed room. They were made up of the usual people: devotees of the occult, mixed with dedicated fans of Elvis, and, of course, those who were simply curious. Each and every person who walked into the room eagerly anticipated the possibilities that awaited them. Would Dooley really be able to contact the long deceased King of Rock and Roll? Would the King actually make an appearance, and if he did, which version of Elvis would they see—the young heartthrob clad in leather, or the older, heavier, jump-suited version? Dooley planned on contacting Elvis at 2:01 p.m., because he knew the King was an avid believer in numerology, and 2, 0, and 1 were the King's favorite numbers.

The King's tunes played hauntingly in the background as the chosen few spectators took their seats around the table set up for the event. Tricks of the trade—tambourines, bells, candles, and a crystal ball—lay atop the round table. The goateed Dooley took his place at the head in the ornate chair that set him apart from the rest of the participants. He welcomed everyone and delved into the many mysterious experiences that awaited them on this special day.

"Let us all hold hands," he said, speaking into the microphone in front of him and taking the hands of the person on either side. "We must all close our eyes and concentrate, not just those sitting here around the table, but all of us in the room."

The eager crowd did as they were told. With hands clutched and a crystal ball at the ready, Dooley channeled the ghost of Elvis while speaking into the microphone strategically placed in front of him.

"Elvis, we know how much you loved Las Vegas," he began. "You performed right across the street," he said, referring to the Las Vegas Hilton. "Are you here today?"

The crowd drew a collective breath and held it, waiting. A deep silence hung heavily over the room.

"Elvis," Dooley tried again. "If you're here with us this afternoon, please give us a sign."

At the very moment Dooley called on the King, a lightning bolt came out of the sky, accompanied by a loud crack of thunder. Being on edge already, the participants jumped in their seats. One person even let out an involuntary scream.

The Greek Isles Hotel and Casino was one of the smaller, older properties in Las Vegas and the roof was probably not in complete repair because the ceiling began dripping water and continued dripping throughout the remainder of the séance. Dooley tried several more times to contact Elvis, but had no luck.

The séance ended and the participants left the casino, disappointed. That is, until they walked outside and found that it was once again a bright and sunny day. According to Dooley, "The Elvis fans and the occult fans determined the lightning bolt was Elvis's symbol. He used to wear a necklace of a lightning bolt, and it said TCB—Taking Care of Business."

Elvis's first visit to Las Vegas was much less spectacular. Almost fifty years earlier, on April 23, 1956, before he became "The King," Elvis opened for comedian Shecky Greene at the New Frontier Casino. He was booked as the "Atomic Powered Singer" in an attempt to cash in on Las Vegas's fascination with the nuclear testing that was filling its skies with mushroom clouds. As Elvis gyrated his hips, bent his knees, and lifted himself onto his toes, the audience was shocked. They were not ready for this young upstart who appealed more to the teenage element than he did to this older, more sophisticated crowd, and they let him know it. Elvis bombed.

While Elvis may not have impressed the crowd, he did catch the attention of an up-and-coming piano player named Liberace who came to see him perform one night. When the show was over, Liberace went backstage with his brother George and took some publicity photos with Elvis. In one photo Liberace held a guitar while Elvis stroked the keys of a piano. Although the two entertainers enjoyed each other's company, neither had any idea of the impact they would both have on the Las Vegas culture.

Although Elvis may have bombed on his first visit to Las Vegas, he would eventually make up for it. Almost eight years later, in 1964, at the height of his movie career, he made a movie with starlet Ann-Margret called *Viva Las Vegas*. Elvis may have been more than a little apprehensive about returning to the town that rejected him. However, his good looks and singing combined with Ann-Margret's tight pants and sweaters brought in hordes of moviegoers, both male and female. The movie was a huge success and started what would become Las Vegas's lifelong fascination with the King of Rock and Roll.

Elvis returned to the town a third time in 1967, but on this occasion it was not to perform. Instead, he was there to attend a wedding—his own wedding. On May 1, 1967, Elvis Presley and Priscilla Beaulieu were married at the Aladdin Hotel in Milton Prell's suite. According to the *Las Vegas Sun*, "Presley wore a black brocade silk tuxedo and Western boots, while Priscilla wore a floor-length wedding gown of her own design: white silk chiffon, with beaded yoke, trimmed in seed pearls and topped with a three-foot tulle veil secured by a rhinestone crown."

Priscilla's maid of honor was her sister Michelle. Two members of the "Memphis Mafia," Marty Lacker and Joe Esposito, stood in as best men. The gangster-style name was given to the group of "friends," associates, and employees because they never left Elvis's side.

Elvis first met Priscilla in Bad Nauheim, Germany, when she was only fourteen years old. Elvis was eleven years her senior. They would have an eight-year courtship before they married; in fact, the courtship would last longer than the actual marriage. The wedding, too, was short, lasting only eight minutes. It was followed by a press conference and a breakfast reception for their approximately one hundred guests. At the reception Elvis and Priscilla cut the six-tier wedding cake and reportedly danced to "Love Me Tender." Brian Mills, an Elvis impersonator and manager of the Viva Las Vegas Wedding Chapel, once said that "Elvis made it hip to get married in Las Vegas."

Maybe Elvis would have actually appeared at the séance if Dooley had held it in the right place. In 1969, Elvis signed on for a four-week stint with the International (later called the Las Vegas Hilton). If the King was at all apprehensive about performing one more time in the town that so long ago rejected him, that apprehensiveness would prove to be unfounded.

Elvis did two shows a night and set Las Vegas attendance records, selling out the 2,200-seat showroom for fifty-eight nights in a row. He also set a record for gross receipts, with more than $1.5 million in revenue. By 1970, Elvis had switched from leather pants to what would become his trademark—leather jumpsuits, open to his chest. His signature hairstyle now included long sideburns and he routinely wore thick, gold-rimmed sunglasses. He also began to perform the martial arts moves he had learned in private lessons. Elvis played Las Vegas every year for the next eight years, ending his run on December 12, 1976. He died a little more than eight months later, but he may have never left.

Elvis sightings are common in the backstage area of the Las Vegas Hilton. One evening an employee was polishing the floor of the stage at about 3:00 a.m., on what is appropriately called the graveyard shift. As he was humming a tune to himself, something made him look up. He saw a man who looked remarkably like Elvis walking toward him.

"At first I thought it was one of the impersonators. I have seen hundreds of Elvis impersonators, some good, some not so good. When I saw him I thought, Man, if this guy's not a dead ringer for Elvis, I don't know who is."

This Elvis, according to the employee, had the same mannerisms and the same way of walking. If this man was an Elvis impersonator, he was the best the employee had ever seen.

"I was fixing to tell him so when he got up to me. We got within a foot of one another, and all of a sudden I felt so cold, like the heat had gone off or something."

The employee started to ask the man if he noticed the change in climate when Elvis just dissolved, right there in front of him. "I know it sounds crazy, but that's the best way I can describe it."

Elvis had a close connection to the Las Vegas Hilton, most likely because it was the site of his greatest success. Several employees have reported seeing Elvis walking around the wings of the showroom and in the backstage freight elevator. When performing, Elvis would frequently take the freight elevator to the upper floors, hoping to avoid the screaming fans that were all too eager to molest him.

On one occasion after the King's death, a guest room attendant entered the elevator with her supply cart when she noticed a man standing in the elevator.

"Oh, hello, Mr. Presley," she said politely, having seen the King of Rock and Roll many times before.

"Hello," the ghost responded.

It was at that moment she realized whom she was talking to—a deceased Elvis Presley. According to Las Vegas legend, the guest room attendant slammed the red button, bringing the elevator to a stop at the next floor. She ran out of the elevator and continued running until she had left the building entirely. She never returned.

Elvis has also been seen running to the stage in his white jumpsuit, vanishing if anyone tries to talk to him. Others have reported seeing him driving his signature Cadillac out by the parking garage. Many have mistaken the ghost for an Elvis impersonator—that is, until Elvis drives the Caddy into a concrete retaining wall and vanishes.

Another place where the King is frequently seen is in the penthouse suite he stayed in while performing at the Las Vegas Hilton. The suite, now called "The Elvis Suite," is on the thirtieth floor. Rumor has it that the King used to ride around the suite in a golf cart so that he could get around faster. He is often seen there in the golf cart, or simply walking around the suite.

Probably the most famous sighting of the King comes from another Las Vegas legend, "Mr. Las Vegas Wayne Newton." Before Elvis Presley was a name known by anyone but his immediate family and friends, Wayne Newton had already released his first record and toured with a Grand Ole Opry road show. He arrived in Las Vegas his junior year in high school and has been performing in one capacity or another in the town ever since. Wayne Newton, along with Elvis and Liberace, make up the three names most closely associated with Las Vegas entertainment, outside of the Rat Pack. Newton was in first grade when he performed in a USO show for President Truman and just eight years old when he won a chance to compete along with his brother in the national talent show, Ted Mack's *The Original Amateur Hour.* He would lose, as did Elvis when he entered the show.

Another thing Newton had in common with Elvis was the Las Vegas Hilton. Newton had performed there on the very same stage as Elvis. One night Newton was on that stage, performing where Elvis had performed and singing a song Elvis had sung, when he looked up into the balcony and saw the King. Elvis was wearing the same outfit he had been immortalized in by a statue the Las Vegas Hilton had placed outside the showroom in his honor back in 1978. Newton was only ten years younger than the King and had known him well. When Newton saw the man in the balcony, he knew what he was looking at. He was looking at the King of Rock and Roll. He was looking at Elvis Presley.

While Elvis has been dead for more than thirty years, the town that first rejected him has held firmly to its adopted son. In 2008, on the anniversary of his death, the Las Vegas Hilton placed another statue at the entrance of the hotel. Elvis poses in his famous jumpsuit, guitar strapped around his neck, microphone in hand, forever performing to the crowd.

A Las Vegas psychic once confirmed that the King still walks the Earth, "because he has unfinished business to do." The psychic also said that Elvis would eventually move on once that business was finished. Elvis died on August 16, 1977. According to the *Las Vegas Sun*, "About 150 mourners gathered outside a Las Vegas mortuary to pay their respects at a service that featured Presley's music played through large speakers."

Las Vegas has never forgotten its King. His image is everywhere and impersonators are found in many stage shows and on the streets trying to lure people into businesses. But probably the best tribute to the King is the Cirque du Soleil tribute show, *Viva Elvis*. While his first effort in Las Vegas may have been less than stellar, the lasting impression Elvis left has never been equaled. In fact, in Las Vegas it can truly be said that Elvis has never left the building.

Every year sightings of Elvis increase as the anniversary date of his death draws near. Records show that on the actual day Elvis died Las Vegas was struck by an uncommon rainfall. According to the *Las Vegas Review-Journal*, the rain fell for three hours, coming down so hard that it caused the roofs of "countless businesses and homes [to] collapse under the weight of constant rainfall."

Maybe that séance worked after all.

THE MAN WHO INVENTED LAS VEGAS

Notorious crime mobster Benjamin "Bugsy" Siegel was determined to live in a luxurious resort in the middle of the Las Vegas Strip. He envisioned himself as the center of attention in the most elegant hotel on Earth. Although his vision didn't come true in his lifetime (in fact, his vision was instrumental in his death), he is said to still inhabit the halls of the Flamingo Hotel, making his dream come true . . . even from beyond the grave.

Even though they weren't crazy about going out that late at night, the two ladies boarded the bus in front of the Royal Resort. Virginia Ridgway, curator of the historic (and reportedly haunted) Goldfield Hotel in nearby Goldfield, Nevada, and her daughter were on one of their typical adventures. This adventure took them to Las Vegas, or "Sin City," as it was called. While they were here more for business than for pleasure, there was no reason they couldn't enjoy a few shows, some fine dining, and possibly a luxury spa treatment.

It was 9:30 at night when the two stepped onto the tour bus. Virginia had talked her daughter into going on the Haunted Vegas Tour. She knew the owner, Robert Allen, and he had invited her to take the tour. As the ladies settled into their seats on the bus, they noticed a man just about to sit across the aisle.

"I don't remember seeing him in the lobby," Virginia said to her daughter.

"I don't think I saw him either. Maybe he came at the last minute."

"Or was hiding in the bathroom," Virginia said, causing the two women to chuckle.

"Mind if I sit here?" the man asked.

"Not at all," Virginia replied. The man sat down in the seat and asked the women where they were from. They told him and he smiled, nodding his head as they talked.

"It looks like he's alone," the daughter whispered to her mother.

"Maybe he's hoping we'll keep him company," Virginia told her.

"We could do that. He's kinda cute." The two women smiled at each other.

Excitement arose as everyone filed onto the bus, which seemed to be filled with a nervous energy and anticipation. Once all were on board, the tour guide entered the bus. He was dressed almost completely in black. He wore a black suit, black shirt, and a type of black ascot. Atop his head was a black stovepipe hat.

"I know he's supposed to look like an undertaker," said Virginia's daughter, "but I think he looks more like a chimney sweep." This comment was obviously overheard by the man next to them, who suddenly chuckled out loud.

The tour guide welcomed the people onto the bus and began to describe the mysteries and haunts that awaited them. "This tour has been featured on both the Discovery and the History Channels," the tour guide said. He went on to list the places where they would be stopping, explaining that ghosts typically hang out only for six to seven seconds.

"Las Vegas is the suicide capital of America," he said, "and not everyone who comes here leaves here. Sometimes, what happens in Vegas *truly* stays in Vegas." It was a corny joke, but the man sitting next to the two women laughed louder than anyone—something he did every time the tour guide told a joke.

"I think our friend may have had one too many," Virginia whispered to her daughter.

The tour made its way to some of the supernatural hot spots in Las Vegas, including the Las Vegas Hilton and the corner where Tupac Shakur was gunned down. As the bus approached the Flamingo Hotel, the man next to the two ladies seemed to take a sudden interest in what the tour guide had to say about the hotel's famous owner Benjamin "Bugsy" Siegel. The man laughed at times and even said that the tour guide was wrong about a fact he attributed to Siegel.

The tour bus stopped outside the famous hotel and all on board got off the bus and headed to an area by the hotel rooms and wedding chapel, commonly known as "Bugsy's Garden." The man stayed behind the two women as they walked through the garden. He was laughing as the tour guide spoke. The group eventually gathered around a monument to the slain gangster as the tour guide continued talking. The monument consisted of a large bronze plaque that had a depiction of the original Flamingo at the top and a carved face of the mobster at the bottom. The plaque was encased in stone.

"What do you think of the mon . . . ?" Virginia's words were cut off as she turned to the man only to find he was not there. She looked around but he was nowhere in sight.

"What happened to that man?" she asked the tour guide.

"What man?" the tour guide said.

"The man who was standing right here," she said, pointing behind her. "The man who was sitting next to us on the bus—you know, the one who was laughing a little too hard at your jokes?"

"He must have gone to the restroom. We'll wait a few minutes for him to come back."

After five minutes the man had still not returned. The tour guide waited as long as he could, but he had a schedule to keep and if the man didn't want to continue on with the tour, that was his own business. He told the group to get on the bus and they left the Flamingo without the man.

"What do you think happened to him?" Virginia asked the tour guide.

"Guess he just didn't want to finish the tour."

"Don't you think that's strange?"

"This is Las Vegas. Everything's strange," he said.

Suddenly one of the other guests spoke up. "You don't think he was . . . ? I mean, he did get off at the Flamingo. You don't think he could have been Bugsy, do you?"

So many stories swarm around the deserts of southern Nevada that it's hard to sift fact from fiction. If you listen to some people, Bugsy Siegel was the man who invented Las Vegas. Of course, to believe them you would have to deny every event that occurred during the ninety years of history that had already filled the valley by the time Siegel arrived.

Benjamin Siegel was born in Brooklyn, New York, in February of 1906, the son of Jewish immigrants. As a young man, Siegel teamed up with his best friend Meyer Lansky. The two hoodlums-in-training put together a string of illegal gambling events they called "floating crap games," so named because they were held in a different location every night. Switching spots nightly made it difficult for the police to find them. This was ideal because neither Siegel nor Lansky wanted to deal with the police, both having already had their time behind bars.

One night, as the game was in full swing, a local police officer named Sergeant Hearn surprised the men by dropping in on the gathering. After a slight panic, Lansky thought on his feet. He handed the dice to the sergeant, offering him very generous odds. The lucky sergeant won ten dollars, but it didn't stop him from shutting the game down for the night—although he did ask where the two would be holding the next event.

As the policeman departed, an angry Siegel, feeling like he had been made a fool of, followed him into an alley. There, he hit the policeman over the head with a lead pipe, taking back the ten dollars and Hearn's gun. When Lansky discovered that Siegel had the moxie to kill a cop for ten dollars, he said that Siegel was as crazy as a bedbug, leading to Siegel's nickname, "Bugsy." Though born out of a lighthearted moment with a trusted friend, Siegel eventually grew to hate the nickname because of the comment it made on his violent temper. Those who dared to call him by this nickname to his face, reportedly, did not live to repeat the offense. "My friends call me Ben, strangers call me Mr. Siegel, and guys I don't like call me Bugsy—but not to my face."

Siegel and Lansky gained notoriety in the underworld, eventually becoming known as "The Bug and Meyer Mob." The two became involved in bootlegging in New York, New Jersey, and Philadelphia. In 1930, they teamed up with Albert Anastasia and Lucky Luciano in a gang led by Joe "The Boss" Masseria. A year later, Siegel allegedly killed Masseria on orders from Lucky Luciano, a move that ended the war for control of the New York Mob and created "the Syndicate."

In 1931 a very important event happened on the other side of the nation: Gambling was made legal in Nevada. Both Luciano and Lansky wanted to get their foot in the door of the gambling scene, but avoided moving the Syndicate to Las Vegas because of the heat. They both did a small amount of business from long distance, making brief trips to the new mecca, but the majority of their business remained in New York and New Jersey.

By 1937, Bugsy's temper had angered several powerful people. Luciano decided it would be best to send Siegel to the West Coast to escape the wrath of his enemies and to avoid the numerous contracts that had reportedly been taken out on him. Lansky and Luciano had worked their way into three Fremont Street properties, using men with no records as fronts for the operations. They decided to get more involved with the race and sports book operations in the downtown Las Vegas casinos, so they sent Siegel and Moe Sedway to investigate.

Siegel helped the Syndicate take greater control over the race and sports book, until it had a complete monopoly. Siegel had the charm to "convince" Las Vegas casino owners they needed the protection the Mob could provide. Many of the casino owners were starting to complain about the Mob's involvement, even going so far as to make formal complaints to Carson City. However, with the onset of World War II, the state capital was involved in doing its part for the war effort.

Most of the government's attention was focused on the conflicts in Europe and the Pacific. This opened a door for the Mob, one it gladly stepped through.

Siegel was handsome and quite the gentleman. He was also charming with the ladies, who thought he and Hollywood would make a perfect match. "I've never met a more courtly, a more gentlemanly man in my life," recalled singer Kay Starr. "I thought to myself, 'Well, if this is a gangster, I'd like to know more of them.'" Siegel agreed and soon developed a fascination with the film industry. While in California, Siegel was in his element. He loved the whole movie-industry scene. Siegel even dated actress Virginia Hill, although it didn't stop him from chasing other romantic interests.

While in Los Angeles, Siegel made the short trip to Las Vegas many times on behalf of his boss. At the time, Las Vegas was nothing more than a few casinos in the desert. Siegel was a frequent guest in one of the two outlying casinos, the El Rancho and the Last Frontier. He stayed at these two casinos because he didn't care for the smaller, less-sophisticated casinos downtown. It was during a stay in the El Rancho that Siegel got the idea for a luxurious resort hotel and casino on Highway 91, a highway that would eventually be known as Las Vegas Boulevard, or, more famously, as "the Strip."

Although some would say that Siegel saw the opening and operating of a hotel casino as a way of becoming a legitimate businessman, Siegel was a sociopath, and it is more likely that he simply saw the resort as a way of moving Mob operations closer to his beloved Hollywood. To his credit, Siegel had a vision of taking the Las Vegas resort to the next level. In an attempt to emulate the resorts he stayed at in California, Siegel wanted his resort to be a posh, luxurious place where the Hollywood elite would come to play.

By 1945 Siegel had managed to raise $1 million toward the building of his new Flamingo Club—it was later changed to "Flamingo Hotel" for licensing purposes. Siegel was able to convince Lansky to allow him to build the resort. He found a property out on Highway 91 that was already struggling. Billy Wilkerson, a known gambler, had put more money than he could afford into a resort that he wasn't able to finish. Siegel came on board and quickly took over the project.

It turned out that building an oasis in the desert was far more involved than Siegel could have foreseen. Construction was taking way too long, something noted by Luciano, who was impatient to see some return on his investment. Luciano insisted Siegel open the Flamingo before it was ready. Because they were used to seeing immediate results on their investments, The Syndicate bosses held a meeting in Havana, Cuba, the day before the opening of the Flamingo. If the Flamingo turned out to be a success, Siegel would be given a chance to pay back the loan. If not, he would be eliminated. The grand opening proved to be a disaster and the money didn't flow in as expected.

On a cool June evening in 1947, Benjamin Siegel, accompanied by associate Allen Smiley, arrived at the bungalow he shared with Virginia Hill in Hollywood. He had just gotten a haircut and a manicure. He sat on the chintz sofa in the living room, reading the *Los Angeles Times* in front of an open window. At about 10:30 p.m., a hailstorm of bullets from a .30 caliber military M1 carbine shattered the quiet Hollywood night. Two bullets found their way through the open window into Siegel's head, two more into his ribs, and one into his lungs. Three shots missed. Benjamin "Bugsy" Siegel was dead at forty-one years of age.

Even though Siegel's demise was front-page news across the country, only five people, all family, attended his funeral. His boyhood best friend and trusted partner, Meyer Lansky, was in Havana and couldn't make it back in time. His lover, Virginia Hill, was in Switzerland. Not one of Ben's new Hollywood buddies found the time to attend. For a man who had such grandiose visions of himself, it was a sad, embarrassing end.

Ever since the day Siegel was killed, there have been thousands of reports of appearances by his ghost. Some of the most common have been reported in his personal suite. Before the suite was demolished in 1993, the green toilets, bidet, and linoleum in both bathrooms were original, having been personally chosen by Siegel. While he stayed at the hotel, Siegel was an avid pool player, and it is by that pool table that guests have reported seeing a ghostly man standing.

The demolition of Bugsy's suite has not stopped him from haunting his beloved Flamingo. Another report comes from a couple on their honeymoon. They met up with two other couples who all sat by the pool one warm summer night. At one point they saw a man standing near the pool in a pair of slacks and an old-style, yet pristine smoking jacket. The man seemed to be looking at the women, one of whom commented that it was odd to see a man wearing a smoking jacket in the 1990s and especially on such a warm night.

Moments later, when the men returned from swimming, the bride went to point out the man, but when they all looked, he was gone. She described him to the men as "a handsome man with intense eyes, wearing a smoking jacket and slacks." The next day, when the newly married couple was reading about the history of the hotel, the two saw a drawing of Bugsy. The bride told her husband, "That looks like the man in the smoking jacket."

Bugsy is most often sighted in the rose garden, near his memorial plaque. This is where a couple from Iowa saw the ghostly apparition. "We saw him over by the fountain and thought he was one of the Bugsy tour guides, the way he was dressed. It was around ten at night and still almost a hundred degrees. We felt sorry for him having to wear that shirt, tie, and wool jacket. As other people started coming up to the fountain, no one seemed to notice him. Then this woman walked right through him. . . . It was the scariest thing we ever saw. I don't think the woman even saw him. She was posing for a picture and smiling. . . . No, I'm sure she didn't see him."

While Bugsy may not have lived to see the success of the resort he envisioned in the desert, his ghost seems to be happy with the work he started, as none of the sightings ever report the ghost being anything but cordial. While he may have earned the moniker of "Bugsy" in life, he may have mellowed to just good old "Ben" in death. Interestingly, the Flamingo doesn't allow the Haunted Vegas Tour to visit the hotel anymore, although officials don't say why. Maybe it's because the Flamingo, according to the Haunted Vegas Tour, was listed as one of the ten most haunted sites in America by the *Wall Street Journal*.

SEEING REDD

Redd Foxx made a living from his portrayal of a lovable, grumpy old man who said what he wanted, when he wanted. His Las Vegas home, while not a mansion, was his pride and joy—so much so that he refused to leave, even when the IRS took it away.

Norma wasn't sure she believed in any of this, but she was tired of the things that were happening at work. She hated typing out a report only to have the font color change to red on its own in the middle of her document. She was sick of the cold breezes and the sounds of a party coming from the backyard area where the pool used to be, especially when no one was there. So if a séance would help, Norma was all for it.

She never understood why they had to make these things so spooky. Were the candles and the dim lighting really necessary? Still, she took her place at the round table, decorated with the séance tricks of the trade and watched as her fellow employees sat down with her. The medium entered the room and sat at the head of the table.

"Before we begin," the medium said, "I need everybody to clear their mind of all doubt and fear. In order for us to be able to contact the other side, we all need to allow ourselves to be open to the possibility of contact. In just a moment I will invite the spirits from the other side to come join us."

It all seemed so theatrical that Norma was having a hard time keeping the "open mind" the medium had requested. But she did her part, taking the hands of the people on either side of her, as instructed by the medium, and closing her eyes.

"Redd," the medium continued, "are you here with us this evening? Are you in your house? Can we speak with you?"

She watched as the medium seemed to go into a trance. *If her eyes roll into the back of her head,* Norma thought to herself, *I'm leaving.* The medium started to sway back and forth, almost as if she were listening to some inaudible music. The medium's mouth opened wide and Norma swore she heard the medium say, "This is my house and I'm never leaving it."

John Elroy Sanford was born in St. Louis, Missouri, on December 9, 1922, into extreme poverty. By the time he was four years old, his father had left the family. When he was thirteen, Sanford moved to Chicago and joined a band. He and three of his friends formed the washtub band they called the Bon-Bons, with Sanford playing the washboard. After three years together in Chicago, the trio eventually disbanded. This left Sanford to make his own way in the entertainment world.

As a kid, Sanford had a bit of a ruddy complexion, which gave way to his nickname of "Redd." Sanford flirted with the name "Chicago Redd," because he was living in Chicago at the time. He used the name when he moved to New York and took a job as a dishwasher. It was while working as a dishwasher that he met a young man by the name of Malcolm Little. While the two worked together, washing dishes, Little adopted the name "Detroit Red" as a joke. Little would eventually change his last name one more time, choosing the simple letter X. Malcolm X, as he was known, called Chicago Redd "the funniest dishwasher on this Earth" in his autobiography.

Sanford wouldn't keep the name Chicago Redd for long. While reports differ on when the change took place, Sanford would eventually settle on the last name of a famous baseball player by the name of Jimmie Foxx. When he added the baseball great's last name to his own nickname, Redd Foxx was born. Foxx started working in comedy clubs in New York, on what was then called the "Chitlin' Circuit" because the audiences were mainly Black.

It was while working the Chitlin' Circuit that Foxx met Melvin "Slappy" White. Foxx and White developed a lifelong friendship while working comedy clubs as a team all across the country. Their comedy was adult-oriented, often causing them to be booked with the tagline "Redd, White, and Blue." Longtime friend and entertainment writer Joe Delaney once said, "Redd was basically a very funny guy and he was as dirty as he felt he had to be."

On one of his trips to Los Angeles, Foxx was approached by executives of the Dootone record label who wanted him to record a series of comedy albums. Foxx and White took to records with a fury, recording many albums that were called "party records." It was through these recordings that Foxx began to make a name for himself. It was also during this time that Foxx first arrived in Las Vegas.

In the 1950s Las Vegas was a very modern town with a strong Southern presence. This meant that it still remained a stalwart supporter of segregation. Even though Black people made up more than 10 percent of the town's population, they were still banned from many downtown casinos and clubs.

Foxx, however, was a perfect fit for Las Vegas. He was a comedian whose vulgarity drew a line in the sand, you either loved it or hated it; there was no in-between. He started his Las Vegas career at a small casino called the Sans Souci Hotel Casino. The Sans Souci boasted one hundred deluxe rooms and advertised refrigerated air-conditioning, a snack bar, and a telephone in each room. It also had a swimming pool and a restaurant called Dinah's Original Pancake & Chicken House. The hotel would later change its name to the Castaways before eventually being destroyed, with the Mirage opening on the land where it once stood. Foxx continued to perform at the Castaways in the Samoa Room with then unknowns Tony Orlando and Kenny Rogers, before eventually moving to the Hacienda Hotel and Casino.

Foxx would be the first Black comedian to perform in front of an entirely white audience, paving the way for other comedians like Flip Wilson, Richard Pryor, and Eddie Murphy. In 1970, Foxx signed a three-year contract with the Sahara Hotel for $960,000. The contract guaranteed him thirty-two weeks a year and allowed him to build his cherished Las Vegas home. Foxx loved the home, once saying, "This is my house and I'm never leaving it."

Foxx also loved Las Vegas and while living here he took to gambling, specifically keno. "He was a dyed-in-the-wool keno player," recalled John Boni, then vice president of casino operations for Sahara Resorts. "We had a special chair and window for him. He'd even have one of his staff play his numbers when he was performing." Boni claimed that Foxx used keno and small-stakes poker as a way to relax. A longtime Las Vegas resident remembered seeing Foxx at the keno lounge. "He could be the nicest guy you ever want to meet, and generous, or foul-mouthed and rude. It just depended on how his luck was going that night."

By the 1970s segregation was no longer a factor in Las Vegas. Frank, Dean, Sammy, and the rest of the Rat Pack had helped to further promote the rights of Black entertainers, and a new television show called *All in the Family* was breaking down boundaries and changing stereotypes. A year earlier Foxx was approached by Ossie Davis and offered a small role in his film *Cotton Comes to Harlem*. Foxx played Booker Washington Sims, better known as "Uncle Bud," an aging junk dealer.

While the film received mediocre praise, it did catch the attention of Norman Lear, the creator of *All in the Family*. Lear was looking to create an American television show based on the British comedy *Steptoe and Son,* about a middle-aged man and his elderly father who run an unsuccessful junk business. Foxx was cast in the lead role and his original last name was used in place of Steptoe.

Sanford and Son debuted three days after the one-year anniversary of Lear's wildly successful *All in the Family*. The sitcom was a huge success and Foxx became an overnight sensation. His character, like *All in the Family*'s Archie Bunker, was a bigoted man who refused to see life in the modern world. Unlike Bunker, Fred G. Sanford was always coming up with get-rich-quick schemes that frustrated his son Lamont, played by Demond Wilson. Foxx became famous for his fake heart attacks on film, which he used when the scheme went awry or when Lamont threatened to leave. "This is the big one," he would say, one hand over his heart and the other arm outstretched wide. "I'm coming, 'Lizabeth," he'd say, referring to his character's dead wife.

The show ran from 1972 to 1977, with more than 130 episodes. It was a financial windfall for Foxx, who spent freely on cars, jewelry, and keno. Foxx was also loyal to his friends, giving Slappy White a recurring role on the sitcom as his friend Melvin, in five episodes. During the run of *Sanford and Son,* Foxx continued his Las Vegas performances. In 1976 Foxx and NBC reached an impasse over financial compensation for *Sanford and Son.* Foxx left Hollywood and returned to his beloved home in Las Vegas. He then sent a telegraph to the NBC executives, saying, "I'm sick in Las Vegas and I'm going to stay sick until the man from NBC comes up with the money to make me well." A settlement was eventually reached in 1980, and Foxx returned to the set of *Sanford and Son.* Unfortunately, Wilson chose not to return to the show and without him, it failed to generate sufficient viewer interest and was canceled. Foxx then had a short run on CBS with *The Redd Foxx Comedy Hour.*

In 1989 Foxx starred with Eddie Murphy and Richard Pryor in Murphy's movie *Harlem Nights.* As a result, he was sued by Las Vegas talent agent Jackie Baskow, for $50,000. Baskow claimed that she had negotiated Foxx's contract with Murphy and was due her 10 percent commission. Foxx told district court judge Thomas Foley that he hadn't used Baskow's services. "I can hustle my own jobs," he told the judge, adding that he had handled his own affairs since the 1950s. Foley agreed and dismissed the case.

Foxx was right. He had been handling his own affairs since the 1950s, and that would prove to be his downfall. Even though he had made millions of dollars, in 1983 Foxx had reached such financial difficulties that he was forced to declare bankruptcy. The only bright spot was that he was able to keep his home, many of his cars, and much of his jewelry. Foxx probably thought he had dodged a bullet, but that bullet would return in 1989 when early one morning Foxx got a knock on the door of his home. Foxx was face-to-face with agents of the Internal Revenue Service who claimed that Foxx owed $2.9 million in back taxes, penalties, and interest. The IRS agents seized eight of his cars, much of his jewelry, and other valuable items. They also took a portion of his current earnings.

Foxx made many attempts to settle the debt, but nothing seemed to work. In an interview with *People* magazine, Foxx stated that the agents didn't even treat him like he was human. "He was extremely patriotic and I think it really bothered him that some people thought he was trying to avoid taxes. I personally believe that put a strain on him," said Boni. According to Marc Risman, Foxx's attorney, "The IRS put a real dent in him, but he showed a lot of courage and a lot of class to try and work through it." Foxx's troubles seemed to stem more from his incompetence as a businessman and less from any desire on his part to cheat the federal government. Still, he had a large debt to pay and Foxx was not the type of man to give up easily.

In 1991 Foxx signed on for another television series with his friend Della Reese, with whom he had worked on *Harlem Nights*. The sitcom, called *The Royal Family*, starred Foxx and Reese who played a married couple entering their retirement years when their daughter and three grandchildren moved back into their home. Foxx was not excited about the prospect of doing another television show. "I can't work the hours I did on *Sanford and Son*," he told the *Las Vegas Review-Journal* in 1989, before he had signed on with *The Royal Family*. "I'm an older man than I was then and if I'm going to give up five years in the twilight of my life, then I want a payday." Foxx added about his Las Vegas home, "I'm comfortable here. I have no regrets."

Foxx felt a great burden from the IRS debt, and by all accounts this seemed to be the only reason he returned to situation comedy on television. On October 11, 1991, at around 4:00 p.m., Foxx was rehearsing a scene for *The Royal Family* when he suffered a heart attack on set. The cast members initially thought Foxx was doing his old *Sanford and Son* routine, but quickly realized it was no act when the comedian went down. He was rushed to the hospital and died at 7:45 p.m., the entire cast by his side.

More than seven hundred friends and family attended Foxx's funeral in Las Vegas, including his friends Slappy White, Eddie Murphy, George Carlin, and Della Reese. Foxx was buried in Palm Memorial Park in Las Vegas, a bright red fox decorating the upper right corner of his tombstone. The IRS immediately seized his Las Vegas home and while Foxx may have no longer owned the site on Eastern Avenue, he refused to leave.

The first owner, an Elvis impersonator, bought the home and lived there with his uncle. The two complained of cold breezes that could never be linked to any source. They also claimed that lights came on at night, doors and windows seemed to open and close on their own, and the floor creaked at night as if someone was walking on it. One of the places that seemed most haunted was not even in the house. Voices could always be heard from the pool in the backyard, as if a party was going on. The back door would even open and close by itself. A vision of a ghostly Redd Foxx convinced the owner that the house was haunted, and he sold it after only nine months of occupancy.

Michael Carrico and fellow investigators from Las Vegas Paranormal Investigations were allowed to enter the residence to conduct an investigation. Once inside they were able to gather electronic voice phenomena (better known as EVP) in the area around the pool house, where they heard laughter and conversation.

A group of real estate agents bought the building and remodeled extensively, filling in the swimming pool and turning the backyard into a parking lot. However, Foxx's ghost was not deterred. One employee recalled seeing the ghost. "I think he meant to tell me something. He walked right up like he was going to speak to me, then turned and was gone." While doors continued to open, items continued to be moved, and Foxx's ghost continued to be seen—especially around his bedroom—no one felt the ghost meant any harm. Still, the ghost made work difficult at times and the business decided to do something about it, so a séance was held.

When the séance was over, the medium told the owners that Foxx was very proud of his Las Vegas home and wanted everyone to know it was his. The new owners agreed to place small red foxes on the business sign that rests on the front lawn. They also placed lighting around the house, making it easier to see. While this seems to have appeased Foxx, he still shows up every once in a while, pulling pranks such as making coffee cups disappear and teasing the ladies. The IRS may have taken his home, but it couldn't force him to leave.

AT THE CORNER OF FLAMINGO AND FOREVER

Popular rapper and actor Tupac Shakur was gunned down after attending a prize-fight at the MGM Grand. For various reasons, the killers have never been brought to justice—although a video made just before his death suggests that Shakur might have known the murder was going to happen.

It was a typical Las Vegas evening, 5:00 p.m. and 110 degrees. LeRoy had gone to the airport to pick up his friend Lamont. It was Lamont's first visit to Las Vegas and LeRoy had to admit, he was a little excited to show him around the town. LeRoy pulled the car up the ramp on his way to passenger pickup. Lamont was waiting there, plaid shorts and all, a smile growing on his face as he approached.

"Nice shorts," LeRoy said, getting out of the car to help his friend with his luggage. "Very gangsta."

"Funny. Did you get it?"

"You're not even in the car yet," LeRoy said, closing the trunk and moving quickly back to the driver's seat.

"So, did you get it?" Lamont asked again once he'd gotten into the car.

"Didn't I tell you I'd get it?"

"Yeah, you did. So you got it, right?"

"I got it."

"Then let's go!"

"Hold your horses, there's plenty of time," LeRoy said, pulling the car out into the flow of traffic. He drove down the exit ramp and circled onto the road, then turned left onto Swenson Avenue. The pair traveled north until they reached Tropicana Avenue, where LeRoy took another left. They were partially up the street when Lamont saw the emerald-green building on the right side of Tropicana.

"There it is!" Lamont yelled, turning himself sideways in his seat. "That's the MGM!" he said, poking the glass window with his finger. "That's where he was right before it happened!"

"Yeah, I know that."

The car reached Las Vegas Boulevard and turned left. When they started to pass the black glass pyramid, Lamont yelled out a second time. "Look at that!" he said, again poking the glass. "That's the Luxor! That's where he was staying the night it happened."

"Yeah, I know that too."

"That means he traveled down this very street," Lamont said, without removing his gaze from the Luxor. "Same street we're on right now."

"That's what it means, all right."

"So c'mon man, take me to the house," Lamont said, righting himself in his seat. "I want to see the house."

"Okay, okay, I'm going," LeRoy said, turning the car east on Sunset Boulevard, just south of McCarran International Airport, the place where he had just picked up Lamont. Traveling on Sunset, just past the airport, they came upon Tomiyasu Lane and turned right. This area of the Las Vegas valley was known as Paradise, Nevada, and it sure lived up to its name. The homes were mansions, surrounded by large walls with ornate gates. The mansion they were looking for was a few houses down on the right. LeRoy pulled the car up to the dark ornate gates.

"There it is," LeRoy said to his friend, "Suge's Las Vegas mansion." He was referring to Marion "Suge" Knight Jr., CEO and producer at Death Row Records. Lamont had asked him to find the address of the home.

"Wow!" Lamont exclaimed as they both leaned into the windshield to get a better look at the large house laid out before them. "So this is where Tupac stayed when he came to town. Man, this is some place all right. Drive around the block."

LeRoy started the car and was beginning to pull away when his friend yelled out, "It's him—it's Tupac! It's really Tupac!"

"What're you talking about?" LeRoy asked, stopping the car suddenly.

"Right there on the balcony. It's him! It's Tupac!"

LeRoy turned his head quickly to look at the house. Sure enough, standing on the balcony was a young Black man in his late twenties, the spitting image of Tupac Shakur. He was standing there looking contemplatively into the grounds of Knight's estate. Wanting a better look, LeRoy backed up and spun the car around quickly. Lamont never took his eyes off the balcony.

"He's gone!"

"What?"

"He's gone. He's just gone."

Looking up at the balcony, LeRoy could see that the young man was no longer standing there. "Where'd he go?"

"He just disappeared."

"You mean he went inside."

"No, I mean he just disappeared."

Tupac Amaru Shakur was born in East Harlem in New York City on June 16, 1971. His early years were made of multiple changes of addresses, attending political meetings, and scary dealings with the Federal Bureau of Investigation. This was because both his mother and father were members of the political organization "Black Panther Party," known more commonly as the Black Panthers. The Black Panthers were made up mainly of Black Americans and were seen by the FBI as a radical organization. In fact, Chief J. Edgar Hoover once stated that the Black Panthers were "the greatest threat to the internal security of the United States."

Shakur's mother, Afeni Williams (originally Alice Faye Williams), was one of the party's most fervent activists. She once said, "From the day, the moment, I was arrested from my sleeping bed on 117th Street, the fight was on." Afeni gave speeches, started a free breakfast program for children, did fund-raising, and worked as hard as she could for Black freedom. During the late sixties, she met Lumumba Abdul Shakur, who had changed his name from Anthony Coston. In 1969 Afeni and Lumumba, along with several other members of the Black Panthers, were arrested on thirty counts of conspiracy.

Afeni faced 351 years of incarceration and had no reason to believe that either she or her husband, Lumumba, who was still in jail, would ever be acquitted. Afeni desperately wanted a baby. While out on bail she started seeing fellow Panther Billy Garland and promptly got pregnant. "I got pregnant while I was out on bail," she said. "I never thought that I wasn't going to spend the rest of my life in jail. I was never getting out and that's why I wanted to have this baby."

Afeni was pronounced not guilty after a two and a half hour jury deliberation. One month later she gave birth to her first son—listing his name as Lesane Parish Crooks on the birth certificate. Afeni gave her son the name to protect him from the FBI. However, she would later change his name to Tupac Amaru Shakur, in honor of the last emperor of the Incan people who led an uprising against Spain but was ultimately beheaded.

Even from the start, Shakur had an ominous future. He once said, "I was cultivated in prison, my embryo was in prison." While this wasn't entirely true, it did seem to leave a mark on him, one that would affect him his entire life. Strangely enough, had Afeni not been arrested, Shakur may never have been conceived and certainly wouldn't have been born. "If I thought I was getting out," his mother said, "I never would have had the baby. I probably would have gotten an abortion."

The man who, as an adult, tattooed thug life on his abdomen, was quiet and withdrawn as a child. "I read a lot. I wrote poetry. I kept a diary," he said. He would have a great deal of material to write about. Not only was he poor, but his mother had stayed an activist and was becoming addicted to crack cocaine. He was also ruthlessly teased for his fine features (he had long lashes and high cheekbones). Shakur became a master at hiding his true feelings; however, he would soon be given an outlet for his emotions. When he was twelve, his mother enrolled him in free acting classes. He took to acting naturally and was chosen for the role of Travis in a community production of *A Raisin in the Sun*. "[W]hen the curtain went up, I just caught that bug," he said.

In 1985, the family moved to Baltimore. It was then that Shakur, at fourteen years old, caught a break and was accepted into the Baltimore School for the Arts, and it was there that he cultivated his talent. In 1988 Shakur moved with his mother and younger sister to Marin City, California, a crime-ridden city that had earned the nickname "the Jungle." Shakur rapped everywhere he could and to anyone who would listen. It was through rapping that he started to truly make a name for himself. By the time he met music promoter Leila Steinberg, she had already heard of him.

Shakur and Steinberg formed Assemblies in Motion (AIM), an organization that brought talented performers to high schools in the area. Steinberg once said of Shakur, "As Pac entered the group he took a lot of my infantile thought processes to the next level." Shakur worked with recording artist Gregory E. "Shock G" Jacobs and his group, Digital Underground, acting as a roadie and dancer, and continued rapping whenever he got the chance. Shock G allowed Shakur to rap onstage with one of his songs, but his real break came when the artist allowed Shakur to have a solo on their next album, *This Is an E.P. Release*.

In 1991, Shakur began his career as a solo artist with the song, "Brenda's Got a Baby." He started spelling his name 2Pac and recorded his debut album, *2Pacalypse Now*. While his first album did well, it was his second album that brought him two Top 20 pop chart hits, "I Get Around" and "Keep Ya Head Up." The two songs sent the album platinum, selling more than a million copies. It was at this time that Shakur tapped into the bug that had bitten him as a youth. In 1993 he played the romantic lead opposite Janet Jackson in *Poetic Justice*. Shakur received critical acclaim for his role in the film, as well as for his musical talent. However, he was also receiving just as much condemnation for his often-violent lyrics.

During the early 1990s Tupac was both the perpetrator and the victim of violence on more than one occasion. Shakur had signed on with Death Row Records, and in so doing became embroiled in a feud between East Coast and West Coast rappers. He was also known to insult his enemies on his tracks. In 1993 he was arrested on a sexual assault charge. In 1994, he was convicted of assaulting director Allen Hughes and spent several days in jail. Later that year, he was shot five times in the lobby of a recording studio during a mugging. This incident happened on the day before he was sentenced to four and a half years in prison for the sexual assault case from the year before. After serving eight months in prison, he was released on bail. He was reportedly released after Death Row Records CEO Suge Knight paid a bond of more than $1 million.

On the evening of September 7, 1996, Shakur and a number of his associates, including Knight, attended a Mike Tyson fight at the MGM Grand in Las Vegas. Tyson and Shakur had developed a friendship, and Tyson had invited his friend to see him fight Bruce Seldon. Shakur had written a song called "Wrote the Glory," which Tyson used during his entrance into the ring. Even with all the buildup and the drawn-out opening bouts, it was an early evening. With one minute and nine seconds remaining in the first round, Tyson scored a knockout, ending the fight only moments after it had begun.

As the crowd left the area and headed to the casino, Knight and Shakur went to congratulate Tyson. When Tyson took too long, the group decided to leave, knowing they would see him later at the party being held for him at Knight's Club 662, over on Flamingo Avenue. As the group entered the casino, a member of the Death Row posse whispered something in Shakur's ear, causing him to run over to a man, later identified as Orlando Anderson, and start beating on him. Shakur and his entourage were seen "punching, kicking, and stomping on the man for unknown reasons." The altercation, which was caught on security surveillance tapes, resulted in a "pretty bad beating," according to Las Vegas Metropolitan Police. Shakur and his party quickly departed the area as security descended on the scene.

Tupac got in the passenger seat of Knight's black BMW, with Knight behind the wheel. They were one car in a large convoy, including many in Shakur's entourage. After two quick stops, one at the Luxor Hotel to change clothes and a second stop at Knight's Las Vegas home, the entourage headed to Club 662. The streets around the MGM are always crowded on a fight night and this night was no different. As Knight's BMW crawled along, they had to stop at a red light. At about 10:55 p.m., while stopped at that light, Shakur rolled down his window at the request of a photographer, who took the last known photograph of the popular rap star.

As Knight's BMW crawled along, they were again forced to stop at a red light, this time at the corner of Flamingo and Koval Lane. The mood in the BMW was light and they were excited to get to the party. This is probably why no one noticed the white, late-model Cadillac that had pulled up alongside the BMW on the passenger's side. According to a number of the occupants of the car behind Shakur and Knight, the rear window of the Cadillac rolled down and an arm appeared, holding a gun. As they watched in horror, shots were fired through the rear and front doors of the BMW.

As cars began to scatter, Knight, knowing Tupac was badly wounded, tried to get Shakur to safety. He gunned the engine of the bullet-ridden BMW and made a sweeping U-turn, heading toward the Strip. He hit a number of curbs, flattening the tires and bending the rims, but made it to the Strip before turning toward Harmon. Near the corner of Harmon and Las Vegas Boulevard, the BMW stopped and was immediately surrounded by the police.

They initially thought the occupants of the BMW might be the perpetrators and not the victims. Knight was pulled from the BMW and forced down to his stomach on the street, where he was quickly handcuffed. When the bodyguard car arrived moments later, the bodyguards informed the police that Knight was the CEO of a record company and that he was in the car that had been shot at. The police officers immediately removed the handcuffs and, at Knight's urging, rushed to help the injured Shakur. After initially fumbling to get the passenger door open, the police pulled Shakur from the car and put him into an ambulance, which took him to University Medical Center.

Shakur had been hit by four rounds: One bullet hit him in his right hand; another struck his pelvis and ended up in his abdomen. A third bullet struck his thigh, and the fourth and final bullet entered his body under his right arm, into his chest. Knight had suffered a head wound.

Shakur was injured badly, and although he had been shot two times before, he would not survive this shooting. On the afternoon of September 13, 1996, nearly six full days after being shot, Tupac Shakur died of internal bleeding. He was officially pronounced dead at 4:03 p.m.

Impromptu candlelight vigils took place on the corner of Flamingo and Koval, the stoplight where the slain rapper was gunned down. Attendees claimed that the vigils were held not only to remember Shakur, but also to promote "peace and love at a time when gang violence is grabbing headlines."

Since that fateful day in 1996, many people have reported seeing Tupac standing on the corner of Flamingo Road and Koval Lane, the corner where the killing took place. On many occasions, people walking in the area have noticed a young man, head shaved, wearing the same clothes Tupac wore in the picture taken just twenty minutes before he was shot. He is standing, looking at the road, as if trying to see into the white Cadillac that pulled up next to him. Those people who have approached the young man say that as they near him, he disappears. Shakur's ghost is also reported to have been seen on the balcony of Suge Knight's old Las Vegas mansion.

Interestingly, more of Tupac Shakur's music has been released since his death than while he was alive. In all, ten albums were released after his 1996 death, every one of which has gone platinum. Many people have wondered if Shakur knew of his death before it happened. A month before his death, Shakur filmed a music video for the song, "I Ain't Mad at Cha." In the video Shakur is shot six times before dying in an ambulance. Later, as a spirit, he's seen riding around in a limo that resembles Knight's car. When he arrives in Heaven, he is met by comedian Redd Foxx and is invited into a jam session with Miles Davis, Billie Holiday, Marvin Gaye, Nat King Cole, Louis Armstrong, and Jimi Hendrix, among others. As Shakur sings along with the heavenly hosts, it does make a person wonder: Was the video a premonition, or just a strange coincidence?

IN THE PRIME OF HIS LIFE

A young man on top of the world and a world-class poker player both meet their end at a motel in the forgotten part of Las Vegas. One of the two would have an extended stay.

This wasn't the best part of town, but a job was a job and she was happy to have one, even if that job was at the Oasis Motel. The Oasis was located on the Las Vegas Strip—not the glitzy, well-lit part of the Strip that everyone visits when they come to Las Vegas, but the seedy, prostitute-ridden, junkie-strewn, wino-infested habitat tourists only find themselves in when they've strayed too far from the domed canopy of Fremont Street. This area of town was affectionately known as the "Naked City."

The Oasis was by all accounts a run-down, pay-by-the-hour, adult-themed motel nestled between liquor stores, pawnshops, quickie wedding chapels, and similar adult-themed establishments. The sign outside the hotel welcomed guests to the Oasis Fantasy, boasting rooms and adult videos. Cheri Alvarez not only worked as a clerk at the hotel, she also lived there with her husband. Not something she was particularly proud of, but again, a job was a job.

It was a Sunday evening around 9:00 p.m. Cheri was sitting at the front desk, leaning out the window used for evening guests, while talking to one of the lower-end ladies of the evening who went by the name Jasmine. Out of the corner of her eye, she noticed a young man entering the parking lot. He was wearing a khaki shirt, jeans, and black tennis shoes. He had on glasses and was carrying an armful of the escort magazines available for the taking in racks along the Strip.

He smiled as he approached, asking, "Can I get through here?"

"It's not a good idea," Cheri told him. "This area of town isn't the best. It's called the 'Naked City' because there's a lot of crime here. What are you doing in this area anyway?"

"Oh, I'm just out walking," he said, smiling.

"Well, this isn't the safest place you could be."

"You look like a movie star," Jasmine piped in.

"Not me," he answered quickly.

The young man opened one of the escort magazines he was carrying and started looking at the advertisements.

"You won't find anything in there," Jasmine told him. "Those girls are all hookers and the services are nothing but a rip-off."

The young man smiled but continued to look at the girls on the pages.

"Why don't you just give me the money?" Jasmine said. "I'll take care of you, honey."

Cheri thought it best to leave the two alone. Jasmine was just plying her trade and she didn't need anyone hanging around while the price was negotiated, so Cheri went into the adjoining office while the two spoke. Of course, officially, the motel didn't rent rooms to prostitutes; prostitution was, after all, illegal in Las Vegas. Still, everyone knew the score. After a few minutes Jasmine went into the office.

"I need a room," she told Cheri. Cheri took Jasmine's twenty dollars and handed her the key to room number 4. "Look, do me a favor and call me in about ten minutes," Jasmine said, taking the key. "This one's acting a little weird."

Cheri didn't know how Jasmine did it. How she was able to be with so many different men, without knowing anything at all about them. Every time Jasmine took someone into one of the rooms, Cheri just cringed.

When the ten minutes had passed, Cheri called room 4 to check on Jasmine.

"I'm okay," Jasmine said.

Five minutes later Jasmine and the young man exited room 4 and went their separate ways.

Some seven hours later, the young man reappeared at the front desk. This time he was met by Cheri's husband, Juan.

"Can I get one of your fifty-eight-dollar rooms?" the young man asked.

"Sure," Juan said, getting the key to room 20. "How 'bout I give it to you for fifty-five dollars, seeing as it's so late."

"That would be nice, thanks."

The young man didn't appear to be under the influence of drugs or alcohol, but he did seem a little strange. Despite Juan's many attempts to engage him in conversation, the young man didn't respond. He simply took the key, paid the charge with a credit card, and went to his room. A few minutes later Juan watched as the young man walked across the street and entered the nearby 7-Eleven. When the young man returned, he was carrying a white plastic bag. The two made eye contact and a chill went down Juan's spine as the young man looked at him with no expression and entered room 20.

It would be the last time anyone would see David Strickland alive.

They were all set up in room 20, the very room in which David Strickland had been found hanging from a bedsheet. The room hadn't changed much in the intervening years, and the motel had done little to discourage the room from being rented. In fact, as soon as the coroner had completed his work and the police had released the room, it had been cleaned and made available for rent once again—by the hour, of course.

Zak Bagans, one of the stars of the Travel Channel's popular show, *Ghost Adventures,* had gotten permission to film there. He wanted to find some evidence, something that could prove Strickland's ghost still haunted these parts.

The filming crew looked around the room. The bedspread was soiled. The carpet was not one they would want to walk on barefoot. Two large mirrors hung on the wall, by the side of the bed. A television was squirreled away inside a faux-wood cabinet located at the foot of the bed. The beam Strickland had used to hang himself stretched across the ceiling of the room.

"Are you ready?" the cameraman asked.

"I think so. Let the camera run," Zak said.

The cameraman clicked the button on the recorder and pointed it toward the dirty tiles that lined the shower stall. The lights were off in the room, the only light coming from the video recorder itself. He had no sooner started the recording when an orb rose from the bottom of the shower and climbed the wall partway before disappearing.

"Did you see that?" the cameraman yelled out. "I got him! I got Strickland."

David Gordon Strickland Jr. was born on October 14, 1969, in Glen Cove, Long Island, New York, but moved to Princeton, New Jersey, with his family when he was young. While still in high school, Strickland moved to California, landing in Pacific Palisades, a Los Angeles neighborhood. By all accounts Strickland had no intention of getting into acting before he moved to California. However, like so many before him, the lure of Hollywood soon took hold of the six-foot-two Strickland, who joined a theater company instead of going to college.

It was there that the stage called. He started by performing comedy sketches and soon worked his way into parts in *Biloxi Blues, Bye Bye Birdie, Danny and the Deep Blue Sea, Pizza Man,* and *I Won't Dance.* As a member of the theater company, he also worked on a number of student films and soon found that he had a bit of talent in front of the camera. In 1988 he was able to land a guest-starring role on *Roseanne* and another on *Dave's World* in 1993. In 1992 he landed a recurring, five-episode role on the popular sitcom *Mad About You,* playing Hollis, a coworker of Paul Reiser's character, Paul Buchman, at the Explorer Channel. Hollis turns out to be a villain on the show, stabbing Paul Buchman in the back. In 1994 Strickland landed another three-episode, guest-starring role as Dace on *Sister Sister,* a sitcom starring twins Tia and Tamera Mowry.

But Strickland would probably be best known for the role he had at the time of his death, that of Todd Stites, a music critic for the San Francisco–based magazine, *The Gate,* on *Suddenly Susan.* Strickland played a quirky, lovable character who suffered from a short attention span, attributed to his addiction to MTV. The show premiered on September 19, 1996, and was just entering its fourth year when Strickland's body was found. Strickland's character was slated to develop a romance with the show's star, Brooke Shields.

The weekend Strickland hung himself from the beam in room 20, with a king-size bedsheet, a movie in which he had a role opened at the number-one spot. *Forces of Nature* starred Oscar-winning actress Sandra Bullock and Ben Affleck. The film grossed $13.9 million its opening weekend. Strickland played the small role of Steve Montgomery, the hometown suitor of Affleck's fiancée. However, while the role may have been small, his star, as they say, was about to be launched.

But Strickland also had a dark side. On the day Strickland's body was found, he was due to appear in a Los Angeles court to report on his progress in a drug diversion program he had been ordered into. Strickland was arrested on October 31, 1998, and charged with possession of cocaine. He pled "no contest" in December of that same year and was ordered into the program. He also received a thirty-six-month probation. Had Strickland successfully completed the program, the charge would have been stricken from his record.

But drugs were not the actor's only demon. Strickland had been diagnosed with bipolar disorder, a condition which causes severe mood swings that range from the lows of depression to the highs of excessive excitement or enthusiasm. When people are on the low swing, they may feel sad or hopeless. They may lose interest in things that had previously been important to them. In most cases bipolar disorder can be controlled with medications and psychological counseling. Although reports indicated that Strickland was taking the mood stabilizer lithium, it is unknown whether or not he was receiving therapy as well. Unfortunately, when a person is on a high, he or she may stop taking the medication, feeling it is unnecessary. Strickland was one of those people. A few weeks before his death, Strickland was cheerful and eager to discuss his future in an interview he gave.

Strickland arrived in Las Vegas on Saturday, March 20, 1999, but what he did from the time he arrived until he was found dead Monday morning is for the most part unknown. Some reports indicate that he was seen at the downtown strip club, Glitter Gulch, with fellow actor Andy Dick. Dick would later confirm that he had been with Strickland and while he didn't know the young actor very well, Dick said of Strickland "[h]e was fun and he was a great guy."

Checkout time at the Oasis Motel was around 10:00 a.m.—people tended not to stay in the rooms very long. When Cheri didn't see any sign of the young man her husband had checked in the night before, she decided to call the room. The phone rang and rang with no answer on the other end.

"He must be a heavy sleeper," she said to her husband and then decided to go to the room to check on its occupant. Taking the spare key, Cheri walked over to room 20. She stood on the reddish faux stones painted onto the concrete outside the door and knocked loud enough to wake the young man if he was still sleeping. There was still no answer. She knocked again, but this time didn't wait for a response. As she slowly opened the door, Cheri was able to make out a figure, fully clothed, standing in the room. A chair seemed to be knocked over behind him. She was about to apologize for opening the door when she saw the sheet around his neck. As the heavy realization of what she saw gripped her, she screamed.

Juan, hearing the scream, ran to the room, only to find the same sight that awaited his wife. The young man Juan had checked in under the name of David Strickland was hanging from a beam in the center of the room, a sheet tied around his neck. When Juan got over his initial shock, he could see that Strickland was fully clothed and that his feet were still touching the floor.

"He's alive," Juan said, rushing past his wife into the room. Juan ran up to the man hanging from the sheet and started to pull it from around the man's neck. The sheet was tight—too tight—and as Juan tried to release it his hand touched the young man's neck. As soon as Juan touched him, he knew the truth: David Strickland was dead.

"Call the police," he told his wife, who was only too happy to leave the room. While he was waiting for the police to arrive, Juan looked around the room. He saw some empty beer bottles, but could find no sign of drugs, nor did he find a suicide note. The bottles, six of them, were aligned perpendicular to the bed. They were all in line with the base of a table sitting beside the bed.

As Juan entered the bathroom, he saw a sight that made his heart sink. The light fixture that was part of the ceiling fan had been ripped out. Electric wires were dangling and the fixture was still hanging from them. Juan knew the horrible truth: Using the beam hadn't been Strickland's first attempt at taking his life that evening.

Four days later the Alvarezes packed up their belongings and gave their notice to the Oasis Motel. They left town with their four-year-old son, saying, "We came here for a better life, but this is not a good environment."

Strickland wasn't the only famous person to die at the Oasis Motel. On November 22, 1998, only four months before Strickland hung himself, three-time world champion poker player Stu "The Kid" Ungar was found dead in room 6. Ungar was well known for the round, Lennon-like sunglasses he wore while playing. Ungar checked into room 6 on November 20, paying fifty-eight dollars a night. While Ungar had won an estimated $30 million in his career, he also had a severe drug and gambling habit. In 1990 he was found on the floor of his hotel room, suffering from a drug overdose.

While he would eventually recover, his abuse of drugs would take a toll on his body from which he would not be able to recover. "I did coke to keep up," said Ungar in a 1998 issue of *Icon* magazine. "You use it as an excuse to stay up and play poker, but then you take it home with you."

Months after this interview appeared, Ungar was found lying on the bed of room 6, with $800 in his pocket. He had just signed a contract with casino mogul Bob Stupak to assume all his debts and to front his play.

Why would Stu Ungar, a world-class poker player, stay in a run-down motel in the middle of one of the worst areas of town? Then again, why would David Strickland, a young actor with a seemingly bright future, take his own life? "We handle three hundred suicides a year, and you can ask the same question about nearly all of them," coroner Ron Flud said in 1999.

According to some reports, Jasmine whispered something prophetic to Strickland before they parted ways. "Important changes are going to happen in your life," she allegedly told him. The coroner was able to place Strickland's death at around 4:00 a.m.

An employee of the Oasis Motel firmly believes that room 20 is haunted. Whether it's Strickland or someone else, he can't say. What he can say is that every evening he can hear a man crying out from the room. The man starts his cry at around one in the morning and stops promptly at four. The voice says only two words.

"Help me."

THE LAST TIME AROUND

Bobby Hatfield was a successful member of the singing duo the Righteous Brothers. While he had a series of successes, he also had a dark secret—one that would eventually cost him his life. Still, he achieved all his dreams, including the first one he ever had: to be good enough to play in Las Vegas.

It was strange being back in Las Vegas on the Orleans Hotel Casino stage, but it had been Bobby's favorite town to perform in and it seemed fitting to do the tribute concert there. Bill Medley was apprehensive about going onstage without his longtime partner. He wondered if the crowd would appreciate his solo effort, or if he'd even be able to get through the first song. As he stood behind the curtain, waiting to go onstage, his mind drifted back to that day in 2003, when he was first told of the tragedy.

The show was scheduled to start in fifty minutes, and his partner was nowhere to be found.

"This is typical," Medley said under his breath, pacing back and forth. The two had just started their reunion tour and there he was, standing in Miller Auditorium in Kalamazoo, Michigan, on the campus of Western Michigan University, half of the famous Righteous Brothers.

"Has anybody tried to call him?" Medley asked.

"I've tried," their manager David Cohen told him.

"Is he even in the building?" Medley asked.

"I don't think so," David said.

"Well, maybe someone should go to his hotel room and find out where he is!" He remembered being as angry with Hatfield as he had ever been. While the two had gotten back together, Medley wasn't sure that his partner had beaten his cocaine addiction. In fact, he'd had a sneaking suspicion that Bobby Hatfield was still using and that this was probably the reason he wasn't there yet. He remembered growing increasingly worried about Hatfield's well-being.

Medley had paced even more as the auditorium filled with 2,400 anxious fans ready to hear the songs they had grown to love. Hits like "You've Lost That Lovin' Feelin'" and "Unchained Melody." He remembered nervously primping in the mirror, ready to read Bobby the riot act as soon as the concert ended.

It was close to twenty minutes later when Cohen returned. He had a morbid look and seemed to be having a hard time looking Medley in the face.

"What is it?" Medley had asked him.

"It's Hatfield," he started.

"What? Don't tell me he's in no shape to perform," Medley said.

"He's dead, Bill."

The news had struck Medley like a kick to the gut. "What do you mean, 'He's dead'?"

"He's dead. Bobby Hatfield is dead."

And now, years later, here he was again—half of the famous Righteous Brothers—about to go onstage and sing a tribute to Bobby Hatfield. Medley took a deep breath as he was announced. He smiled, said a quick prayer, and headed onto the stage. When he started the first song, the crowd cheered loudly and Medley began to relax. As Medley sang the songs that made the two of them famous, it was hard to believe his longtime friend and partner was gone. In fact, it felt as if Bobby Hatfield was standing there in his usual spot, right beside him. When the show ended, tears came to Medley's eyes as the crowd rose in a standing ovation.

Medley called the entire band to the front of the stage to take their bows. As they waved, acknowledging the cheers from the crowd, they heard a loud pop coming from above their collective heads.

Fearing for their safety, the band members jumped backward as shards of glass fell onto the stage. They all looked up and saw that one of the Par cans had exploded through the gel. A strange feeling fell over the group when it realized it was the Par can that would have been over the head of Bobby Hatfield if he'd been in his usual position onstage.

Robert Lee Hatfield was born on August 19, 1940, in Beaver Dam, Wisconsin. When he was four years old, he moved with his family to Anaheim, California. The entertainment bug bit Hatfield when he was only a third grader, as he sang "Shortnin' Bread" on a local radio show. Hatfield was a gifted athlete and very popular in school. He was student body president and played on his high school's baseball team. Hatfield was so talented that he was even scouted by the LA Dodgers.

Hatfield also sang in his high school chorus. One year he was asked to be the master of ceremonies for his high school's talent show, when a last-minute decision changed his life.

"Two days prior to the show, for some ungodly reason, I decided to sing. I was never so scared in my life and also never so thankful that I had dark pants on! I sang Johnny Mathis's 'Chances Are,' and even though I thought the sound of my knees banging together was drowning out my voice, I managed to pull it off."

In 1959, when Hatfield graduated high school, he decided not to sign up with the Dodgers. Instead, he was determined to pursue a career in entertainment. Bobby Hatfield would meet Bill Medley in 1962 when the two were brought together by Johnny Wimber as part of a five-piece band known as the Paramours. Wimber was the keyboard player. As legend has it, the band was playing one night in a local bar when a Black marine shouted out "That was righteous, brothers!" after one of their duets. The pair took the name and the Righteous Brothers were born.

Hatfield and Medley didn't have dreams of topping the charts, or even of being inducted into the Rock and Roll Hall of Fame. Their only dream was to be good enough to play in Las Vegas.

"When we started out, rock 'n' roll was thought to be only a fad," Medley once said. "Some DJs were even smashing their records of this so-called 'devil music,' so we were always talking about what we'd do next."

As the Paramours they released a single, "There She Goes (She's Walking Away)," on the Moonglow label in December of 1962. Within three months the Paramours disbanded, leaving Hatfield and Medley to carry on as the Righteous Brothers. They were a perfect match. Medley's rich bass and Hatfield's gospel-inflected tenor created a harmonic blend that was not only unique, its depth of soul often made people think they were listening to two Black men. It also helped that they were two of the few white people in California who were into rhythm and blues. "We weren't out there playing surf music," Hatfield once stated in an interview.

They recorded their first album and had a minor hit with "Little Latin Lupe Lu." While it may have been a minor hit, it caught the attention of record producer Phil Spector. The Righteous Brothers recorded two more albums before Spector bought out their contract and signed them to his Philles label. It was with Spector that their fame would be solidified.

The year 1964 was a good one for the harmonic duo. Not only did they open for such acts as the Beatles and the Rolling Stones, they were also regulars on ABC-TV's *Shindig!* It was that same year that the pair's Vegas dreams came true.

They were performing three shows a night in the lounge of the famous Sands Hotel (the place the Rat Pack made famous). They were also spending a lot of time in the recording studio. It was during one of these recording sessions that they produced one of their most famous singles, "You've Lost That Lovin' Feelin'." The song was written by Barry Mann and Cynthia Weil specifically for the Righteous Brothers.

"We had no idea if it would be a hit," Medley stated in an interview. "It was too slow, too long, and right in the middle of the Beatles and the British Invasion." Not only would the song become a hit, it would also have the most important quality a song can have—staying power. The song entered the Top 40 the day after Christmas that same year, hitting number one two months later. Songs at the time were short, typically two or three minutes at the most. However, this song was four minutes long, sparking Medley's concern about the length. To prevent radio DJs from refusing to play the song, Spector listed it on the label with a running time of three minutes and five seconds. The song would eventually be listed as the most played song on the radio, with more than eight million recorded plays.

The group was on a high. They would break the *Billboard* Top 10 four more times in the next fifteen months. In 1965 they became the first act to have three albums in the Top 20 at the same time, with *Right Now* and *Some Blue-Eyed Soul* on the Moonglow label and *You've Lost That Lovin' Feelin'* on the Philles label. Hearing them sing and, after realizing they were white, a radio DJ took the phrase "blue-eyed soul" from their song, and used it to describe their sound.

Spector tried repeating the process that had created the hit, even employing the soulful songwriter Carole King to write songs for the duo. King, with Gerry Goffin, wrote a song called "Hung on You." Spector allowed the duo to proceed, unrestrained, on the call-and-answer portion of the song, which was sung mostly together. While "Hung on You" was masterfully recorded, it didn't catch on with DJs. Instead, they chose to play the B side of the record, which contained a solo Hatfield had recorded. The song, "Unchained Melody," became a huge success, reaching number four on the Top 40 charts.

Hatfield and Medley were the best of friends. Hatfield reportedly had a wonderful sense of humor and took every opportunity available to make his family laugh. One year, after having his picture taken with Elvis Presley, Hatfield used the photo as his Christmas card, writing on the card, "From Elvis and the King."

By the end of 1965, relations with Spector were not going well and the pair decided that a clean split with the record producer was in their best interest. They almost immediately signed on with Verve Records, who allowed them to produce their own work. They released "(You're My) Soul and Inspiration," written by Mann and Weil. The song quickly topped the US charts. They had a string of minor hits before breaking up in 1968.

Hatfield made an unsuccessful attempt at a movie career in the films *Swingin' Summer* and *Beach Ball*, both of which he acted in with Medley. He also appeared in the made-for-TV movie, *The Ballad of Andy Crocker*, with the hopes of it becoming a series. It didn't.

In 1969 Hatfield tried to re-form the Righteous Brothers, asking Jimmy Walker of the Knickerbockers to replace Bill Medley. The new duo released only one album before disbanding. However, in 1974, Hatfield and Medley reunited, signing with Haven Records. While it had been six years since the two had performed together, it was like no time had passed. Their voices were still in sync and they produced a number-three hit with "Rock and Roll Heaven." The duo produced a couple of albums and toured heavily for the next two years.

Hatfield and Medley weren't heard from again until they were asked to perform for *American Bandstand*'s twenty-fifth anniversary. The success of their performance sparked another tour. Then in 1986, the film *Top Gun* brought their hit "You've Lost That Lovin' Feelin'" to a whole new audience. A year later, in 1987, Medley sang a duet with Jennifer Warnes called "(I've Had) The Time of My Life." The song was from the film *Dirty Dancing* and, like the movie, was an immediate hit. The soundtrack from the movie became the most successful since *Saturday Night Fever*, selling fourteen million copies.

The day before Hatfield died, Linda, his wife of thirty-two years, drove him to the airport. She kissed him and wished him a good trip. Hatfield called her later that day, asking her to do him a favor.

"That depends on what it is," she told him.

"Can you please take a minute out of your busy schedule and call our dentist and tell him that I'm in Kalamazoo, Michigan, and I won't be able to make my appointment in an hour?"

She laughed and told him, "I think I can do that."

A couple of hours later, he called her and told her to make sure she watched *Wheel of Fortune* with her mother because he thought it was funny. It would be the last words he would ever speak to Linda.

The next day she got another phone call.

"Honey, it's Bill," Medley said to her.

"Yeah, I know your voice," she said.

Medley then told her the worst news a wife could ever hear. He had previously called friends so that Linda would have a support unit as she tried to deal with the news. Not willing to have her children find out the news through the media, Linda frantically called each of them to deliver the devastating news. "It seemed like it took forever to get in touch with them," Linda said.

Medley called Linda throughout the night. No one in the band would leave Hatfield until they were sure he would be coming home. Medley told Linda, "We have been together for forty-two years and we're not going to leave him here alone." Medley and the band brought Hatfield's body home that Friday. When the band met with Linda, they joked that if Hatfield had any idea he was going to die in Kalamazoo, Michigan, he would have already come up with fifty jokes about it.

Robert Lee Hatfield died on November 5, 2003, at the age of sixty-three. He and Medley had been inducted into the Rock and Roll Hall of Fame by Billy Joel only eight months earlier. The reason for Hatfield's death was originally listed as heart failure due to advanced coronary disease. It was eventually amended to acute cocaine intoxication.

"Bobby and I were like an old married couple. Most of all," said Medley, "what I'm going to miss is looking to my right and seeing my friend."

The services for Hatfield lasted close to two and a half hours. It was held at Mariners Church in Irvine with family, friends, and fellow artists in attendance. "The whole world is a fan of Bobby's music," said close friend Roy Hardick. "But only a fortunate few of us got to know him as a person."

Hatfield's daughter Vallyn spoke of her parents' relationship. "They were perfect for each other," she said, trembling as she spoke. Then, in true Hatfield style, she brought laughter into the mix, saying, "I finally got my dad to come to church with me today," and then after reflecting added, "I thought it would be my wedding, not his funeral. Not so soon. In a way, I'm happy because he's with

God now," she continued. "I will be with him someday. I will always be your little girl, Dad."

Not everybody gets the chance to sing at his own funeral, but Hatfield did. As a nearly forty-year-old video played of Hatfield, singing "Unchained Melody," the crowd was brought to tears.

The night the Par can fell in front of Bill Medley and his band was not the only time Hatfield's presence was felt on the stage at the Orleans Hotel Casino. "I would feel someone walk by and brush my hair," said an employee who worked with the Righteous Brothers. "When I turned around, there wouldn't be anyone there."

Orleans Hotel Casino employees have also reported seeing a man walking down the hallway near the stage in a patterned shirt, much like the ones Hatfield was known to wear. They also noted one occasion when nothing in the showroom seemed to be working properly; this was specifically noted by the lighting person, who couldn't get his board to work correctly. The crew knew the cause of the problems when one of them remembered it was Hatfield's birthday.

Maybe Hatfield took a cue from the film that made his song "Unchained Melody" a renewed success in 1990. The movie, *Ghost*, starred Patrick Swayze, who, coincidentally, played a ghost in the title role.

Before Hatfield's death, he and Medley had discussed making their current tour the last one they would do. They even had a name for it: "The Last Time Around."

STRANGE OCCURRENCES IN SIN CITY

LAS VEGAS IS KNOWN FOR TWO THINGS: entertainment and gambling. In this part of our tour, we'll concentrate on some of Las Vegas's haunted hotel and casinos. We'll spend some time in one of the most haunted hotels in Las Vegas, then return to the showroom, now long gone, where the Rat Pack played to a packed house two times a night. We'll visit a casino, designed in the style of ancient Egypt, with a curse that may have been brought on by its designers. Then we'll hit a haunted Tiki bar before heading to a spot where a controversial casino once stood and a musician never left.

Also in this part of our tour we'll leave the hotel and casinos for a moment and travel to the outskirts of the city to visit Las Vegas's own ghost town. Then we'll head to the oldest high school in Las Vegas and meet Mr. Petrie, a phantom who roams the theater, keeping students in line and playing a prank or two in the process.

So grab your EMF meter, night-vision camera, and voice recorder and get ready to experience some Vegas-style paranormal phenomena.

THE BEST ROOM IN THE HOUSE

In a hotel that once catered to the vices of the men and women working on the Boulder Dam, one room hides the secrets of a sordid past. Even though the hotel was long left vacant, it still enjoyed a thriving clientele; however, not all guests came in through the front door.

Robert had just started in surveillance. A new property meant new experiences and new layouts to learn. So, he decided to take a walk around just to get to know the place. Binion's Horseshoe was actually made up of three different properties: the Eldorado Club, the Mint, and the Hotel Apache. The latter was a three-story hotel built in 1932 to welcome workers from the dam who came to Las Vegas on their days off. The lure of gambling, alcohol, and other vices—all outlawed in neighboring Boulder City—presented an exciting diversion from the hard work and long hours spent building the largest dam in American history.

Robert had checked out most of the property over his first two weeks but had a few more places yet to visit. He left the surveillance room, which led into the hallway on the second floor of the Hotel Apache—then known as the East Hotel—which had been shut down to guests in 2009 due to the recession. As he came around the corner of the dark hallway, something stopped him dead in his tracks.

At first, he wasn't sure he saw it. The hallway was, after all, mostly dark in an effort to save money and avoid a power bill. But he had seen it all right. There in the eerie glow of the emergency lights was a dark shadow in the shape of a body—a human body. It had come out of the wall and was making its way across the hallway. Robert didn't move. Unsure what to do, he simply watched the apparition as it crossed the hall and disappeared into the adjacent wall.

That was when he heard the music.

> *Like the beat, beat, beat of the tom-tom*
> *When the jungle shadows fall*
> *Like the tick, tick, tock of the stately clock*
> *As it stands against the wall*
> *Like the drip, drip, drip of the raindrops*
> *When the summer shower is through*

He started to make his way down the hall, stepping toward the origin of the sound, the music that was echoing down the hall.

Day and night, night and day, why is it so
That this longing for you follows wherever I go
In the roaring traffic's boom
In the silence of my lonely room

He rested an ear on the door of room 227. He was definitely hearing music. But it wasn't normal music; that is, it wasn't music of the times. No, it was music that would have fit right well in the hotel when it was opened in 1932. But there was only one problem: there was no power in the hotel or any of the rooms. Which meant there would be no way to operate a radio, record player, or any other electronic device. So where was the music coming from?

One of the oldest hotels in Las Vegas, the Hotel Apache opened in March of 1932 with the express purpose of giving a break to the workers who were building the Boulder—later called Hoover—Dam. Most of those workers lived in Boulder City, a government run town purposely built to house those very workers. Being a government town, Boulder City did not allow such vices as gambling, alcohol, and certainly not prostitution. Las Vegas, therefore, proved to be a nice diversion to workers after a long and hard week on the job.

Built by dam Cement Contractor P. O. Silvagni, the three-story Hotel Apache was considered luxury in its time. This was likely because each and every one of its 81 rooms came complete with its own private bathroom, the casino floor was carpeted, and the lobby had air conditioning—the first in Las Vegas. It also had an anomaly at the time: the valley's first electric elevator. In 1932, the Hotel Apache was as much a mega-resort as is the Mirage, Caesars Palace, or Resort World today.

But even from it beginning, the Hotel Apache kept it secrets. One of those was a room at the top of the hotel known as room 400. Although listed on the original plans as the "Penthouse," room 400 was not accessible to the general public. In fact, the guests of the hotel wouldn't even know the room existed. This is because the elevator didn't even go to that room. In fact, it stopped on the third floor. When the hotel was remodeled, it was found that room 400 contained a couple secrets of its own, and the front door wasn't the only portal to the room. In fact, there were two additional doors: one in the closet that led to a stairway and the other in the bathroom below the sink that led to an area not included on the original hotel prints. This second door leads to an area that currently houses the heating, venting, and air conditioning units, known as HVAC. Why it is connected to the room is anyone's guess.

One explanation for the extra doors might be that room 400 had once been used for something not in Silvagni's original plans: a count room. At the end of the day, every casino brings all the money that was taken in the that day to one room to be counted and sorted into various denominations. That room is known as the count room. Who is allowed to go in and out of a count room is heavily controlled and these doors may have been used as additional access points. When the mob ruled Las Vegas, the count rooms were where the skim took place. That is, where the mobsters took a portion of the money coming in before it was counted and these extra doors may have been used for the skim.

Room 400 has been hesitant to welcome guests. Though it has seen the likes of Humphrey Bogart, Lucille Ball, and Clark Gable, the room seems unwilling to welcome just any old person. Hotel rooms all over the world typically have locks on the doors to prevent unwanted visitors and to protect the guests inside. Las Vegas is no exception. When the Apache reopened, the management decided to allow guests to stay in room 400, but every time they placed a lock on the room—the same lock they had used for every other room in the hotel—it didn't work. Apparently, something or someone inside the room didn't appreciate the lock, or maybe they just didn't want visitors.

Robert's experience with the second floor "guests" wasn't the only one he had in the Apache Hotel. During the remodeling of the hotel, Robert was in the hallway when he heard a knocking coming from a door. Startled, he took a step back, but had the presence of mind to pull out his phone and begin recording. As he did, the knocking stopped so he stopped the recording, and as he did, he once again heard a faint knock coming from the door. He started recoding again, saying, "Somebody's trying to get out from this door," and as soon as the words left his mouth, the knocking grew louder and more rhythmic. The door was one of those secret doors that led to room 400, which, at the time, was not operational and no construction was taking place in the room.

Those who have stayed there have often reported the door to room 400 creaking, as if being opened, before the handle is even touched or the door moved. But room 400 isn't the only place paranormal activity has occurred in the Hotel Apache. A security officer patrolling the halls on the third floor when the hotel was shut down reported hearing a demonic voice ordering him to "Get out!" The shaken officer went to his supervisor, hoping it was just another of the tricks he liked to play and when that supervisor said it wasn't him, they both returned to the floor where the officer reported hearing the voice. Almost immediately, fear fell upon both men. "You could just feel something here that didn't want us here," said the supervisor, who admitted he was afraid. "We ended up talking out loud and saying a prayer just to say, hey, we're here doing our job. Just leave us alone. We're going to leave now." The supervisor also admitted that every time he is on the floor he gets an eerie feeling.

Another incident happened to the assistant director of food and beverage. It was around 3 a.m. and he was working in his office, which was in the basement of the building, a room that was once used by the hotel's butcher. Suddenly all the computers shut off and then every photo on the walls fell to the floor. None of the photos were broken and all of them left the distinct markings on the wall that indicated they had been in their exact locations for many years. Next to the office is the meat cooler. One day the director of purchasing escorted a medium around the property. When they arrived at the meat cooler, the medium refused to step inside, saying, "No. I'm not going in there."

According to Zak Bagans, owner of Zak Bagans: The Haunted Museum and host of TLC's *Ghost Adventures*, "There are secret tunnels . . . escape routes. It is a hotbed for activity. Deaths, suicides, murder . . . you name it. It happened right up here," he said about the hotel, calling it, "One of the most haunted locations in Nevada."

But you don't have to take Zak Bagan's word for it, you can try it for yourself, since the hotel is currently open and fully functional. If you're the daring kind, you can even rent one of the hotel's ghost-hunting kits and ask to stay in room 400.

A CASINO'S CURSE

Why do bad things keep happening at one of the most notable casinos in Las Vegas? Was it poorly designed construction, or something far more sinister? And why did the hotel almost completely change its theme?

"Two!" he yelled, looking at the drawings on the papyrus scrolls spread out before him. "There must be two Hor-em-Akhet!"

"Two Hor-em-Akhet cost money," the royal bookkeeper explained. "The Pharaoh's coffers are not endless."

"But the pyramid must be protected," the architect protested.

"Yes, and that is what the Hor-em-Akhet will do."

"This one is facing east. Do you understand? East."

"Yes, and facing the east, does not the Hor-em-Akhet represent the circle of life?"

"Of course it does. But two Hor-em-Akhet are necessary. They must be placed here and here," he said, pointing alternately to either side of the pyramid, emphasizing each position with a hard jab of his finger. "The constellation of Leo is rising from the horizon. Do you not see it? It is the first dawning of spring. The *two* lions," he said, "must be placed with one toward the east and one toward the west."

"It took only one Hor-em-Akhet to defeat Seth, lord of the underworld. How many do you think it will take to protect one pharaoh?"

"One Hor-em-Akhet may have defeated the fearful Seth, but he is not the only threat to the Pharaoh. One Hor-em-Akhet will protect against the darkness. But the east is only half of the horizon, half of yesterday and tomorrow. Do you not understand? There must be *two!* Two Hor-em-Akhet are needed to protect the pyramid. You tell our lord Pharaoh Khufu, if he wants to be protected in this earthly existence, as well as his journey through the next, he had better authorize two Hor-em-Akhet. You tell him, if he doesn't, he is only inviting disaster."

It felt like they had waited forever. The line for the Nile River Tour ride had wrapped around half the casino. Security had created makeshift lines by placing stations throughout the floor of the casino. They even had to position a security officer between two sets of stations so that casino guests not on the ride were able to navigate around the lines. But they had heard so much about this ride and they were determined to take it while they were in Las Vegas.

It was finally their turn and the two women found it hard to contain their excitement as they boarded the boat designed to resemble an ancient Egyptian barge. Erin slid into her seat and readied her camera as Katherine slid in next to her. The ride was not the typical thrill ride found at most tourist attractions. In fact, the women didn't even have to wear seat belts. Instead, the ride slowly wound its way around the first floor of the casino, following an elaborate canal that had been cut into the floor and filled with water.

"We are about to enter the temple of Ramesses the second," the tour guide announced as the barge passed replicas of pharaohs sitting on chairs, their hands resting on their own legs. The pharaohs were surrounded by columns.

"Isn't this exciting?" Erin said to Katherine, who quickly agreed. "I know these artifacts are replicas, but they are simply amazing!"

The two women took pictures and pointed out the images to each other as those images were explained by the tour guide. The barge made its way around the casino, through the Temple of Amun and around toward the dark tunnel. As the barge entered the tunnel, Erin suddenly felt a chill and involuntarily wrapped her arms around herself. "Did it just get cold in here?" she asked.

"It sure seems like it," Katherine replied.

"It's probably just the water and the tunnel," Erin said to herself more than anyone.

It was at that moment she saw him. He was floating just above the water and as the barge drew closer, he reached out to her. At first she didn't realize what was happening; after all, why would a man be standing in the water? But as the man came closer, Erin leaned back against Katherine to avoid his grasp, and as she did, Katherine turned toward her. When Katherine saw the man floating in the water, she screamed.

On October 15, 1993, at 4:00 a.m., the Luxor opened, eighteen months after ground was broken. The resort cost $375 million to build and, as was the style at the time in Las Vegas, it looked like a bit of Egypt on the Las Vegas Strip, mainly because it was shaped like a pyramid. "You have to give credit to the creative people who suggested a pyramid and those who didn't laugh," Nevada Gaming

Commission Chairman Bill Curran said when the hotel opened. "Lesser people would have said it can't be done."

At the time, the Luxor was the tallest structure in Las Vegas. It is roughly three-quarters scale of the Great Pyramid. It contains more than 2,500 rooms and is thirty stories, making it 350 feet tall, but it isn't the only spectacular part of the resort. The front walkway contains replicas of ram-headed sphinxes just like those located in the Egyptian city of Luxor during King Tut's reign, around 1300 BC. It also has one 110-foot sphinx at the front of the hotel facing the famous Strip, meant to replicate the Great Sphinx at Giza, and a 140-foot obelisk positioned in front of the sphinx. Interestingly enough, the name Luxor came from the Egyptian city of Thebes, which did not have pyramids.

As intriguing as the hotel is on the outside, it is equally stunning on the inside. When it was first built in the mid-1990s, the Luxor featured museum-quality exhibits created by Egyptologists hired by the resort to authenticate reproductions of Egyptian ornamentation. Hieratic-carved light posts throughout the casino contained actual Egyptian writings. The front lobby was a replica of the temple at Abu Simbel, complete with four colossal statues of Ramses. It also boasted the world's largest atrium at the time. On the casino level, a man-made replica of the Nile River—five times as long as the pyramid is high—took guests on a historic tour through ancient Egypt.

The Egyptian theme continued on the 100,000-square-foot casino floor, with more than 2,500 slot machines, 82 table games, a poker room, and a race and sports book. Even the slot machines got into the spirit of things. Guests pulled the handles of machines called "Pharaoh's Gold," "Treasures of Tutankhamen," "Pyramid," and "Valley of Kings." One device even allowed gamblers to place wages on tiny Egyptian barges that raced around a watery oval track.

The Luxor is also a technological wonder. The pyramid shape of the hotel made the installation of standard elevators impossible. Instead, the Luxor uses inclinators, which are a type of elevator that travels at a 39-degree angle. The inclinators move passengers side to side instead of up and down. The top level of the pyramid contains a facade that looks like a modern city, giving the subtle feeling of the ancient Egyptian first floor being an underground archaeological dig. This top floor was complete with a $50 million ride, called "Secrets of the Luxor Pyramid." The interactive ride used movie and motion effects to take passengers on a journey through time to find a stolen, magical Egyptian treasure. The most notable technological advancement, however, is likely the 42.3 billion candlepower light that shines atop the pyramid, blasting upward into the sky. This light is so powerful that it can be seen from space.

But the Luxor faced challenges almost from the beginning—challenges that many believe were the result of a curse placed on the casino from the start. Some place the source of the curse on the life-size sphinx that faces the Las Vegas Strip. While the sphinx is a replica of the one protecting the Great Pyramid, evidence seems to indicate that two sphinxes are needed to truly protect the pyramid. Between the paws of the ancient Sphinx in Egypt lies a *stele*—an upright stone slab—that depicts two sphinxes placed back to back to protect the pyramid. If two sphinxes are necessary, and if one is facing east, shouldn't a second sphinx be facing west? Some Egyptologists believe that a second sphinx once guarded the Great Pyramid along with the first; however, unlike the existing sphinx, the westward-facing sphinx wasn't buried by sand. Instead of being protected by the elements, as was the case with the eastward-facing sphinx, the westward-facing sphinx was, over the years, destroyed by erosion.

Others believe the ground that the Luxor sits on is cursed. The Luxor is built on a swampy piece of land, one which would eventually cause its sister property, Mandalay Bay, to partially sink after it was built. Many old-time residents of Las Vegas claim the land was routinely used by the Mob as a dumping ground for those who found themselves on the wrong side of a Mob-related conflict. This may explain the middle-aged man in the striped brown suit who has been seen wandering the hallways of the upper floors. According to those who have encountered him, if you don't get out of his way, he will simply walk right through you, leaving you feeling frigidly cold. Others claim he will simply disappear. However, all agree that the man seems angry and deep in thought.

No matter what the cause, the Luxor experienced setbacks and tragedies almost from the start. The County Commission—who, according to Circus Circus Enterprises Chairman William Bennett, didn't know how to build a pyramid—changed its requirements for fire precautions after twelve floors of the hotel had already been built. Bennett estimated that the county's requirements cost the resort an extra $7 million. "If the county had required those safety precautions from the start, it would have only cost $1.3 million," Bennett said.

In 1997 the Luxor, in an attempt to make its black-glass pyramid stand out at night, signed an agreement with Bee Inc. to install lights that would illuminate the four corners of the Luxor's pyramid. The system suffered from "numerous design flaws, construction flaws, and unscheduled power shutdowns," according to Luxor executives who complained that the system wasn't completely operational and that it suffered from faulty equipment. They eventually filed suit against Bee Inc. in 2003.

At least one worker lost his life while building the pyramid and several others were injured. Many workers who arrived on-site during construction refused to go back once they had spent time in the pyramid, because they considered the property jinxed. In fact, guests have complained that the property seems to have a strange feeling, one that lifts once they walk outside. This feeling might possibly be caused by the ghost of the construction worker who is the most notable permanent resident of the hotel.

In fact, death seems to be a constant visitor to the Luxor, in the form of suicides and murders. Not long after the hotel was opened, in 1996, a young woman rode the inclinators to the twenty-sixth floor of the hotel. The unique shape of the structure afforded her a view of the entire casino below. The woman climbed onto the railing of the balcony, sitting with her feet dangling off the edge. She gazed down at the people below and then jumped to her death, landing directly in front of the all-you-can-eat buffet. Many have reported seeing a sad young woman dressed in red walking around the area where the buffet once stood.

Another death occurred when a young man either committed suicide or was simply unlucky. According to some reports, the man was showing off to his girl-friend by hanging onto the outside edge of the balcony railing. Because most people don't look up, he wasn't noticed as he teased his girlfriend, threatening to jump if she wouldn't marry him. Whether that was the case or not is unknown. What is known is that the young man did fall, landing on the floor in front of the reservation desk. This young man's ghost is said to walk the casino floor.

In 1997 a California man was arrested and charged with killing a sixteen-year-old prostitute in his room at the hotel. According to police reports, Michael Hathaway met Sara Gruber at the bar. He took her to his room where he sexually assaulted the underage girl and eventually strangled her. She was found at 9:00 a.m. by the guest room attendant who had entered the room to clean it. Gruber had a false Arizona ID in the name of Alana Alvarado, which showed her to be twenty-one. An autopsy determined that Gruber died from asphyxiation by strangulation.

In 2004 MGM Mirage bought the Luxor and the rest of the Mandalay Resort Group, once known as Circus Circus Properties. It almost immediately funded an estimated $300 million makeover of the resort, removing many of the artifacts and the Egyptian-themed decor that had decorated so much of the casino. The Nile River Tour, whose initial purpose was actually to transport guests to the inclinators, was removed completely, some say because of the number of guests who reported seeing ghosts at the entrance to the tunnel.

Many claim that the makeover was an attempt to remove the curse that seemed to loom over the casino. However, Luxor President and Chief Operating Officer Felix Rappaport, who helped oversee the property's makeover, stated, "The competition has just moved by it. You didn't have to be a rocket scientist to realize that it needed to be freshened up."

While the casino kept its Egyptian theme on the outside, almost 80 percent of the interior was changed. However, the changes do not seem to have had an impact on the curse. In 2005 famous musicians Frankie Valli and the Four Seasons cut short their three-week engagement at the Luxor, saying, "Some people just don't live up to the deals they create."

In 2007 a man placed a bomb on a car in the parking garage, hoping to kill his ex-girlfriend and the man she was currently dating. Caren Chali was walking with her boyfriend to their car in the parking garage when the boyfriend noticed that something had been placed on the hood. Not realizing it was a bomb, the boyfriend removed the device and, as he did, the bomb went off, taking half of the man's hand with it and sending a metal fragment into his head, killing him. Chali was not harmed in the incident.

In June of 2010 a University of Nevada, Las Vegas football player was killed in an altercation with a mixed martial arts fighter in one of the rooms at the Luxor. The two friends were staying in a suite at the hotel when twenty-five-year-old Jason Sindelar got into a confrontation with his girlfriend at a party being held in the suite. DeMario Reynolds approached Sindelar and asked him to leave. The drunken Sindelar slapped his girlfriend and attempted to grab her by the throat. That was when Reynolds grabbed Sindelar in a bear hug, telling him, "I don't want to fight with you; I love you." When Sindelar calmed down, Reynolds let him go, only to be attacked by Sindelar. While the fight was broken up, Sindelar, after a short rest on the couch, again attacked Reynolds, this time dragging him to the ground as he hit him. Reynolds would not recover from the incident.

Also in 2010, a dancer in the Luxor's "Fantasy" show didn't show up for practice one Sunday. A roommate reported thirty-one-year-old Deborah Flores-Narvaez missing and contacted her sister when Flores-Narvaez didn't show. While Flores-Narvaez stated in her online biography, "I'm blessed with a substantial amount of common sense," she would eventually be found dead at the hands of her volatile boyfriend, who encased her in concrete after he killed her.

It would appear that removing the Egyptian artifacts and the overall theme has done little to change the curse. Bad things continue to happen and ghosts can still be found on the property. During the renovation process the buffet was moved to an entirely different location; however, the ghost of the lady who leapt to her death can still be seen wandering around the area where the buffet was originally located.

Many believe that the source of the curse is the missing westward-facing Sphinx. Others claim that the curse won't be released until an artificial eye is placed at the capstone of the pyramid. They believe that the Eye of Providence, or all-seeing eye, would represent God watching over the resort.

ONE LAST SOLO

On the night of the opening of the first desegregated hotel casino in Las Vegas, a young saxophonist who dreams of stardom is found dead. It would be an ominous opening for a hotel that seemed doomed from the start.

It was finally going to happen. He was finally going to make it big—and in Las Vegas of all places, the town the world was just starting to discover. It was opening night of the Moulin Rouge, Vegas's first Black casino. If he could make it here, the world would be his oyster. He had been playing the saxophone almost since he was able to move his fingers and blow into the mouthpiece. Everyone told him he had a gift and he was going to make the most of it. He had been playing nightclubs all across the country, some of them nice, many of them seamy, but none that would launch him into the spotlight he so wished for.

It wasn't easy for a man of color to make it in America in 1955. While the civil rights movement was starting to gain momentum, in most cases he was only allowed to play to Black audiences. While some whites might sneak in to see the performances, they were not in any way the norm. In just another month a photo of two Black showgirls from this very casino would grace the cover of *Life* magazine. Jazz was making its presence known, and the young musician dreamed of following in the footsteps of Louis Armstrong, Henry "Red" Allen, and Clarence "Frogman" Henry, who were blowing audiences away nightly in New Orleans.

Looking in the mirror, he tightened the shiny black tie around his neck and slid on his black suit jacket over his white shirt. He was happy that he had good eyesight and didn't have to wear those thick black-framed glasses that were so popular. He was brushing back his hair when a knock came at the door.

"It's opening night," the young Black man said. "You ready?"

"Man, I was born ready."

"You were born cocky, that much is for sure." The young man was a fellow member of the band. He was dressed in the same clothes, right down to the shiny black tie. "You done any relaxing?" he asked.

"Ain't done nothin' yet. You got some?"

"Don't I always?" he said, holding up a bag that was partially filled with a green, leafy plant.

"Well, get on in here," he said, rubbing his hands together.

"No can do. We got a party to get to."

"Now? Is there time?"

"There's always time for a party. C'mon. A bunch of us are getting together over at Sheila's room. We can do our relaxin' there 'til it's time to go on."

The two men walked over to the back side of the hotel and onto the top floor. They could hear the music even before they got to the door, which sat partially open. As they stepped inside, they found the room full of musicians, singers, those who loved to hang with musicians, and those who were just there for the marijuana. A smoke-filled haze, a mixture of pot and cigarettes, permeated the room, making it a little hard to recognize faces until they got close. A woman walked up to the musicians, smiled, and handed the saxophonist a joint. He put it up to his lips and took a long drag, filling his lungs before exhaling slowly.

He handed the joint to his fellow musician and headed over to the table where all types of liquor were displayed. He picked up a glass, twisted the cap off a bottle of rye, and poured himself a full glass. His friend came back, poured a drink, and the two went out to the balcony to enjoy the Las Vegas night air.

They were smoking and drinking on the balcony, trying to chase away opening-night jitters, when an altercation erupted. The crowd backed away from the commotion, pushing right toward the two young men. The saxophonist tried to get out of the way as the crowd rushed over, but he wasn't successful. Instead, he was pushed closer and closer to the railing of the balcony and without anyone seeing it, he went over the edge.

On May 24, 1955, the Moulin Rouge—the first casino targeted to the Black community—opened its doors to a Las Vegas fanfare. The luxury casino was billed as a "truly cosmopolitan hotel," with mahogany-lined walls and crystal chandeliers. Strip casinos placed "Welcome to town" ads in the local newspaper. Entertainers such as Sammy Davis Jr., Pearl Bailey, Nat King Cole, and Harry Belafonte were headliners. It seemed the resort was destined for an almost immediate success. But as is often the case in Las Vegas, the success of the Moulin Rouge did not last.

From the moment it opened, the Moulin Rouge, or Red Mill, attracted both a Black and white clientele, many of whom were the entertainers performing on the Las Vegas Strip. Heavyweights in the entertainment industry such as Cary Grant, George Burns, and Frank Sinatra were frequent patrons. "It was the place to meet," recalled former Moulin Rouge entertainer Bob Bailey. "It was exciting and different, a breakthrough in the social mores of the town. An atmosphere you could only get at the Moulin Rouge."

Heavyweight boxing champion Joe Lewis was brought in as a host and given a percentage of the hotel. The late-night review "Tropi-Can Can" in Club Rouge was a resounding success, making the June 20, 1955, cover of *Life* magazine. "The whole Strip emptied out," recalled Anna Bailey, one of the showgirls to grace the *Life* cover. The show was so popular that management added a third 2:30 a.m. show.

While the Las Vegas casino industry supported the new casino, that support was based on hopes that the Moulin Rouge would prove to be a home for Black patrons, eliminating their desire to be in the white casinos. In 1950 Las Vegas was a very modern town with a very strong Southern presence. Las Vegas had gained a reputation as an "all-American vacation town," and America at that time was not looking to see Black dealers, Latino bellmen, or Asian hosts. However, at the same time, west Las Vegas in the 1950s had a strong and growing Black presence.

World War II had come to an end and the country was looking for a place to forget about death and destruction, a place to have some fun. Las Vegas became that place. In the 1950s, Vegas gained its reputation as Hollywood's playground. Every major entertainer performed in Las Vegas and it was the only place outside of Hollywood where you could find Jack Benny, Frank Sinatra, Dean Martin, Bob Hope, and Mae West all in one spot.

While such landmark cases as *Brown v. Board of Education* and incidents such as Rosa Parks's refusal to give up her seat on a bus changed how the rest of America viewed their Black neighbors, Las Vegas remained a stalwart pillar of segregation. Even though they represented more than 10 percent of the town's population, Black people were banned from many downtown casinos and clubs. This ban included the very entertainers those establishments sought to perform at their venues.

Sammy Davis Jr., Nat King Cole, and Lena Horne, although welcomed as entertainers, were unable to enjoy the same benefits as their white counterparts. In fact, not only were they not allowed to book rooms in the hotels where they performed, they weren't even allowed to walk around the place and have a look. Black entertainers were forced to seek lodging in west Las Vegas, in houses run by "people of their own kind." It was an area that entertainer Sammy Davis Jr. likened to *Tobacco Road*.

Black business owners knew that Black entertainers were forced to seek lodging from them, and, proving that greed knows no color, these business owners felt no remorse in taking advantage of them. Many were charged higher rates than other Black customers renting the same rooms. Not only did these business owners charge more for the same room, they even charged more than the resorts. While the El Rancho was charging $14 a night for what was considered a first-class hotel room, one business owner was charging the Black entertainers who stayed at her place $15. The entertainers were outraged—not only at being taken advantage of, but at being unable to stay in the hotels of the casinos where they performed. Nat King Cole was "disgusted and dismayed" that he could not even look around the casino that bore his name on its marquee. Most upsetting to these entertainers was that before 1947, they had been allowed to stay in the very casinos that now banned them. Other Black leaders agreed, and in January of 1954 a lawyer and a National Association for the Advancement of Colored People (NAACP) representative by the name of Franklin Williams was hired to force the city to pass a civil rights ordinance.

Las Vegas residents and city commissioners packed a small room on the west side of town. Tensions increased as Williams argued for the right "to have a cup of coffee or throw a few nickels in the slot machines," adding, "[Y]ou don't have to sleep with [me] or let me into your home." Many cries filled the room in protest to Williams's speech, while others yelled out their support. Williams's attempts were unsuccessful, but the city was forced to realize that something had to be done to curb the rising tide of uneasiness in the Black community. Therefore, in 1954, city officials approved the construction of a large new gaming property in west Las Vegas.

Before the casino even had a name, it sparked controversy. Neighborhood casinos, although a mainstay of modern Las Vegas, were almost unheard of in the Las Vegas of the 1950s. White residents in the nearby communities banded together to protest the construction, but their protests were in vain and the Moulin Rouge was given the green light.

Despite racial differences, the Moulin Rouge was actually intended as an interracial resort. It was built on property owned by Will Max Schwartz, located on a perfect spot between the Black-populated west side and the predominantly white area of downtown. The $3.5 million it took to build the hotel casino would come from New York restaurateur Louis Rubin and Los Angeles broker Alexander Bisno. The Moulin Rouge consisted of two stucco buildings that housed a hotel, casino, and theater. The hotel's name was written in stylized script above the entrance to the casino. The sign was designed by Betty Willis, the creator of the famous "Welcome to Las Vegas" sign on the south end of the Strip. The outside of the building was painted with murals depicting scenes of dancing and fancy cars.

While the Moulin Rouge opened to fanfare, the success did not last. Within six months of opening, the hotel was out of business and in December of 1955, it declared bankruptcy. There were many theories regarding why the hotel closed, ranging from oversaturation of casinos (four casinos closed that year) to jealousy on the part of the established Strip casinos, whose Mob presence pressured them to run the business out of town. Most likely it was poor management and a lack of understanding by its owners regarding what it took to keep a gaming establishment afloat. James B. McMillan, a civil rights activist who was married in the hotel, recalled, "When the hotel closed . . . it was not because of not having any business; it closed because the partners just couldn't get along and they decided not to pay any more bills."

While the flame of the Moulin Rouge burned brightly, it extinguished quickly and was never able to regain its light. Through the years it passed between a series of hands, at one time being owned by Sarann Knight Preddy, the first Black woman to hold a gaming license. A tower was built on the property in 1956 and for many years the resort sat vacant.

Hauntings at the Moulin Rouge began to be reported in the mid-1970s, when guests often reported seeing apparitions in their rooms. The area where the Moulin Rouge was located had become one of the bad parts of town. Killings and overdoses were not uncommon.

One couple, who had come to Las Vegas on a budget, reported seeing a ghost in their room late one evening. They had come back later than expected from a show at the Tropicana and collapsed almost as soon as they hit one of the two beds in their room. The wife was awakened by someone saying, "Please no . . . please don't." The voice made her sit straight up in the bed, and when she did, she saw a young woman in the bed next to her and her husband. "I could see right through her, so I had a pretty good idea that I was either dreaming or she was some kind of ghost or something. She was crying softly and saying over and over,

'Please no, please don't.'" The woman told the ghost to "just go away," and fell back to sleep.

The next morning she called her mother, who was horrified that the couple had chosen to stay in the Moulin Rouge. "That Moulin Rouge is a rough place," she told her daughter. "There's lots of dope and killings; why, just last week a girl was murdered there in one of the rooms." When the woman asked her mother if there was a picture of the woman who was killed, she answered, "I don't think so. Why?"

"Just curious," she answered.

In 1992 it was placed on the National Register of Historic Places, a move that, oddly enough, made it even more difficult to make a successful go of it because of the Register's restrictions on renovations. On May 29, 2003, the Moulin Rouge met an unceremonious end when a fire burned the property to the ground. On June 4 of that year, Las Vegas fire investigators ruled the cause of the fire as intentional. No one was ever arrested.

Like many Las Vegas landmarks, the Moulin Rouge no longer stands, but that doesn't stop the wild parties that went on every weekend from continuing. While the building itself may be gone, people who walk around the property at night report hearing laughter and music coming from the spot where the once-popular casino stood. The guests and musicians who found a home at the Moulin Rouge seem to have chosen to remain there . . . and one in particular. A saxophonist— one who fell from a balcony so many years before—plays solos nightly, solos that would bring the residents of New Orleans to their knees.

A TRAGEDY THAT STILL HAUNTS VEGAS

In the early hours of one November morning, a fire swept through the MGM Grand Casino, killing eighty-five people. An outdated fire code combined, strangely enough, with air-conditioning to destroy a large part of the building. In true Las Vegas style, its residents pitched in wherever they could, coming to the aid of complete strangers. But while the fire may be gone, there are those who still can't let it go.

It was a busy Friday night. His table was full of players eager to lay down wagers in the hopes of a huge payback. Adam was always amazed at how much money people were willing to part with while chasing a big payday. Sure, there was always the chance that someone would make it big, but there was an even better chance that they would lose everything. Huge casinos weren't built on guests' winnings.

He dealt the cards: an ace to spot one, a five to spot two, a ten to spot three, and a three to spot four. Adam knew what each person would do before they even told him. The man in spot one would take another card. He'd play that ace like it was gold, taking hits until he went over, messing up the rest of the table. The second spot would also take another hit. The third spot, adding a ten to his queen, would double, but it wouldn't do him any good, because the first player had already messed up the hand. The fourth player would stay on his thirteen, hoping the dealer would go over.

Adam looked at spot one and smiled.

"Hit me," the man said.

The player was new and new players always said, "Hit me." Adam dealt a six. Now the man had a four, a six, and the ace. He watched as the man struggled to count the cards, confused over whether the ace was now a one or still an eleven. He was about to say "Hit me" again when the lady next to him leaned over.

"You have twenty-one, dear," she said.

"Are you sure?" he asked her. "I always get confused with these aces. I can never remember if they are ones or elevens."

"They're always elevens until you go over twenty-one. You're not over twenty-one."

"What the heck is that?" the woman in spot three said suddenly. "There, right there. What the heck is that?"

The players at the table turned to look at what the lady was pointing to. Adam didn't. Thieves often tried to distract dealers, hoping to palm chips when the dealer looked away. If your chips got taken, you got fired. Adam kept his gaze on the chips, but then he noticed that every one of the players was staring at something . . . staring intently at something.

Despite himself, Adam looked up. It was then that he saw what the players were seeing. A group of people were moving past the tables, only these people weren't walking—they were floating. And not only were they floating, but Adam could see right through them.

It was going to be a busy morning. Her station was already full, plus there were at least twenty more people waiting in line and it was only 6:45 a.m.

"Be right there," she said to the man who was waving to get her attention. She set the drinks down on the table, one in front of each guest.

"What can I get you?" she asked. She took their orders and then walked over to the man who had gotten her attention. "What can I get you, sweetie?" she said.

"How 'bout a cup of coffee and two eggs, over easy."

"Bacon or sausage?"

"What do you recommend?" he said, smiling, and then added, "How come you're a waitress and not a showgirl?"

"Bacon," she said, smiling back, "and I don't have the legs for it."

"Bacon it is," he said. "They look good to me."

"You're sweet," she said. "Toast?"

"Wheat. Dry, please."

"Have it for you in a jiffy," she said, and turned toward the kitchen. She had made it about halfway across the restaurant when she saw the flames. It was at that time she heard someone yelling "Fire!"

The restaurant erupted in panic. She couldn't tell where the fire was coming from. All she could see was thick black smoke pouring into the restaurant. People were running all around her, many of them screaming, most of them coughing . . . choking. She tried to help them get out, but the cloud of smoke was growing. It had already filled the entire restaurant and she was finding it harder and harder to get air into her lungs. Every breath she took was labored and when she did get air, it burned inside her.

As the black cloud filled the restaurant, she became disoriented and stumbled. She put her hand out to catch her fall, but nothing was there. She hit the floor hard. Trying to get her bearings, she crawled until she came to something she could recognize. If she couldn't figure out where she was . . . well, she didn't want to think about it.

She patted the floor, feeling for anything familiar. She put her hand on something soft—softer than the metal chairs and table supports she had been bumping into. As she crawled closer, she saw a face, the face of a man. She tried to scream, but nothing came out.

It was then that she recognized the face. It was the man who had flirted with her only moments ago. He was unconscious and she could tell right away that he wasn't ever getting up. If she couldn't get out of here, she would be just like him.

With renewed energy she turned and crawled toward the front of the restaurant. Minutes passed like hours as she crawled across the carpeted floor, coughing violently. As she came to the entrance of the restaurant, she was finally able to stand. People were running in every direction, Security trying to calm them down and direct them to the exits.

The black smoke was filling the casino. It was hot, and she felt like she had just stepped into an oven, but the firefighters had already arrived, and their presence made her feel calmer. She coughed again as she moved toward the exit doors, where fresh, clean air awaited. As she stumbled toward the doors, she noticed the firemen staring at something, wide-eyed . . . something behind her . . . right behind her. She turned her head and it was at that moment she noticed the ball of fire rushing toward her.

On the morning of November 21, 1980, guests awoke to a crisp 38-degree Las Vegas morning. The MGM Grand Hotel & Casino was the jewel of the Strip. It was a modern, twenty-six-story, two-million-square-foot building. Employees filed into the casino, ready to start the day shift. More than five thousand people had already filled the hotel and casino, fifty of whom were in the Orleans Coffee Shop. As guests were served their coffee and eggs, the second-largest life-loss hotel fire in United States history was already under way.

The Deli, located next to the coffee shop, was one of the few restaurants that had not yet opened. Unbeknownst to anyone, two friction-damaged wires in a display case had been rubbing together for quite some time. The rubbing was caused by a machine that powered a refrigerated display case. The display case was in the Deli and the wires, located in the wall, went unnoticed. As the wires worked against each other, they eventually wore thin—so much so that on this November day, the wires touched together causing an arc, and then a spark, which started the fire.

Fire codes in the 1970s, when the MGM was built, were vastly different from modern-day fire codes. Codes at that time did not require sprinkler systems or readily available fire extinguishers. Because no sprinklers went off when the fire first started, the flames found a ready supply of fuel in the plastic, paper, and wood building materials.

It was around 7:00 a.m. when the fire was first noticed by MGM employees. Chef Oborn grabbed a nearby wall-mounted fire hose from the kitchen and rushed toward the flames. He was saved from certain death by a fellow employee, who stopped him from using it on the fire. The hose Chef Oborn had grabbed was filled with water. Had the chef used water on an electrical fire, he would have been electrocuted. Given a constant supply of fuel and little resistance, the fire spread quickly, often at a rate of fifteen feet per second, and easily reached temperatures of over 2,000 degrees.

The Clark County Fire Department was contacted at 7:13 a.m. and responded at 7:17 a.m., only four minutes later. By then, thick black smoke was already billowing from the building. The firefighters no sooner entered the building when they were met by a fireball rolling toward them from the Deli.

Faced with the ball of fire rushing toward them, Captain Rex Smith ordered his men to evacuate the casino. It took Captain Smith and his crew twenty-five seconds to run out of the casino and reach their fire trucks. They were closely followed by the fireball, which came shooting out the front of the building, destroying everything in its path. The ball of fire had traveled a distance of 336 feet in only twenty-five seconds.

The employees of the MGM put the lives of their guests ahead of their own. Not only Security, but every employee who could, pitched in to help guests reach the exits. Employees were shocked to find that even as the fire spread, guests would not leave the slot machines they were playing, no matter how much they were begged. As the fire swept through the casino, many of the guests were more concerned with saving, or stealing, the small round pieces of plastic representing the money they had won than they were with saving their own lives.

One guest would not leave until the pit boss personally vouched for the amount of chips he had in front of him. Another continued to pull the handle of a slot machine even though the guest was warned by an employee that "people were dying over there." As employees helped guests to evacuate, Security struggled to gain control of the situation. Looters rushed in to grab what they could get—money from the gaming tables, jewelry from the guest rooms—and some did not make it back outside.

Strangely enough, the very thing that allows Las Vegas to be an entertainment mecca in the scorching desert heat would be the cause of the MGM Grand's demise. If it wasn't for the invention of air-conditioning, nobody in their right mind would have ever endured the scorching, 100-plus degrees that hit Vegas every summer. It is air-conditioning that allows Las Vegas to be a resort in the desert, and it was air-conditioning that allowed the deadly smoke to spread throughout the casino and into the hotel.

The air-conditioning return ducts funneled the deadly smoke from the casino into many of the rooms in the north wing of the hotel. In some cases, the smoke was filtered, but even then, toxic carbon monoxide was still pumped into the rooms. Some guests ran from their rooms into the stairwells only to find them engulfed in smoke. Once in the stairwell, any guests who allowed the door to slam behind them found that door locked when it closed, trapping them in the thick smoke. Screaming was no use, as there was no one to hear them. Their only choice was to climb higher and try to outrun the rising cloud. Many became quickly disoriented. Trapped with no escape, they died in the stairwell.

As the heavy black smoke passed through the ventilation system and seeped under the doors of the guests' rooms, many took their chances and jumped out of the windows. They chose to leap to their deaths rather than face an inevitable suffocation. Some guests simply died in their sleep, unaware of the black death that had rolled into their rooms. Television cameras responded immediately and broadcast the disaster nationally. Many residents, seeing the melee playing out in front of them, chose to get involved. The owner of a local helicopter business rallied his pilots to the scene. As the helicopters circled overhead, guests pleaded to be rescued. Unfortunately the length of the helicopters' blades prevented the pilots from getting close enough to rescue guests from their rooms.

Instead, pilots took their helicopters to the roof, where they were able to land. They rescued guests and employees stranded for more than two hours in the upper levels of the hotel. Helicopters were also provided by the Las Vegas Metropolitan Police Department, Nellis Air Force Base, and services as far away as San Diego, California.

A local trucking company donated two refrigerated semi trailers that were quickly turned into a makeshift morgue. Three deputy coroners were sent to the scene to identify bodies. All totaled eighty-five people died as a result of the fire, or fire-related injuries. Seventy-nine of those deaths were a result of smoke or carbon monoxide inhalation. More than seven hundred guests and employees were injured. Three hundred firefighters reported symptoms of smoke inhalation and fourteen were hospitalized.

When the smoke cleared, the north end of the casino was completely destroyed. Twenty-four floors of the hotel, untouched by the fire, were damaged by thick, heavy smoke. Strangely enough, the south side of the casino came through relatively unscathed. And in true Las Vegas fashion, a day after the fire, MGM Grand Vice President Steve Booke proclaimed that the showroom showed little damage and could easily house a show that night. Most of the restaurants on the south end experienced little damage as well.

The hotel was eventually sold. The MGM Grand relocated to the corner of Tropicana and Las Vegas Boulevard, where it is currently located. Bally's Las Vegas now occupies the spot where the MGM fire took place. Since the fire, employees at Bally's have reported guests calling the front desk, claiming to see such things as dismembered feet floating in their rooms. When the employees check the room numbers, they are always located in the tower where the fire took place. Guests also report seeing ghostly apparitions of people in the halls who appear and then suddenly disappear before their eyes.

The employees of Bally's are all too familiar with that portion of the hotel, known as the Emerald Tower. Guest room attendants (GRAs) who work on the appropriately named "graveyard shift" on the upper floors (nineteen through twenty-four) frequently report seeing shadowy figures lying on the beds in many of the rooms. Some of these GRAs are known to carry rosary beads as they attend to the rooms on those floors. Several employees also refuse to use one of the service elevators in that tower because, as the story goes, room service employees lost their lives in that elevator during the fire. While no ghosts have been reported in the elevator, some employees aren't willing to take any chances.

The ghosts of people who perished in the fire are not limited to the Emerald Tower. Many guests have reported seeing people floating through the casino, and for some unexplained reason, this seems to occur only on the casino's busiest nights.

Faced with a decision to either burn to death in a fire or die from a nineteen-story drop, it's easy to see why those who perished in the fire at the MGM Grand can't seem to let go. As a result of the fire, building codes throughout the United States were updated to mandate sprinklers, fire extinguishers, and emergency warning systems. While devastating, the fire helped Las Vegas to become a city that has the most advanced fire protection systems available. Even still, the fire is often one of the most talked about events when the subject of Las Vegas is raised. It is an event that, to this day, still haunts the city.

WE'LL LEAVE THE LIGHT ON . . . THE GHOST LIGHT, THAT IS

Some people believe that ghosts are simply residual energy that remains in an area long after the people have gone. If that is true, there is no greater source of energy in Las Vegas than what once existed in the Sands Copa Room. Although the building that once housed this famous showroom no longer exists, in true Las Vegas style, the crowds still seem to roar.

"Ladies and gentlemen," the announcer began, "direct from the bar—Mr. Dean Martin."

The people sitting at the tables in the famous Copa Room at the Sands Hotel and Casino clapped loudly as Martin walked onstage, cigarette in hand. The small room was packed with men in suits and ties and women clad in elegant dresses. They had all come to the famous showroom to see the Rat Pack perform and that performance started with Dean Martin.

"Thank you," Martin said to the cheering crowd and then broke into song, singing the way only Dean Martin could. When he finished, the crowd applauded its approval, to which Martin smiled and bowed graciously. As the clapping died down, Martin spoke.

"I'd like to have you meet my wonderful pianist," Martin said, looking over and pointing to the older, balding man sitting at the piano. "Not only is he a fine piano player, a wonderful composer of songs, a great musician—this young man," Martin said, turning to the crowd, "has been a communist for thirty-two years." The crowd roared with laughter and Martin smiled at his own joke.

"But I'm very fort-unit in having him," Martin continued, deliberately stumbling over his words and pausing to let the crowd laugh, "with me because he's responsible for our great big hit, 'Everybody Loves Somebody.' He wrote it. Mr. Ken Lane."

With that, Martin again pointed to the man at the piano as the crowd applauded.

As Lane started playing the song, Martin said to him, "Just one chorus and we'll get out, because I left a drink." The crowd laughed again as Martin turned to them and began singing his hit song.

Three Las Vegas locals—Zak Bagans, Nick Groff, and Aaron Goodwin, stars of the Travel Channel's *Ghost Adventures*—arrived at Madame Tussauds Wax Museum at The Venetian Las Vegas Casino, Hotel & Resort. Their purpose was to spend the night in the museum and record whatever they experienced. They had with them recording devices, both video and digital, as well as an array of handheld electronic equipment designed to capture all manner of paranormal activity.

The museum stood on the site of the old Sands Hotel and Casino, a portion of which now occupies the same place where the famous Copa Room once hosted the hottest acts in Las Vegas. Some of those same entertainers, including the Rat Pack, now occupy the museum, forever immortalized in wax. Maybe it's because the museum is located in the exact spot where the Copa Room once stood, or maybe it's because of the history of Madame Tussaud herself (she once had a job making death masks for victims of the guillotine in eighteenth-century France), but many of the employees at the wax museum have reported hearing and seeing ghosts.

Kurt Mayne, an employee in the scream maze at the museum, has experienced several paranormal events while working there. On one occasion an older man dressed in overalls came out of the bathroom and walked right through him. On another occasion, while he was sitting in a part of the museum meant to resemble a morgue, he had another encounter. "I heard a man's voice. Just kind of *Ohhhh*," Mayne related, imitating the voice. "The next thing I know, something taps me on the back of my bald head."

Mayne, along with other employees, also claims to have seen an old man dressed in a 1970s-style white shirt and green pants walking up the stairway going to the second floor of the museum. The man is frequently seen walking up the stairs, when he suddenly disappears.

Chris Mayes, the show manager of Madame Tussauds, who himself has reported hearing laughter and glasses clinking in the area of the old Copa Room, opened the back doors to the museum and wished the *Ghost Adventures* team good luck as they stepped inside to start their investigation.

"Thank you very kindly," Sammy Davis Jr. said to the crowd as Dean Martin and Frank Sinatra carried a long table onto the stage. The table was draped with a white sheet, under which were hidden items of different sizes.

"There's another show that falls beyond . . . ," Davis tried to continue as the two men carried the table across the stage, bringing it directly in front of Davis, before setting it down.

"I have another number to do fellas," Davis protested.

"You *think* you have another number," Martin said, commandeering Davis's microphone, "but it's over, o v a u r, over." While the crowd laughed, Martin continued, "You've been here since Friday, get out of here."

Zak, Aaron, and Nick set up two static night-vision cameras, one in the Viva Las Vegas Room and one covering the staircase where the man with the green pants had been seen by employees. They also set up REM-Pods on the stairs. These paranormal research tools were designed to flash a light when the presence of electromagnetic energy was detected.

Zak suggested that the group start off by moving around so that their bodies could be used to try and pick up on any energy that might be in the room. When this had happened in the past, the group had been able to record electronic voice phenomena (EVP) almost immediately and Zak was hoping that would be the case this time as well.

The museum was completely dark and while their camera equipment was recording on night-vision, the three men could barely see anything. They made their way up the stairs and onto the second floor of the museum, where they encountered the wax figures of several stars who had recently passed away. They wondered if the spirits were possibly coming back to see themselves as they used to be, in another time.

As they continued to make their way around the wax figures, they suddenly heard a noise. It was a noise that sounded like someone laughing.

"That laughter is what we're trying to capture," Zak said, looking into the camera. His theory was that the laughter being heard in the hallways of Madame Tussauds Wax Museum was a residual from the crowds at the Copa Room laughing at a joke made by Sammy Davis Jr., Frank Sinatra, or Dean Martin. "That's the laughter we may just have heard," he said.

In the 1960s Las Vegas showcased the most famous talent in the world, and the Sands Hotel and Casino was the hippest place to be.

While Jake Freeman had made his money in Texas oil, gambling brought him farther west to Las Vegas. In 1951 he purchased a plot of land for $15,000. His intent was to build a world-class resort, and he had $600,000 at his disposal with which to do it. His partner and co-owner, Jack Entratter, was an imposing figure, more than six feet tall with a deep, baritone voice. Before moving to Las Vegas, Entratter had been general manager of the famous Copacabana club in New York City.

The two men made the Sands a rousing success from the moment it opened on December 12, 1952. Right from the start, the Sands was considered the most luxurious resort on the Strip, if not the world. It had copper light fixtures and an Italian marble entrance, as well as many other lavish features. Entratter had managed to bring the entertainers he booked in New York to play in the Sands's showroom, called the Copa Room, loosely named after the New York club.

Jerry Lewis, a regular at the Copa Room, once said, "We wouldn't go anywhere in Vegas but where Jack was. The performers that played the Copa—Sinatra, Lena Horne, Tony Bennett—he got all of them to play the Sands."

But probably the most notorious of the people who performed at the Copa Room were the infamous Rat Pack. Consisting of Frank Sinatra, Dean Martin, Sammy Davis Jr., Peter Lawford, and Joey Bishop, the Rat Pack, as they were called, became synonymous with Las Vegas itself.

Sinatra, being the oldest and arguably the most famous at the time, was crowned the leader. The group often referred to themselves as "the clan," but the press started to call them the "Rat Pack," reportedly because Judy Garland once told them they looked like a pack of rats after seeing them emerge from an all-night party. The name stuck.

Amongst themselves, however, the group referred to their meetings as "the summit," the name given by Sinatra who didn't like the racial implications associated with the word *clan*. Because Sinatra began using "the summit" as the name of the group, they started to call him the "Chairman of the Board."

One evening during an especially long summit meeting, the chairman had an idea. He proposed that the five should appear onstage at his regular haunt, the Copa Room. The men agreed and Sinatra arranged the event. On the first night the Copa Room presented the Rat Pack, it was filled to capacity. Guests and celebrities alike had gathered to see the group perform. Nervous energy filled the room as the excitement of seeing their favorite performers grew. When the boys walked onstage, drinks and cigarettes in hand, they were met with cheers and resounding applause.

The secret to the Rat Pack's success was not just their entertainment ability. Rather, what made the group so famous was their ability to create a mystique—one that every member of the audience wanted to be a part of. As is the case with most entertainers, the Rat Pack went to bed when most people were waking up and getting ready for work. But these boys made it sound like they were doing it by choice, not just because it was the schedule that best fit into the lifestyle of the typical entertainer. They also managed to blur the lines between work and play. In fact, Davis would often say, "Ladies and gentlemen, what happens here onstage happens offstage."

As the decade came to an end, the time of the Rat Pack ended with it. In 1967 the Sands cut off Sinatra's line of credit. Frank responded in true Sinatra style by throwing furniture at pit boss Carl Cohen. Sinatra left the Sands and signed a contract with the year-old Caesars Palace. The rest of the Rat Pack did not follow.

Being in a building at night with all the lights off, hunting for ghosts, can be a little off-putting. Being in a building late at night that is occupied by hundreds of wax people just standing there can be outright spooky! Especially figures created with the groundbreaking process originated by Madame Tussaud.

Marie Tussaud was born in Strasbourg, France, on December 1, 1761. Tussaud's father was killed in the Seven Years War only months before her birth, causing her mother to take up work as a housekeeper in order to feed herself and her child. She ended up working for a physician named Philippe Curtius, who was not only a talented doctor, but was also skilled in modeling wax. Curtius used his ability to create models that illustrated anatomy.

Tussaud was fascinated by the process and Curtius was happy to teach it to her. She took to modeling wax naturally and quickly became very skilled. In 1789, Curtius, and therefore Tussaud, became involved in the French Revolution. He seized the opportunity to create wax models of the events of the revolution to keep the Parisian peasants updated. Tussaud helped Curtius create two wax busts of revolutionary heroes Jacques Necker and the Duc d'Orléans. The busts were taken by a group of protestors who wrapped them with black crepe, a symbol of a funeral, and speared them on long pikes. The protestors then marched through the streets with the heads, two days before the attack on the Bastille.

Soldiers responded to the protest and killed the man displaying the head of Necker, which was hacked to pieces in the process. Two days later the real heads of both Necker and the Duc d'Orléans were taken by the guillotine. It was a fate slated for both Curtius and Tussaud when it was discovered they had created the busts. Tussaud was arrested and readied for the block underneath the guillotine's heavy blade. However, Curtius was not unknown or ill respected in French society, and because of this, Curtius had support—support which saved him, and by proxy Tussaud, from certain death. After their release Curtius was hired to create death masks of those killed by France in the Revolution. Most often this task fell to Tussaud.

Throughout the years she improved upon the techniques taught to her by Curtius and invented many of her own. She traveled through France and England and became famous for her ability to re-create the likenesses of famous figures and historical events. The processes invented and used by Tussaud are still in use today in her museums, and are held in strict secrecy.

In his hand Zak held a new piece of equipment that the trio had brought to use on this adventure. Called the Ovilus II, it was designed to allow spirits to manipulate a phonetic generator inside the unit, so that they can choose specific words by using their energy.

"Is there someone in this room?" Zak asked.

Suddenly a word appeared on the digital screen of the Ovilus II, which then repeated the word out loud in an eerie digital voice: *Noah.*

Zak asked if the spirit's name was Noah, but got no answer. He then asked a series of questions trying to get the spirit to answer, even asking who his favorite entertainer was in the Copa Room. Finally he asked the spirit if it could say something else.

As the three men kept walking, a digital voice said the word *play.* The Ovilus II then said the word *corner,* followed by the words *tied, contract, cave, dig, throat, lash,* and *alive.*

Throughout the history of the Sands, the Copa Room has been remodeled many times and even relocated within the casino. However, 1996 would see the end of the famous showroom, as well as the Sands itself. In November of that year, the Sands Hotel and Casino was imploded to make room for the multi-billion-dollar resort, The Venetian Las Vegas, which opened almost three years later on May 3, 1999.

After being locked in the museum from dusk till dawn, Zak and his *Ghost Adventures* team managed to record laughter on the stairway where the man in the green pants was seen by Mayne and other employees. One of the pods placed in the stairs lit up right after the camera recorded the laughter. The team was also able to capture a voice that appeared to say *singing in the rain,* as well as a photo of a transparent figure standing behind the rail at the base of a different set of stairs in the museum. The figure is wearing what looks to be dark pants and a white shirt. There were no wax likenesses in or around the area. Why does this man haunt this particular portion of the museum—and is he the spirit who spoke on the voice emitter, suggesting that maybe he had met with a nefarious ending in the 1970s when the Mob ruled Las Vegas? Or was he just a fan who never wanted to leave the engaging atmosphere created by the entertainers in the Copa Room all those years ago?

While not all of the people who perform in Las Vegas believe in ghosts, when the lights onstage dim for the night, a single light is routinely left on. This light, called the "ghost light," is left on just in case any spirit feels the need to perform one more time.

SO VEGAS HAS A GHOST TOWN?

The Clark County Museum is home to some of Las Vegas's most cherished posses-sions, including many of the houses that were once part of its fascinating history. In a town that routinely demolishes its past, these buildings provide a rare peek at the Las Vegas of yesteryear. It does seem, however, that the houses aren't the only parts of Las Vegas's past that have remained.

"Why'd you sit on the bed?"

The two employees were in the bedroom of the Beckley House, straightening things and cleaning up after the tourists who had walked through the day before.

"I just made that bed," she said, a bit annoyed as she straightened the antique quilt the museum used as a bedspread.

"I didn't sit on the bed," her fellow employee said, dusting the antique vanity against the wall across from the bed.

"Really? If you didn't sit on the bed, then how do you explain this butt print?" she asked, pointing to the circular indentation. "I certainly didn't do it."

"What're you talking about?" he said, turning to face the bed.

"There. Right there. See it? A butt print. Your butt print."

"You're crazy! Why would I sit on the bed after you just made it? Especially when I have a chair right here to sit on?" he said, pointing to the old chair posi-tioned in front of the vanity.

She mumbled to herself as she pulled the edge of the quilt, removing the indentation. She straightened the sides of the quilt and left the room, still talking to herself under her breath. He just ignored her and continued dusting the room. When he finished dusting, he went into the front room to get the vacuum. As he wrapped the cord around the holder, she went back into the bedroom.

"Oh . . . my . . . gosh!" she said, emphasizing every word. "I can't believe it!"

He shook his head, lifted the vacuum, and walked into the bedroom. "What now?"

"That!" she said, pointing to the indentation in the quilt. "Really?"

"Okay, how did that get there?"

"What do you mean, 'How did that get there?' Obviously you think you're being funny."

His eyes were wide and he seemed glued in position, stiff as a board. "I didn't sit on the bed," he said.

"You're serious, aren't you?" she said, looking into his eyes.

"I'm very serious. I didn't sit on that bed."

The Beckley House is part of the Clark County Museum, also called the Clark County Heritage Museum. The thirty-acre site features "a collection of restored historic buildings that depict daily life from different decades in Las Vegas, Boulder City, Henderson, and Goldfield." The homes were all relocated from around the valley to become part of the museum. They line both sides of a street called the Heritage Street of Historic Homes.

Heritage Street is home to five houses, a print shop, and a silver Spartanette travel trailer with a motor court cabin. The small, but elegant, wedding chapel—the Candlelight Wedding Chapel—is located to the rear of the Babcock and Wilcox House, just east of the Museum Guild Gazebo. All of the houses are on the Directory of Historic House Museums in the United States. They are each decorated in the theme of a different time period, and each has been made to look as if it was built in its current location, complete with manicured lawns. In fact Heritage Street could look like any street in hometown America. But four of these homes have something in common, besides their mannequin residents: They are also home to ghosts.

The Beckley House is the first house on Heritage Street. Located on the west side of the street, the Beckley House is a California-style bungalow. It was built in 1912 at a cost of $2,500 and was originally located at South Fourth Street in downtown Las Vegas. The house was owned by Will Beckley, who immigrated to America in 1883, landing in Illinois. He moved to Las Vegas in 1908 at the encouragement of his brother and initially lived in a tent house.

The Las Vegas of the early 1900s was a dusty town consisting mostly of tents and hastily constructed wooden buildings. William Clark and his younger brother J. Ross had commissioned John T. McWilliams, a Canadian immigrant, to survey land they had bought from Helen J. Stewart, a wealthy ranch owner. Stewart was willing to sell the land in hopes of enticing the railroad to come to the valley. The two brothers, who owned the San Pedro, Los Angeles & Salt Lake Railroad, were a perfect team. In 1905 the brothers held a public auction to sell plots of land and Las Vegas was born.

When Beckley moved to Las Vegas, he opened a clothing store on the land that is now occupied by the Golden Gate Hotel. The store faced the railroad depot that is now occupied by the Plaza's high-rise hotel. The store was a success and in 1910 Beckley proposed by letter to Leva Grimes, an Illinois schoolteacher. She accepted, and Beckley brought his new bride to Las Vegas and had the house built in 1912. The Beckleys were very wealthy and the house was the center of social activity in bustling Las Vegas.

In the 1920s the Beckleys had the home renovated, adding a brick fireplace that burned coal instead of wood. They also had the kitchen extended, placing a dining room in the original kitchen. Even though electricity was available, the Beckleys kept the wood-burning stove they had installed in the kitchen originally. An oak telephone was mounted on the wall so the Beckleys could call their store anytime they needed simply by lifting the receiver, cranking the handle, and dialing "27." A calendar from the Beckleys' own store hung on the wall of the home. A trapdoor in the kitchen floor led to a small room that was most likely a root cellar.

Through the years, the Beckley house became a local landmark, being known as the last pioneer home in Las Vegas. Will lived in the home up until his death in 1965. Leva remained in the home until 1978, when, at the age of ninety-three, her ill health no longer allowed her to stay in the house alone and she moved in with family members.

Las Vegas is a town that always looks to tomorrow, and the lure of development threatened the Beckleys' beloved home. It was clear to everyone that the house would not be able to be kept in its original location. Enter the Clark County Museum. The Beckleys donated their home to the museum, and in 1979 it became the first house on Heritage Street. The museum decorated it in the time period of the 1920s, the heyday of the Beckleys' ownership.

Many of the items in the home are original, owned by the Beckleys themselves, including the entire bedroom set, the articles in the closet, and the quilt that lies on the end of the bed. Employees have claimed that no matter how many times they straighten the antique quilt, an unexplained indentation appears. "It looks like someone had just sat down on it," an employee stated. Some employees have also reported having the bedspread mussed up after it had just been straightened.

The home had only one bedroom, so the Beckleys' two children slept in the attic room or on the rear porch (which was covered in the remodeling) when the summer heat rose to unbearable heights. Some have reported seeing an elderly man and a little girl standing near the staircase that leads to the attic. Others have claimed to hear moans coming from the house.

Sitting right next to the Beckley House is the Goumond House. Built in 1931, the home looks more like something that belongs on the Swiss ski slopes than the Las Vegas desert environment. The Goumond House is the only two-story home on Heritage Street. It is a yellow, chalet-style Tudor house, decorated in the Swedish/Scandinavian style, with green trim and a cobblestone entryway and chimney. It has a steep gabled roof, a covered front porch, and heavy exposed timbers. A portion of the house extends on the right side to create a covered carport.

By 1930 the population of Las Vegas had grown to more than 5,000. Even still, Las Vegas had been struggling since the Union Pacific Railroad pulled its repair shops out in 1922, forcing the town to find another source of commerce. Hundreds of railroad employees left along with the railroad. The loss of residents had a ripple effect on all of the businesses in the area, so when the director of the Reclamation Service, Arthur Powell Davis, proposed a canyon near Las Vegas as the place to build a dam that would tame the Colorado River, the town took hope.

The dam brought a great deal of wealth to the valley, and Prosper Jacob Goumond was one of the people who benefited from that wealth. Goumond was part owner of the Boulder Club, a casino on Fremont Street located next to the Apache Hotel. He also owned Tule Springs, a recreation area he bought from John Herbert ("Bert") Nay. The area had served as a watering hole for the Native Americans of the region. In 1916 Nay filed for water rights to the property, eventually adding a blacksmith shop and a storage room as he gained more land. Goumond bought the property and quickly took advantage of Nevada's lenient divorce laws, which only required a six-week residency to file. Goumond opened a ranch that became a resort for movie stars looking for a quickie divorce.

Tule Springs was also a self-supporting ranch where Goumond grew alfalfa and raised cattle on over a hundred acres. It had a large vegetable garden as well as a variety of animals that were raised and sold. Many of the ranch's wooden buildings still exist.

The Goumond House was originally built by the firm of Warner and Nordstrom for Haken "Jake" Hagenson. It was originally located on South Seventh Street near the Las Vegas High School. Goumond bought the house from Hagenson shortly after construction was completed. The house had a full basement, which was very uncommon in Las Vegas, as the ground is made up mostly of caliche, a substance as hard as concrete and almost completely impervious to water. Goumond moved into the house along with his wife, Gertrude, and granddaughter, Margo. The Goumonds were wealthy enough to have a maid and a cook. They also had one of the first residential swimming pools in Las Vegas.

In 1981 the Clark County Preservation Association obtained the house, donating it to the Clark County Museum in 1984. The home had to be moved in two parts and took a great deal of restoration before it was able to be opened to the public on February 14, 1999. Clark County Commissioner Bruce Woodbury officiated at the opening. While the house is decorated in the style of the late 1940s and early 1950s (it is the only home on the street with a television), the museum preserved many of the original elements of the home, including gingerbread molding, an arched doorway, and a fireplace with flanking windows and bookcases.

Guests to the museum have reported seeing a slender young woman standing at the entryway to the home. If anyone tries to speak to the woman, she vanishes. Others have reported seeing a black cat roaming the hallways of the home. People who have tried to pick up the cat have come away with empty arms. There have also been reports of doors opening and closing by themselves, and a psychic once claimed that there was a sadness in the house, something not reflected by the house's colorful decor.

Right next to the Goumond House rests one of the smallest houses on Heritage Street. The Giles/Barcus House is a cottage-style home built in 1924 that is only twenty-six by twenty-four feet. Originally located 186 miles north of Las Vegas in Goldfield, Nevada, the home was purchased by Edwin Schofield Giles, a mining engineer, consultant, and surveyor. Giles moved from Colorado in 1907 to the booming mining town with his wife and daughter, both of whom were named Edith. Gold had been discovered in Nevada and when the Giles family moved to Goldfield, it was the largest town in the state. It boasted thirty thousand people, three newspapers, five banks, a mining stock exchange, three railroads, and four schools.

The Giles family's first residences consisted of wagons, tents, and various hotels. However, through it all, they always tried to maintain an air of gentility in their home. They had Persian rugs and a rubber-lined bathtub. They purchased the home in 1928. By then, the town of Goldfield had dwindled to a mere 1,500 residents. At the time, most of the homes in Goldfield still used an outhouse for restroom facilities. But the Gileses' home was an exception. It has an indoor bathroom, complete with a pedestal sink, tile counter, walk-in shower, and, most important, a toilet.

Despite its modern conveniences, the house was basically one main room with a bathroom. The house itself was constructed of wooden boards covered with tarpaper and cloth. It remained in Goldfield until 1955, when daughter Edith, who married Clyde Barcus, moved with her husband to Las Vegas, taking their beloved home with them. The home was relocated to the corner of Hacienda and Giles Street, where it was used as an antiques and collectibles store called Odd Shop Antiques.

Edith died in 1984, but not before she had made arrangements for the home to be donated to the Clark County Museum. The home now rests at the end of Heritage Street and, strangely enough, has an outhouse behind it. A visitor to the museum once noted a piano being played in the home.

"I walked in and distinctly heard the sounds of someone playing the piano," she said. While the woman thought the music was simply coming from the museum's sound system, she remarked, "When I said something about the particular song, my husband shook his head. He hadn't heard any music in there."

Another visitor reported seeing an elderly lady in a heavy, dark velvet dress sitting and doing needlework. Thinking she was a period-costumed employee, the visitor waved and commented on how hot the costume must be. The old woman didn't respond, so when the visitor went back to the gift shop, she shared her experience with the woman at the counter. The woman told the visitor that there was no one like that working at the Giles/Barcus House. It was then that the visitor realized she had just seen a ghost.

Interestingly enough, while Goldfield, Nevada, was once known for its gold production, it is now best known for being a ghost town. This just goes to show that you can bring the house out of the ghosts, but you can't bring the ghosts out of the house.

At the southeast end of Heritage Street is a house that was instrumental in the war effort during World War II. In 1940, when Hitler was running amok in Europe and the United States was just getting into the war effort, the US government was looking for a place to mine magnesium. Nevada Senator Patrick McCarran was intent on convincing President Franklin D. Roosevelt that Nevada would be the perfect place to mine the magnesium needed for bombs. Germany's relentless bombing of Britain made it difficult for a factory to be built in Europe, and magnesium was plentiful in the hills at Gabbs, Nevada, just three hundred miles north of Las Vegas.

In 1941 the US government signed a contract with Basic Magnesium Inc. Once the contract was signed, the largest magnesium plant in the United States was constructed, employing 14,000 construction workers. While the magnesium was mined in Gabbs, the plant was located just outside of Las Vegas, in the valley between Las Vegas and Boulder City. It was here that the US government built homes, creating a townsite for the employees of Basic Magnesium. The townsite was complete with stores, schools, churches, a library, a theater, a hospital, and even a bowling alley.

The houses were meant to be temporary. The interiors were constructed of quarter-inch plywood, with batten strips covering the seams. The exterior was made up of redwood siding, because it was weather resistant. Windows were strategically placed to provide cross ventilation, and a small six-sided evaporative cooler, commonly called a swamp cooler, provided the only relief for the sweltering summer heat. Cool air entered the house through one vent located at the entrance of the house. Fans could be used to circulate the air into other areas of the house.

The house also had a "thermador" wall heater for the winter months. The kitchen contained open cupboard shelves, a Gibson refrigerator, a cast-iron sink, and a Westinghouse stove. The house also had a washing machine and a small pantry. While the house may have been basic, it did contain three bedrooms, two closets, a bathroom, kitchen, and a living room.

Some sensitives claim that the Townsite House is the one with the most energy on Heritage Street, and, according to them, not all of it is positive. A sensitive is a person with heightened sensitivity to his or her environment. One sensitive was reportedly overcome with sadness upon entering the Townsite House and had to leave. The sensitive claimed to have picked up "a strong negative feeling" in the vicinity of the child's room. The sensitive explained that the house "holds some dark secrets." These secrets may never be revealed, as the Townsite House is actually made up of six different original townsite houses, which means that no single family ever actually occupied this particular building.

It does make a person wonder if bringing all these homes together inspired the ghosts to come and reside here. Or was it the ghosts who inspired the museum to acquire these particular homes, putting them together to create one big, old, Western ghost town?

THE TIKI BAR BE OPEN

A pirate with a hunger for gold steals an idol from a land that can't be reached by boat—even by those who know how to find it. Only instead of controlling the idol, it controls him. Now the artifacts of that golden theft have found their way into a Las Vegas Tiki bar, but something may have very well come with them.

"Now there be five of 'em, captain," his first mate called out.

"Let the scalawags come!" the captain responded. "Let them come, if they think they can catch the Black Falcon."

William Tobias Faulkner was the terror of the East Indies, swooping down on the unexpecting and stealing their goods with impunity. His favorite target: the East India Trading Company. They could hardly get a ship across the Indian Ocean without meeting up with Captain Faulkner and his men. Finally, the East India Trading Company had had enough and sent a fleet of mercenary ships to find the captain and remove him from the seas—by any means necessary.

A decoy vessel had been set as a sacrifice. Filled with spices and fabric from the Orient, it would be too much for Captain Faulkner to resist. They were right, he didn't, but just as he and his crew had plundered their bounty, three ships appeared on the horizon—three ships bound for the Falcon.

Finding the Falcon was one thing, catching her was a completely different task all together, for the Black Falcon was the swiftest schooner on the waters. Its double mast and shallow draft allowed the Falcon and her crew to outrun many a Dutch Fleut or Spanish Galleon, especially in the hands of a captain like Faulkner.

When Faulkner took the sacrificial vessel, he was on his way to find the greatest bounty of his career. During a game of bones in Tortuga, Captain Faulkner had become the proud owner of a map to Skull Island and the treasures it held. He hadn't won the map as much as acquired it. According to legend, the island had once been home to an ancient mythical race of one-eyed giants who mined gold ore from deep inside the mountains of the island paradise. They smelted the ore in the rivers of lava flowing from the island's active volcano. Expert craftsman, these giants, they turned the gold into precious pieces of jewelry, chalices, and such. But their crowning achievement was a golden idol said to possess mystical powers.

Faulkner wanted that gold, and even more, he wanted that idol, for with it, he could truly rule the seas. He pulled out his map and pointed the Falcon toward the island, the mercenary ships hot on his trail. As he drew near, the water turned to mist, so thick the human eye could not navigate through. Faulkner stuck to the map, as one by one, his pursuers fell to the coral reefs or the Sirens who hunted in these waters.

With the help of the map, Faulkner brought the Falcon to the shores of Skull Island, where he and his crew disembarked. As they headed to Mermaid Cove, the local headhunters captured and beheaded Faulkner's crew, one or two at a time. Beaten and battered, and the only remaining member of his crew, Faulkner found himself at Mermaid Cove, where a group of Sirens took pity on him and brought him back to health.

The Sirens, Faulkner noticed, all sported hand-crafted amulets make of fine gold. When he saw them, he knew he had found what he was looking for. After he had regained his health, he furtively followed the Sirens as they made their way to their secret temple hidden by a glossy waterfall, which he later described as Diamond Falls. There he found the objects of his desire. He gathered all the trinkets and baubles he could carry, and as he did, he found—perched upon a golden pedestal—the Golden Tiki idol. Towering over the glimmering idol were two figures carved in stone, each sporting one eye in the middle of the forehead.

Faulkner grabbed the Golden Tiki, rushed through Diamond Falls, and scurried back to his ship—somehow making it past the island's headhunters. All the way he could hear the Sirens wailing, warning him to return the idol or suffer its consequences. He didn't listen. By the time he climbed the gangway, he realized that he had lost all the trinkets and baubles along the way, but it didn't matter, he still had the idol.

He set the idol on the table in his cabin, then he locked the door, took his seat, and stared into its glowing eyes. He spent the next several days and nights staring into the thing. He didn't eat and didn't drink, but as he drifted off into madness, he managed to scribble his story on the back of a nearby map. Faulkner's bones were eventually found, still sitting in the chair of his cabin, but the idol was gone.

So goes the legend of the Golden Tiki, the namesake of a bar on Spring Mountain Road in Las Vegas' Chinatown. A bar that is said to be haunted. The owner, Branden Powers has filled his Exotic Tiki Bar with hundreds of artifacts, taxidermy, mummified remains, island art, and, of course, all manner of shrunken heads. Powers opened the bar in 2015 and almost immediately started noticing unexplainable anomalies, such as floating orbs and moving shadows. Ashtrays slid across tables on their own so often that Powers hardly even noticed it anymore. One such movement was shown on the Travel Channel's *Ghost Adventures*, when Zak Bagans and his crew investigated the place.

Powers was sitting one night in a booth he often used to conduct business when the ashtray suddenly moved on its own. Powers pulled out his phone and when the ashtray did the same trick again, he caught it on video. That video was shown on *Ghost Adventures*. According to Powers, he once had a psychic come into the bar who told him that the ghost of his deceased father liked to hang out in that booth. Powers' father, according to him, was a smoker and Powers had placed a photo of his father under the glass that protects that very table, so the revelation by the psychic came as no surprise.

The Golden Tiki seems to have become the haunt of many a ghost. "There are six regulars," Powers said, "but I think there are hundreds more." The six include an old man whose ghostly profile has been captured in at least one photo and two little girls, one of them Asian, that like to photobomb people's selfies. One time one of the bar's designers, Peter Pryor, was doing some plumbing work in the women's bathroom when he heard a little girl's voice. He went out into the bar, which was vacant at the time except for a female bartender, and asked if a child had been let in. He was told that he and the bartender were the bar's only current occupants, but when he returned to the restroom, he saw the shoes and legs of a little girl in one of the stalls. He pushed the stall open, but there was nothing was there.

Stall doors in that restroom seem to have a mind of their own. Guests have reported doors to the stalls shaking back and forth, as if someone were trying to get inside. The stall doors have even locked by themselves, forcing an employee to have to slid underneath to release the lock. Besides ashtrays being moved, glasses have flown off shelves, and once a sheave that held ropes which were strewn across the ceiling gave way and came crashing down, almost hitting a bartender. The sheave, which had been properly secured, could not have come down on its own.

Powers takes it all in stride. "Ghosts just like to come here," he said. "Probably because we are so welcoming." One of the ghosts they believe haunts the place is that of Vinnie Paul, Las Vegas resident, drummer, and co-founder of the band Pantera. Paul, who passed away in 2018, spent his last night alive in the Golden Tiki. He gave the drummer, a friend of his, a one-finger salute as he left the building. He died later that night. When Zak Bagans and his crew investigated the bar, they recorded what they believe where voices of some of the ghosts. Powers believes one of those recorded was Paul, based on what he said in the recording—something inappropriate for television. Paul's shrunken head now resides in the booth he occupied when he visited the Golden Tiki.

Paul isn't the only person whose shrunken head decorates the walls of the Golden Tiki. Many other celebrities, authors, poets, and all manner of people who have inspired or influenced Powers have found themselves with shrunken heads. Nicolas Cage, Evil Knievel, Devo, Ernest Hemingway, Debbie Harry, and Rob Zombie have all had their heads shrunk. Even Powers and his wife Lisa have taken their place on the wall of shrunken heads. Las Vegas Mayor Goodman and his wife are represented, as is Walt Disney, which is appropriate because a trio of hula girls who once danced for millions in Disney's Small World ride now dance above the bar. Several employees are included in the group of shrunken heads, including the original builder Billy the Crud and bartender Ivana Blaze.

Included in the bar is a mummified mermaid—who, by the way, is pregnant—and a headhunter who guards the front door just in case anyone gets out of line. An actual machete used by actual headhunters is on display at the bar, as is a witch doctor's medicine bag. Skulls line the wall of the bathroom and if you look closely enough, you can find a skull from one of those mystical one-eyed giants who roamed Skull Island. And of course, there is the requisite TV playing clips from island-themed shows, many of which are wonderfully obscure.

Placed strategically around the bar are tributes to people—often first responders—who have suffered tragedies. On a wall toward the back of the bar is a photo of Powers' grandparents appropriately dressed in island attire, and ghosts—lots and lots of ghosts. "There's so many orbs," Powers explained, "That sometimes it feels like it's snowing." And why wouldn't they come here? Quite frankly, it's a great place to hang out, have a flaming drink, and get your head shrunk.

In the back of the place is the Pirate Room, which gives the feel of being in the captain's quarters on a ship at sea. But not any old captain, no, this is Captain Faulkner's quarters, though he is no longer there—at least not in the flesh. And what about that Golden Tiki idol? Well, if you keep a weather eye open, once you enter the front doors and have adjusted to the dark, you might just spot it on a lava stone shelf to the right. The idol resting there may or may not be the one found by Captain William Tobias Faulkner. Still, when the Sirens call, it's best not to take the chance and look into its eyes.

THE LITTLE CASINO THAT COULDN'T

Some places just can't seem to get off the ground, no matter how hard they try. Las Vegas has one of these places—a casino that just couldn't fit in on the Strip. But while it may not have found its place in the world, it did manage to find its own ghosts.

"I can't believe you bet that much," she said, taking hold of his arm. This was Melissa's first time in Las Vegas and her boyfriend Tony was showing her a good time . . . a very good time. The two were dressed to the nines. She was wearing a shiny silver dress that hugged her even more tightly than he did. His attire consisted of a dark suit, red shirt, and a tie that matched her dress perfectly.

"Why?" he said, smiling. "I won, didn't I?" Tony clasped her hand in his and walked over to the elevator.

"Sure, but you could've just as easily lost."

"But I didn't," he said, "and that is why we got this suite." Tony pushed the button for the elevator, waiting for it to arrive on the casino level.

"I can't believe they just gave you this suite," Melissa said as they stepped into the mirrored compartment.

"They didn't just give it to me," Tony said, pushing the button for the seventh floor. "I had to earn it."

"With that bet?"

"With that bet. The casino knows that the longer they keep me here, the more chance they have of getting their money back, and, trust me, they want it back."

"So they comped you a room and food? How does that get them their money back?" she asked. "And," Melissa said, smiling, "isn't it your money?"

"It is now," Tony said as the elevator doors opened to the small foyer.

It was called the Panorama Suite because it provided a 180-degree view of the Las Vegas Strip and it was beautiful.

"Oh my gosh!" Melissa said as she entered the main room. The suite was larger than her home, close to 1,800 square feet in all, and seemed to be all windows. The furniture was rich, solid wood, except for the chairs and couches, which were all dark leather.

As Melissa stood at the window, Tony closed the door behind them and made his way around the suite. Their luggage had already been brought up and placed in the bedroom; the bed had been turned down, and a chocolate placed on each pillow. In the main room, at the bar, was a basket of fruit. On the right side of the fruit, a welcome note rested against a bottle of champagne—Ruinart Blanc de Blancs. Two fluted glasses and a corkscrew were conveniently placed next to the bottle.

"Want some champagne?" Tony asked.

"Why not?" she answered.

As Tony uncorked the bottle, he heard a noise at the door to the suite.

That's strange, Tony thought to himself, *that sounds like a key.*

Melissa had heard it too.

"Is someone trying to get in?" she asked. "That sounds like keys in the door."

"That's what I thought," Tony said. "But that's impossible; hotels don't use keys anymore. They haven't for a long time. It's all plastic cards now, and plastic cards don't make that kind of noise." He had put the bottle down and was walking over to the door when he heard the doorbell ring. "I guess someone is there after all," Tony said. When he opened the door, the foyer was empty.

"Who is it?" Melissa asked as Tony stood in the doorway looking out.

"It isn't anyone."

"What do you mean it isn't anyone?" she asked, turning and walking to the door.

"I mean, no one's here. The foyer's empty."

"Maybe they got on the elevator."

"I'd be surprised—I didn't see the doors close. Besides, why would someone ring the doorbell and then just leave?"

"Who knows?" Melissa said, turning to go back inside. "Besides, didn't you offer me champagne?"

"I did at that," Tony said, and shut the door. It was then that he heard the voices. They were coming from the foyer. There were two of them and while he couldn't quite make out what they were saying, Tony clearly heard two voices. He turned sharply and swung the door to the suite open wildly, but the foyer was still empty.

The Tally Ho opened its doors in 1962. The English-themed casino cost its owner, Edwin Lowe, close to $12 million. The Tudor-style country club had leaded windows, a gabled roof, and thick, heavy timber. The property housed thirty-two villas, four swimming pools, and six restaurants. It also had a nine-hole golf course that many claimed was one of the most challenging in the West. What it didn't have was a casino and being surrounded on three sides by hotels with casinos, it was the kiss of death. Lowe went bankrupt and the hotel closed within two years.

In 1964 the Tally Ho got a new owner and a new name, the King's Crown. Unfortunately, the new owner applied for and failed to get a gaming license. The King's Crown closed six months after opening.

Enter casino mogul Milton Prell.

Prell had made his name with the Sahara and the Mint, both successful hotel casinos. In 1961 he decided that the sunshine and ocean mist of Los Angeles was a better fit for him than the desert of Las Vegas and he sold the two properties to real estate developer Dell Webb. However, his self-imposed exile lasted only five years and by 1966 he was ready to come back to his true love, the casino business.

Prell had a grand idea of building a $40 million resort next to his old digs, the Sahara Hotel and Casino, on the site of the defunct El Rancho. Unfortunately, billionaire Howard Hughes beat him to the punch. So Prell simply looked elsewhere. His search brought him to the King's Crown and he wasted no time in purchasing the property.

There hadn't been a new hotel casino built on the Strip in eight years (the Stardust in 1958 was the last). Prell would change all that. His first step was to change the look of the hotel. He said good-bye to the English Tudor and hello to a Middle Eastern–themed resort based on the tales of Aladdin and his forty thieves. Knowing how Las Vegas operated, the first thing Prell built was a casino. He then built a 500-seat theater, which he named the Baghdad Theater showroom. He added an Olympic-size swimming pool and a 150-seat gourmet restaurant, as well as nine more holes to the golf course, making it an eighteen-hole, par-three course.

Like the Dunes, which built a massive genie that stood at the entrance of the hotel over the porte cochere, Prell had a fifteen-story electric sign built, complete with a giant lamp, for the front of his resort. He paid the Young Sign Company $750,000 for the lamp and sign, which needed forty thousand lightbulbs to keep it lit. On April 1, 1966, Prell opened his Aladdin Hotel and Casino. As guests entered the casino, flower petals rained from the ceiling.

From the moment it opened, the Aladdin was a success. Prell put three different shows in the Baghdad Theater showroom and had them perform twice nightly, something unheard of in Las Vegas—then, and now. It worked. Within a year, the Aladdin was the toast of the Strip. It even hosted what was probably the most secret event in the history of Las Vegas—the wedding of Elvis and Priscilla Presley.

Prell knew how to run a casino and he also knew whom he needed to help him do it. He hired Carl Wilson, a man who had worked for him at the Sahara and the Mint, as casino manager. Along with Wilson, he hired an experienced staff and he let them do what they did best: run a successful resort. Unfortunately, Prell's return to the Las Vegas desert may not have been his best bet. While his precious Aladdin thrived, Prell's health began to decline—so much so that shortly after its opening, Prell was forced to sell the Aladdin.

At this point the casino began to take a turn for the worse—one that would soon lead to the property being labeled as "jinxed." In 1969 Prell sold the property to the Parvin/Dohrmann Company, who owned the Fremont. In 1971 they, in turn, sold it to a group of investors headed by Peter and Sorkis Webbe, Sam Diamond, and Richard L. Daly, for $5 million. The new owners dumped $60 million into the resort, expanding the casino and adding a twenty-story tower. They also expanded the showroom into a 7,500-seat theater where the golf course once sat, which they named the Theater for the Performing Arts. The new theater hosted concerts, plays, boxing matches, and even high school graduations.

The original lamp-themed electric sign also got a makeover. The new sign towered 140 feet over the Strip. It cost $300,000 to build and the 40,000 light-bulbs were replaced with state-of-the-art neon and huge attraction panels. When the renovations were complete, the new owners had a grand reopening, paying Neil Diamond a reported $750,000 for two shows.

Although the Aladdin seemed primed for success, it succumbed to one of Las Vegas's most famous obstacles—organized crime. Amid reports of skimming and Mob involvement, Nevada state investigators came calling. Fearing they would lose their gaming license, the owners decided to sell the hotel on their own before the Nevada Gaming Commission forced them to sell.

The 1980s would prove to be a rough decade for the resort. It seemed like the Nevada Gaming Commission wanted the hotel to fail. "I told the Nevada Gaming Commission—and it is part of the record—please do not close the property," said Mr. Entertainment and Las Vegas resident Wayne Newton. The reported ties to the Mob had made the Aladdin an embarrassment to the commission, which simply wanted it gone. But Newton had other ideas. Not only did he want to preserve a bit of Las Vegas history, he was also concerned for the thousands of employees who would suddenly be out of work if the casino failed.

"I was working hard to close the deal to buy the Aladdin, because I didn't want to see the employees out on the street," Newton said. "It was so irritating. They gave us thirty days to meet their requirements. When we did, they put in new ones. They wanted the Aladdin closed."

Nevada Senator Harry Reid, then chairman of the Nevada Gaming Commission, confirmed Newton's supposition. "We also wanted the employees to remain working, but there was nothing we could do because the place was being run by a bunch of gangsters and the whole world was watching," he said in an interview with the *Las Vegas Sun.* "We really felt compelled to do something drastic."

Something drastic was indeed necessary. In August of 1979 the state of Nevada closed the hotel only to have it ordered opened immediately by federal judge Harry Claiborne. Eleven months later it was closed again by the Nevada Gaming Commission. In September Newton stepped in and bought the hotel with his partner Ed Torres, the former chief executive officer of the Riviera, for $85 million.

It was a sale that was almost thwarted by another entertainment giant, *The Tonight Show*'s Johnny Carson. According to Newton, Carson and gaming veteran Ed Nigro were poised to purchase the hotel. "Mr. Carson and Mr. Nigro all but had the Aladdin," Newton recalled. "The previous stockholders had gotten into trouble and had to sell the place, and they were being squeezed."

However, the deal was not to be. According to Newton, just about every time the owners thought they had made a deal, Carson and Nigro would change the terms. The owners became frustrated and contacted Newton to see if he was still interested in the property.

"I was coming off stage at the Sands at two o'clock one morning and a friend called and said, 'Is your offer still on the table?' I said it is, and he said to meet him and the Aladdin stockholders at 8:00 a.m. at the Aladdin," said Newton in an interview with the *Las Vegas Sun.* "I met Sorkis Webbe that morning, and he said, 'Kid, we want you to have the Aladdin.' But it was not so much that they wanted me to own the Aladdin. It was that they were frustrated and wanted anyone but them [Carson and Nigro] to own it. I wanted the Aladdin because I thought I could put a face on it."

Unfortunately, Newton and his new partner were never able to see eye to eye. Almost from the beginning he and Torres had "philosophical differences," as Newton called them. The two disagreed on even the simplest things, like the size of the shot glasses in the showroom. Torres also wanted to fire some of the longtime employees and Newton, loyal to the end, wouldn't hear of it. In 1982 Newton sold his portion of the Aladdin to Torres for $8.5 million.

The Aladdin would be sold many more times throughout the years until finally closing for good on November 25, 1997. On April 27 of the next year the property was imploded, except for the Theater for the Performing Arts, which was spared from the wrecking ball—or in the case of Las Vegas, the dynamite charge.

Like a phoenix rising from the ashes, the New Aladdin opened on August 18, 2000. But like the old Aladdin, the casino still seemed to be jinxed. On opening day more than a thousand protestors gathered outside the resort, upset that the hotel had opened without a union contract. The hotel would fail one final time, and on June 20, 2003, it was sold in bankruptcy to a partnership of Planet Hollywood and Starwood Hotels & Resorts Worldwide. It was reopened on April 17, 2007, as Planet Hollywood Resort and Casino. The property is currently owned by Caesars Entertainment, who officially acquired the property on February 19, 2010.

It would seem that ghosts don't really care who owns the property. Guests who stay in the Panorama Suite have reported hearing voices in the foyer, keys in the door, and the doorbell ringing with no one there. One guest who stayed there recently reported having the television turn on and off on its own. On one occasion two hotel guests told the guest room attendant they didn't need the room cleaned; they only wanted fresh towels, which she gave to them. When the guests returned to the room later that day, they found that, contrary to their request, the room had been cleaned, but not by the maid. Instead, the main bathroom had been serviced, ghost-style. "The washcloths were laid out on the counter with all the little soaps, lotions, and shampoo bottles in a perfect circle around them." The guest also reported waking up to the sound of someone sweeping the carpet.

No one knows the source of these ghostly occurrences, but it would appear that whoever the spirit is, its main concern is simply playing pranks on those who stay in the room. The ghost does not appear to have any bad intentions, much to the delight of those who have encountered it. The experience is best described by one of those guests: "That place was spooky, to say the least, but we did feel welcomed."

Welcomed indeed! Some ghosts are spooky, some are scary, and some are just . . . well, some are just playful. That seems to be the case with the spooks in the Panorama Suite. If you are lucky enough to stay there, your best weapon against the spirit who dwells within its walls may simply be a good sense of humor.

MR. PETRIE

In some Las Vegas high schools, "school spirit" takes on a whole new meaning. One school in particular is home to a well-dressed man who can be found in the auditorium, watching over the school and playing tricks on the students who perform there.

They had snuck into the auditorium after lunch. It was, after all, the best place to talk about boys, and they already had one in mind to dish on.

"Did you see what he was wearing?" she said to her friends as they gathered around, taking the seats on either side of her. One girl placed her feet against the back of the seat in front of her, sinking down to a near-reclining position. Another sat on the back of the seats facing her friends. She placed her feet on the cushion of the seat she was facing.

"I know! As soon as he walked into the classroom, I was like, wow, where did you get those pants?"

"I think you all are being too hard on him," said the girl who sat on the back of the seats. "Maybe he just doesn't have mirrors in his home."

"Oh, you're terrible," the first girl said, causing all the others to laugh. As their giggles filled the auditorium, echoing through the empty seats, they continued to talk about the strangely dressed boy. It was at this point that the girls saw an older man coming toward them. He was dressed well, in a suit and tie, and the girls assumed right away that he was a teacher, there to bust them—not only for being in the auditorium, but also for making so much noise. The girls tried to stifle errant laughs as the man raised one finger to his lips.

"Did anyone else just get cold?" one of the girls asked.

"Yes," another confirmed, hugging her arms to her chest.

As the man came closer to where they were sitting, the girls noticed that he had no feet. In fact, the man they had assumed was a teacher was actually floating a few inches off the ground. Floating, right there in front of them. As the realization swept over the group, the girls screamed loudly and sped out of the auditorium, running just as fast as they could move.

Opened in 1931, during the Great Depression, Las Vegas High School, as it was then known, was built during the construction of the most ambitious government project in many years—the Hoover Dam. Originally called the Boulder Dam, the Hoover Dam was authorized by President Calvin Coolidge in 1928 and was designed to tame the mighty Colorado River, reducing its frequent floods and providing power to both Nevada and Arizona.

While many of the workers who built the dam lived in the newly created Boulder City, others chose to live in the nearby town of Las Vegas, where the rules were much less stringent. As the workers and their families moved in, the small town of Las Vegas grew rapidly, rising to a population of more than five thousand people and prompting the need for a high school. Though it was originally thought to be too far out of town (it was located way out on Seventh Street), Las Vegas would eventually grow around and encompass the beautiful art deco–style school.

When it was built originally, the school consisted of three buildings: the three-level main building, the gymnasium, and a third building that was torn down in 1950. That same year a 1,427-seat Performing Arts Center was built near the school. At some point after the school opened, students began reporting lights turning on and off by themselves and doors slamming with no one around. Many also claimed to see an older gentleman who seemed only to appear in the school's auditorium.

Conflicting stories abound regarding the origin of the ghost, nicknamed "Mr. Petrie." Some say he was an elderly man who died when the house he lived in near the school caught on fire. Other stories have him murdered by his wife, who then buried his body in the house's foundation. While these stories place Petrie in a house in the area, available evidence would seem to indicate that this may not exactly be the case. The most compelling proof is an aerial photograph of the area surrounding the high school, taken in 1930—the year the school was built. In the photograph only a few buildings can be seen in the surrounding area (remember, people complained that the school was built so far out of town). While one of the buildings was a house, it belonged to George E. Harris, former principal of Las Vegas High School, not anyone named Petrie.

Some stories report Petrie as a person who suffered from psychotic episodes, one of which caused him to fall into a hole dug by construction workers who were building the school's theater. Other rumors claim that he was a former student or possibly a former teacher who watches over the school. When one of the girls who saw him in the auditorium that day was asked, she said, "Oh yes, he was a teacher. He had that air about him."

Many of these stories seem not only far-fetched, but well-embellished versions of a tale originally told by another source. Truth is, while no one with the last name of Petrie has ever been directly connected to the school, another man who bore a name similar to Petrie's was remotely connected to the land the school sits on. According to the Clark County Assessor's Office, a man named Frank *Partie* once owned the parcel of land the school's theater is built upon. Partie was an electrician who worked for the city of Las Vegas. In 1933, he and his wife, Sylvia, sold the parcel to E. A. Clark, a local realtor and business owner. The Parties kept the land they owned on Ninth Street, across from Fremont Street, two blocks away from the school.

Although many ghosts seem shy, even reserved, this is not the case with Mr. Petrie. This ghost not only likes to been seen, he also likes to have his picture taken, as is evident in the 1968 Las Vegas High School yearbook, which some claim contains a photo of Mr. Petrie himself. In 1986 Las Vegas High School was placed on the National Register of Historic Places, and in 1993, the school was reopened as a performing arts school and renamed the Las Vegas Academy of International Studies, Performing & Visual Arts.

While the school may have changed its name, its most famous resident remained, reminding students that their unofficial mascot wasn't going anywhere. Almost immediately after the name change, students reported doors opening by themselves. Two students rehearsing in an enclosed hallway saw a door swing open. The students went to the door, closed and locked it, and then continued rehearsing—that is, until the same door swung open a second time. "We latched the door and it did it again," one of the girls said. "I swear it was Petrie. . . . There's no way wind could have hit it or anything."

Even teachers can boast of their own Petrie tales. Some claim to have turned lights off on the catwalk only to have them come back on when they got back to the stage.

But it is the students who remember him most fondly. "It never scared me," said a 1993 graduate. "Petrie never seemed like a ghost who set out to scare you. He played games, and if you got scared by the games, then I guess he would think it was funny."

"I never felt any fear in that place," said another student. "It was cool."

The Las Vegas Academy isn't the only high school in the valley where ghosts have been spotted. Another high school in the Las Vegas area that has a ghostly

visitor is the Southeast Career and Technical Academy. The school originally opened in 1966 as the Southern Nevada Vocational Technical Center, or "Vo-Tech," as it was called. Vo-Tech was the first magnet school opened by the Clark County School District. As a vocational school, the high school offers programs that satisfy the needs of those students looking for an alternative to the traditional high school curriculum.

It also offers a ghost. But unlike Mr. Petrie, this ghost is only seen late at night, typically around 11:00 p.m. According to several witnesses, an older man can be seen standing near the doors of the gymnasium. One witness in particular reported seeing the old man standing by the doorway.

"He was wearing this brown jumpsuit thing with a name embroidered in yellow on the front of it," said the witness, who assumed the older man was a janitor. While the witness could see the name tag, he wasn't able to make out the name. He walked over to the man he thought was a janitor and asked him a question.

"I asked him what time it was and he just sort of smirked at me . . ."

And then the old man walked through the doors, right *through* the doors.

"He looked as solid as you or I," the witness reported, but when the janitor went through the doors, it gave him the chills. "I tell you, that's something I'm not apt to forget."

UNIQUE PLACES AND GHOULISH FACES

LAS VEGAS IS SOMETIMES SEEN SOLELY AS BRIGHT lights and casinos. People who visit here seem to forget that there is a real town with real people lurking just off either side of the Strip. In this last part of our ghostly tour, we'll visit some of Las Vegas's not-so-well-known haunts. We'll go to a couple of parks—one where a pioneer woman weeps for her lost family and another where a little boy comes to play on a swing after midnight. But beware, for your own good, don't approach him! We'll go to the Scotch 80s, one of the oldest parts of town, and visit a house with a secret room, where lost souls may have met a dastardly demise and ghosts terrorize its owners. We'll visit a museum where all the malevolent spirits are invited to gather and a 50-year-old doll, named Peggy, holds court. Then, in true ghost-hunter style, we'll head to a couple of cemeteries. There we'll meet Stoney, an elephant who met a tragic ending;

and, quite possibly, we'll see the guardian white cat that only shows itself to those it likes.

So keep your arms and legs in the vehicle at all times, take all the pictures you want, and let's get ready for the final show.

DEMON SWING

In a small park next to a school and a church, a child swings alone every night . . . and he prefers it that way. When approached, he makes it very clear that he doesn't want anyone around.

Bruce and Selina had just started dating. They were at that stage where everything was wonderful. The leaves on the trees were a deep, rich green, the air was especially fresh, and the sky was a brilliant shade of blue. All Bruce and Selina wanted to do was spend time with each other and they took every opportunity to do just that. Tonight was no different. They had come to the park where they could sit on the benches under the trees.

It was almost twilight when they arrived and children were still playing soccer in the grassy field. An older man was teaching his grandson how to fly a remote-controlled helicopter on the baseball field, its lights flashing green and red as it lifted off the ground. A middle-aged father struggled to keep up with his teenage son as they kicked a ball to each other. Mothers, keeping one eye on their children, discussed school, teachers, and possibly their husbands as they sat on the stair-stepped terraces cut into the small hill that led to the open field.

Bruce and Selina chose a bench near a tree that had been planted in remembrance of a loved one. The dedication on the plaque was written in another language—possibly German—and, in this stage of their love affair, they found it especially appealing. They sat on the bench hand in hand as they watched the first and eventually the last person leave the park. As the sun set, the two remained on the bench, locked in a lovers' embrace.

Bruce and Selina talked, held each other close, and even kissed on occasion. Before they knew it, the entire day had passed and the next one had begun. "What time is it?" Selina finally asked.

Looking at his watch, Bruce was surprised at what he found. "Oh my gosh, it's after midnight. We need to get you home," he said as the wind rustled the leaves in the trees around them.

He felt a chill and in the distance heard a chain rattle. The sound caused him to instinctively turn toward the swings. There were two swing sets. The one intended for older kids had seats made of thick blue plastic, attached to the metal frame with strong, heavy chain. The other set was designed for those too young to sit only on a small piece of plastic. On this set the seats were smaller and made of molded plastic. Leg holes allowed smaller children to sit in the seat without the threat of falling out.

Each set had two swings and one of the older kids' swings seemed to be moving. At first Bruce thought it was the wind that was making the swing move, but as he continued to watch, he noticed that the movements were deliberate—almost as if someone was . . . well, swinging.

"Do you see that?" Bruce asked Selina.

"See what?"

"That swing. It's moving."

"What swing?"

"That one," Bruce said, pointing to the swing, which was now moving at a slow, steady, rhythmic pace, "right over there. Do you see that?"

Selina saw the moving swing and immediately took hold of his hand. "That's not the wind," she said. "What could be making it move like that? What do you think . . . ?"

Before Selina could get her question out, they saw it. It seemed to suddenly appear right in front of them. In fact, if they hadn't been watching the swing the whole time, they wouldn't have believed it. A white mist appeared to gather around the swing and as it dispersed, they saw it. A boy, it was a boy, swinging in the swing. Right in front of them, a boy was now swinging—and he hadn't been there only moments earlier.

Bruce took a step closer and Selina pulled him back. "Don't," she pleaded. "Let's just get out of here."

"It's just a boy," Bruce said. "What could he be? About six?"

"Yeah, a boy that up until a few seconds ago wasn't even there."

"But he's still a boy," Bruce said, taking another step toward the swing. Selina clutched his arm, positioning herself a little behind him as the two moved slowly toward the boy. They walked along the cement path that led to the swing sets, inching their way, neither of them in a hurry to arrive.

"It's going to be okay," Bruce said aloud, more to calm his own nerves than anything. The boy seemed to hear him and, still swinging, looked over toward the couple.

"Are you lost?" Bruce asked. The boy didn't answer.

The couple continued their approach and were within twenty feet when the boy's face seemed to change. It was subtle at first, but as they drew closer the face continued to distort until it was hideous—demon-like. Selina screamed and clutched Bruce's arm as hard as she could, burying her face. Bruce just stood, mesmerized, watching the scene that unfolded before him. The swing had stopped and the boy was now staring straight at him. Their eyes locked and a chill ran down Bruce's spine. The air around him seemed to drop in temperature. He was just about to turn and run when the boy suddenly disappeared as quickly as he had come.

Many rumors abound about the boy ghost that is said to haunt Fox Ridge Park. Several people have reported seeing the demon boy swinging after midnight. According to some reports the boy was killed by a drunk driver near the park. Other reports have the boy running after a ball into the busy street before being hit by a car. This urban legend is well known by the people who live in the area, as well as the boys and girls who attend the nearby Estes McDoniel Elementary School.

"There were many rumors of the young ghost boy . . . passed around from students at the school," said one former student.

A parent of a student who also attended the elementary school reported hearing the story of the ghost boy. "I have heard this story many times and other accounts of hauntings in the school."

Those who have visited the park, which coincidently sits right across from a church, have reported seeing all manner of strange events. "One of the swings started moving a little bit from side to side," one witness reported. Another told of hearing a child's voice saying "Good-bye" to him and a group of his friends. Still another recalled a time when she visited the park and talked with a man who claimed to have captured a confirming photograph of mist on his camera.

"I went to the park tonight in hopes to see the little boy on the swing," the woman said. "I encountered a man who had come to the park several times. He was taking pictures around the swing set and all the pictures had white smoke in them, which clearly wasn't there when he was taking the picture."

This smoke or mist has also been reported by those who have gone on the Haunted Vegas Tour. One participant of the tour—which no longer goes to the park at the request of the residents in the area—reported seeing a white mist. "A foggy white mist arose right in front of me, and I swear I could see the face of a child in it," the witness said. "I looked over at the swings and they were moving like someone was in them."

At least one local paranormal investigation team is certain that the park is haunted. In a 2009 investigation, the husband-and-wife team reported having contact with the boy. They arrived at the park shortly after midnight on a cool April evening. The moon was full and the wind still. The duo had brought with them a night-vision camera, a voice recorder, an EMF meter, and a token of their friendship for the boy.

"I had brought a basketball with me to offer the spirit child a token of friendship, in hopes of some interaction," said Susi Miller of the Red Rock Canyon Paranormal Society.

Susi placed the ball underneath the preferred swing of the ghost child, after which she placed the voice recorder and the EMF meter on the seat of the swing. "I began to ask questions of him in pleasant conversation," Susi said. "Nothing happened."

They did, however, start to get readings on their EMF meter, readings that seemed to have no explainable source. "We were not under power lines or light poles. In fact, it was fairly dark in the park with just the perimeter being lit by greenish fixtures."

It was about seven minutes into their investigation when the basketball began rolling on its own. "The basketball rolled quickly across the play area! No wind, no one touched it, it just rolled with a positive, definite force about ten feet away from the swing set."

As her husband recorded the event, Susi was certain they had made contact with the ghost boy. She spoke as if she were talking to the boy, asking him if he wanted to play with her ball again. According to Susi, as she replaced the basketball under the swing, her EMF meter went off again. "The K2 meter lit up like a carnival ride! My heart skipped a beat with excitement."

Susi continued to speak to the boy in a motherly tone, the lights on the EMF meter blinking in response to each question. It was at this point that Susi noticed the swing moving in a circular motion, and when she touched the swing, she "felt the presence of some resistance against the chains."

Susi sat down in the swing next to the boy's, removing the voice recorder and EMF meter from his swing so that he could sit down if he so chose. About twenty minutes had passed when Susi asked the spirit if he liked them being there. She also asked him not to fear them and not to turn into a demon. It was at this moment, according to Susi, that she felt a presence take hold of her.

"At that exact moment, a force pulled me by my jacket right off the swing in which I was sitting, next to his swing, directly onto the ground, backward! I was so shocked, not hurt, but definitely, it got my attention."

After Susi's husband, Dave, helped her up, the couple tried to assure the boy that she was okay and that they didn't blame him for the fall. "I was trying to assure him rather than blame him, even though I knew a reliable force had pulled me off the swing," Susi recalled. Their only response was dead lights on the EMF meter.

Susi walked around the park for a while, eventually returning to the swing. Dave had stayed at the swing and when Susi returned he reported no additional interaction. Dave told Susi that the fall off the swing had probably upset the child spirit and scared him away. But Dave was wrong, because as soon as Susi came back, she seemed to be able to reestablish contact.

"I sat back down and began to try to reestablish communication with him. In a short period of time, the K2 meter began to light up again. It was apparent that this spirit wanted only to communicate with a woman, or possibly a mother figure."

However, despite all of their efforts, the boy never appeared and eventually they stopped getting readings altogether.

"We continued to talk with him for a few more minutes, and then, nearing 1:30 a.m., activity seemed to end. I no longer felt his presence as I had from the moment we'd arrived. The hair stood up on my arms and neck as soon as we arrived at the park, and now had stopped. Our session in Fox Ridge Park had come to an end. It was time to head for home."

The next day when the couple reviewed all the evidence they had collected, they were shocked with what they had found. Their voice-recording devices had picked up two very distinctive EVPs of the boy answering Susi's questions. When she asked the boy if he wanted to play with the ball again, he said, "No." He repeated the same response when asked if he liked them being there.

According to Susi, "There is absolutely no question . . . Fox Ridge Park is haunted."

But Fox Ridge Park is not the only park where suspicious activity has been reported. Green Valley Park also has its share of supernatural occurrences. Located on the corner of Pecos Road and Millcroft Drive, the little park has a baseball diamond, basketball court, playground, bathroom, built-in barbecue pit, and picnic tables. It also has ghosts. Just how many ghosts is up to interpretation.

The most common reports are of a woman who, when she appears, seems to be dressed in the clothing typical of a pioneer woman. The woman is supposedly the lone survivor of a family massacre. As the story goes, a family was following the Union Pacific Railroad tracks west in their covered wagon when they stopped in the area that eventually became the park. As the family made camp, they cooked, cleaned up, and bedded down for the night. At some point the family—which included a husband, wife, and several children—were attacked by Native Americans. The wife managed to get away by hiding somewhere among the family's belongings, but the rest of the family did not survive. The woman is seen in only one area of the park: by the picnic tables at the corner where the streets meet, in clear view of the still-existent railroad tracks. When seen, the woman is always sobbing.

But she isn't the only person who reportedly haunts the park. In another tale two brothers were killed there sometime in the 1970s. The brothers, who are reported to be approximately nineteen and thirteen, were killed near the same picnic tables where the pioneer woman sits and weeps. People claim to have taken photos of the brothers, who also are only ever spotted by the picnic tables. Some people also claim to have been pushed when they stood by the mailbox, which is located in the same area.

One visitor to the park was able to snap a photo of what appears to be a person standing by the mailbox. He was there with the Haunted Vegas Tour and took four photos within seconds of each other. The person was not in the first three photos . . . only the last.

Parks are supposed to be family-friendly places where children play, couples coo, and families gather. Yet even the great outdoors can be home to spooks and spirits who find as much comfort in these places as do the living. While we may never know the origin of the boy on the swing, we do know that the swing is where he feels the safest and, apparently, the place where he would rather be left alone.

STONEY'S STORY

It's a tragedy when animals die—especially when those animals are pets. Unfortunately, the tragedy can often start long before the animal has passed on. Stoney was a wonderful, kind-hearted elephant that left this world far too soon and under the worst conditions possible. His ghost still roams the cemetery where he was laid to rest. In another cemetery a small white cat keeps vigil over its eternal residents.

She was their pride and joy. They had gotten her as a puppy and she had come into their lives at the perfect time. They had been unable to have children and while a dog certainly can't take the place of a child, she had brought them the love they had been missing. She had made their family whole again; she was the love of their lives.

So when her life ended, all too soon, they wanted to keep her close—wanted to be able to visit her whenever they could, wanted her not to be forgotten. The Craig Road Pet Cemetery was the perfect place. The ceremony was short but done very nicely. Their friends had come for support, and the headstone they picked out was perfect: our beloved harley, above a photo and two dates.

"I miss her already," she said to her husband through teary eyes.

"I do too." He wanted to say, "She's in a better place," but it just seemed too clichéd. Instead he told his wife that they had picked a wonderful spot. "Harley would've loved it here."

She looked around the cemetery, trying to hold a fragile smile. Pine trees shaded the lush green lawns. A small A-frame chapel with stained-glass windows, where services were held, gave it the feel of a real cemetery. Benches were strategically placed, allowing owners to sit and remember their pets, running, playing, and licking their faces. "It is wonderful," she agreed.

It was at that moment she noticed movement out of the corner of her eye. It was over to her right, and she had to turn her head slightly to see where the movement originated. When she turned, she couldn't believe her eyes.

"Is that what I think it is?"

"What?" her husband responded.

"There! Over there!" she exclaimed, pointing to a large gray figure strolling across the lawn.

"It couldn't be," he said, immediately noticing the immense figure. "But it is. That's an elephant!"

The Craig Road Pet Cemetery is a well-manicured official pet cemetery where the remains of household pets can find their final resting place. The pets of Liberace, Snoop Dogg, Robert Goulet, and Redd Foxx all have prominent spots on the grounds. The cemetery has been in business for more than forty years and in that time has taken in over 6,700 pets. One of those is Stoney.

When the Luxor opened on October 15, 1993, *The Winds of the Gods* was playing in its Pharaoh's Theater. The show was created by Peter Jackson, known for his *King Arthur's Tournament,* a medieval dinner show featuring jousting knights who fight for glory in a Camelot-style showdown at the Excalibur Hotel Casino. *The Winds of the Gods* was an action-packed, variety dinner show with an Egyptian theme.

One of the stars of the show was Stoney, a beautiful young bull elephant with long ivory tusks, who performed acts in a circus-type ring. Stoney was an Asian elephant, distinguished from their larger African cousins not only by their smaller size, but by their smaller, rounded ears and the two bumps on their forehead. Asian elephants are strong, social, and intelligent, which has often made them the perfect choice for use in transportation, labor, and, unfortunately, entertainment. Asian elephants can grow up to twenty-one feet long, weigh up to eleven thousand pounds, and despite their size, are able to walk silently.

Stoney was born at the Metro Washington Park Zoo (now the Oregon Zoo) in Portland, Oregon, on June 17, 1973. Both of Stoney's parents were born in the wild, his mother from Thailand and his father from Cambodia. Stoney was part of the zoo's breeding program that started in 1962 with the birth of Packy, the first elephant born in the Western Hemisphere in forty-four years. The birth was covered by *Life* magazine and started the Oregon Zoo on a journey toward understanding elephant gestation periods and setting standards for the treatment of elephants in captivity.

Unfortunately, Stoney didn't stay long at the zoo. In 1974 Stoney was designated a surplus animal, meaning he had "made [his] genetic contribution to a managed population and is not essential for future scientific studies or to maintain social-group stability or traditions," as defined by the Species Survival Plan (SSP). Less than a year after his birth, on May 6, 1974, he was sold to Ken Chisholm. Less than a year later, Chisholm would sell Stoney to Mike La Torres, an animal trainer, in April of 1975.

Stoney spent his life as a performer in several different circuses worldwide. His trainer, the now-deceased La Torres, reportedly kept Stoney thin because he believed a thinner, less-strong bull elephant was easier to control. He is also reported as having been abusive to the elephant. In 1993, at the young age of twenty, Stoney was signed by La Torres to *The Winds of the Gods* show. According to one report, show officials instructed La Torres to "fatten" Stoney up. Stoney performed nightly, coming out in front of the crowd, rising up on his hind legs, and then doing a type of handstand on his two front legs.

Elephants are remarkable animals; it's an amazing sight to watch an animal that large balancing itself on its two front legs. However, the act isn't natural to them. Elephants in the wild do not support their massive weight on their two front legs, nor do they do such things as balance on small platforms. These "tricks" that elephants are forced to perform typically result in leg and foot problems, which are the major cause of death in captive elephants. It was this fact that caused animal rights activists to protest Stoney's treatment in the show.

One day in September of 1994, Stoney was warming up backstage. He was lifting himself up on his hind legs when he suddenly pulled a hamstring muscle in his rear left leg. The injury was serious. What happened next is a matter of debate, but sources claim that because there was no place to put the injured elephant, Stoney was forced into a dumpster located behind the hotel.

While it is not known for sure if a dumpster was used, it is known that Stoney, being unable to stand, was eventually moved to a strong mechanical holding device called a "cattle crush," commonly used for examination or veterinary treatment. Unfortunately, the cattle crush wasn't able to support Stoney's entire weight and he was forced to spend most of his time trying to support his own weight on his damaged leg, or kneeling with his belly resting on a metal platform.

On August 26, 1995, Stoney was due to be transferred to an elephant-breeding farm in Arkansas. Veterinarians were brought in to tranquilize Stoney for the move and a crane was on the ready to lift him into a specially equipped truck once he was outside of the building. However, there was still the challenge of getting Stoney outside to the crane.

Animal rights activists were present for the move, which was at least partially filmed. On the day Stoney was set to be moved, he tried to stand on several occasions, trumpeting loudly with pain. As handlers tried to figure out how to move

Stoney without causing him further pain, he kept resting his weight on the metal platform. When it came time for Stoney to move, the metal platform was removed and Stoney stood. However, his injured leg was not strong enough to support his massive weight. He cried out in pain as he tried to move, and in the attempt, broke the femur of his other hind leg.

According to one of the crane operators, after Stoney fell, "he was lying on the ground, sort of groaning in pain." When La Torres walked in, Stoney, ever the loyal elephant, called to his trainer, "then he reached out his trunk to the guy like he wanted to touch him." La Torres told Stoney to "cut it out" and pushed his trunk away. Two days later, on August 28, 1995, Stoney was euthanized. He was buried whole in the Craig Road Pet Cemetery.

It is unknown why Stoney was kept so long in the poor conditions behind the Luxor. Responding to a complaint made by the animal protection group, Performing Animal Welfare Society (PAWS), the US Department of Agriculture visited the site where Stoney was kept and saw "a considerable buildup of feces in the animal bar." They also noted "a buildup of flies near the animal's crush." They stated that Stoney was given a diet of grass, hay, and grain, but was not "currently receiving any fresh produce" due to a lack of refrigeration.

Stoney still has a presence in Las Vegas. Not only can he reportedly be seen roaming the cemetery, walking slowly as he grazes happily on the grass lawn, he also has his own Myspace page. His headstone reads IN LOVING MEMORY OF STONEY, A GENTLE GIANT.

While Stoney is probably the biggest ghost Las Vegas has to offer, a much smaller ghost haunts another pet cemetery on the other side of town. Over thirty million visitors come to Las Vegas every year, and many of them choose to take the long journey to Laughlin to experience the flair of Vegas on a much smaller scale. Every one of those people pass by a makeshift cemetery nestled in the low, grassy desert on the east side of the highway.

The cemetery, commonly called the Boulder City Pet Cemetery, is not a real cemetery at all; that is, it isn't a "formal" cemetery. However, it is a place where people have gone to lay their deceased pets to rest for many years. Trouble is, finding the cemetery is not easy, even for those who know where it is.

Legend has it that the cemetery got its start in 1953, when veterinarian Marwood Doud was searching for a place to bury the deceased pets of his clients.

The town of Boulder City wasn't too keen on the idea of a pet cemetery right next to the human cemetery, so Doud looked for a place a bit farther out of town. He chose a spot right in the heart of the desert, a place hidden by natural growing grass, creosote bushes, and mesquite trees.

Another story attributes the site to Emory Lockette, a longtime civil engineer with the federal Bureau of Reclamation, who began offering pet funeral services in 1953. According to one report in *The Nevadan*, "One local pet owner, Elton Garrett, said he was pleased with the way Lockette handled the burial of his dog, Snickle Fritz. The pet was placed in a cloth-lined wooden box and the grave was fenced and marked with a wooden cross. The charge was fifty dollars." In the same report, Lockette said that he'd arrange for someone else to take his place when he could no longer handle the job, so that the cemetery could carry on.

The three-acre cemetery has no official plot sites or grid lines. The graves are laid out haphazardly. There is no map indicating which animal is buried where, when they became a resident, or who their owners used to be. Some graves have elaborate granite headstones while others simply have a name etched on a wooden cross. Many graves are decorated with fancy wrought-iron fences; some have a heavy concrete slab covering the grave; while others are simply marked with a mound of rocks.

Instead of flowers, owners typically leave chew toys, treats, and even bowls of water—because apparently ghosts can also get parched. One owner even built a doghouse on the site to provide his pet with shade in the hereafter. The site on the whole has the flavor of something that might be found at the boot hill grave of any old Western town. In fact, the cemetery has often been affectionately referred to as "Puss 'n' Boot Hill."

In 1976 the State of Nevada decided the cemetery had to go. It asked the Bureau of Land Management—the official owners of the land—to clear out the site. The BLM determined that the site had been established "without official permission" and could not legally remain there. The plan was to have the owners actually dig up their beloved pets and move them somewhere else.

Luckily, a group of concerned pet owners formed the Incorporated Desert Pet Cemetery Association. The group managed to work out a deal with the BLM and the state that allowed the cemetery to stay intact in its current location. In 1995 Boulder City officially bought the El Dorado Valley where the cemetery lay and it officially became city property, although the pet cemetery remained unauthorized.

For the most part, the older sites are closer to the highway, with the newer sites farther into the desert. The cemetery was used more in the 1950s and '60s and not as much in the '70s, '80s, and '90s. In 2009 a proposal was granted to build an official pet cemetery near the city's wastewater treatment plant. However, the old site still remains near and dear to many residents, not only of Boulder City, but of Las Vegas as well.

That may be due to the guardian cat that roams the graveyard at night. According to several reports, a white cat can be seen walking around the site, but only after midnight. The cat will follow visitors around the site—that is, if it likes them. While the cat may at first seem like any other "normal" cat that accidently strayed onto the site, when it suddenly disappears, it's easy to tell this is no ordinary cat. In Las Vegas, people aren't the only ghosts who never want to leave.

HELL HOUSE

New York may have its Amityville, but Vegas has its La Palazza, a house where demonic voices taunt and terrorize those who are unfortunate enough to live there. The house makes you wonder if a person can really become possessed. Can the dark energy of the events the house was forced to endure still remain, long after the people who committed those crimes have passed on to the next world?

He had made it. He was in Las Vegas and now he owned his dream house. This house was going to stand as a symbol of his success. It was going to help him make his mark—at least, that's what he thought.

Chris Martinez was standing behind the bar area of his new home. His beautiful, blonde girlfriend, Heather Gosovich, was seated on one of the stools on the other side of the bar. Seated next to her was her girlfriend and next to that woman was his buddy Tony. The bar was beautiful. It was made of solid wood and had a marble top. Bottles of alcohol rested behind the bar and glass racks were located above the marble top. A full assortment of wineglasses hung upside down in the rack.

Music was playing as the two couples drank cocktails and enjoyed each other's company. Chris smiled with pride as he played host. Suddenly, out of nowhere, a couple of the glasses slid across the rack and came crashing down on the marble top. While many people might have just chalked the event up to a strange occurrence or a misaligned rack, Chris knew what it was. He had begun noticing things when he first moved into the house.

It had all started with his beloved dog, Roxy, a beautiful pit bull who was Chris's pride and joy. Roxy was the first to notice that something was just not right with this new house. Roxy would sit in one position and follow things with her head—things that Chris, at first, could not see. Roxy knew something was in the house and she also knew that whatever it was, it was something to be feared. Roxy hated being in the house. At night this well-trained dog would pee the bed and then start shaking. Chris quickly realized that this behavior just wasn't like Roxy, so he started paying more attention.

It was then that Chris noticed the woman. He first saw her out of the corner of his eye and then eventually saw her fully. She was an older woman wearing a wide-brimmed hat and large Jackie O.–style sunglasses. Every time he saw the woman, she was sitting in the chair in the living room. He soon came to realize that his new house, the one on which he had pinned all his hopes and dreams, was haunted.

When the glass crashed on the marble top of the bar, Chris knew it wasn't an accident. He knew it was the ghost and he had had enough. He walked around the end of the bar, took hold of a large barbarian-type sword he had in the room, and started challenging the ghost.

Chris swung the sword wildly, screaming, "You come in here, break my glasses, scare my friends and girlfriend. Come on!" At that exact moment Chris began choking. Two indentations were suddenly visible around his neck. Chris felt like someone had taken hold of his throat and was squeezing. He dropped the sword.

"Help him!" screamed Heather. "Help him!"

Tony, who had been sitting and watching the events unfold in complete shock, suddenly had his wits about him. He jumped from the stool and rushed over to his friend Chris, taking him in a bear hug and forcing him toward the front door. Heather ran ahead of him, throwing the front door open violently as the two men arrived. Tony threw Chris out of the entrance and as soon as he was free from the house, Chris gasped for air and immediately started breathing again.

"That was the first time when I realized that what you can't see can still touch you," Chris said.

La Palazza, as it is called, is a 4,815-square-foot house with four bedrooms, three and a half baths, and a large porte cochere over the front door. The one-story house sits on a corner lot that is a little over a half-acre in size. It was built in 1959 in an old area of town, just off the Strip, known as the Scotch 80s. It has a U-shaped entrance guarded by two steel gates. At the height of the Las Vegas boom, the house was valued at over $1 million.

The Scotch 80s is an area of town where many of the rich and famous have homes. In fact, comedian Jerry Lewis's home is just on the other side of the wall from La Palazza. When the house was built, the Mob ruled Las Vegas with an iron fist. Although Benjamin "Bugsy" Siegel is credited with having invented Las Vegas, he didn't come to Las Vegas on his own and he certainly didn't come to town with grandiose dreams of opening a resort. Instead, he came to get the Mob ensconced in race betting. Siegel and Meyer Lansky, friends since childhood, both viewed Las Vegas as a prime opportunity.

When Siegel came to the then small town of Las Vegas, he, with the help of fellow Mob member Moe Sedway, established the Trans-America race wire service. Designed to compete with the established Continental Press Service, the Trans-America wire dissemination service provided the results for the race books, as well as for horse racing. This business allowed the two men to run race betting. Siegel was elated! Not only was this new enterprise legal in Nevada, he was also able to charge subscribers enough of a fee to bring in somewhere near $25,000 a month. It was only because this proved so successful that Siegel and Lansky even thought about moving into gambling.

In 1945 Siegel saw an opportunity to get into the casino business, and he took it. A Hollywood nightclub owner named Billy Wilkerson was floundering in debt after having invested all his money into a resort he called the Flamingo. Wilkerson needed an investor, but what he got was a partner who not only took over, but eventually ran him out of his own property. Siegel took over the building of the Flamingo Hotel with a loan from his Mob connections, and in the process got himself killed when the price tag for the resort ballooned from $1.5 million to $6 million. Unfortunately for Siegel, his longtime friend Lansky was convinced that he was skimming off the top and had him killed.

While Benjamin "Bugsy" Siegel had long been eliminated from the scene, in the 1950s and early 1960s, the Mob wasn't going anywhere and most people didn't seem to mind. After all, the Mob took care of things. If someone was caught cheating, he was "persuaded" never to cheat again. If someone was caught stealing, he simply disappeared. Las Vegas was still relatively small then and, strangely enough, the Mob made residents feel safe. From the 1950s well into the 1980s, the Mob controlled every casino in Las Vegas worth controlling, and while the residents may have thought life with the Mob had its benefits, mobsters were criminals and ruthless murderers.

Contrary to popular belief, the Mob didn't run illegal operations in the casinos. Sure, they skimmed off the top and took money whenever and wherever they could, but they also ran legitimate casinos. Games weren't fixed, mainly because they didn't have to be. The odds were with the house and the Mob knew that as long as they made the gaming experience worth coming for, people would come, they would gamble, and, for the most part, they would lose. It is a model still employed in Las Vegas to this day.

Outside the casino, however, was an entirely different story. There it was business as usual. Mobsters and the people who worked for them loved Las Vegas. They fit right into the upper class of wealthy socialites in every way, including where they built their homes. The Scotch 80s was one of those places. Many members of the Mob owned houses in the upscale community and in some of those houses they conducted their business.

La Palazza may have been one of those houses. The more Chris became familiar with the house, the more things he began to find. One day he found a hidden room.

"Nobody knew it was here," Heather said. "Nobody would ever know this room was here unless it got shown to you."

The room was closed off by a solid steel door. Outside the door were two gold towel holders in the shape of swans. One day Chris noticed that one of the holders seemed to be loose. As he grabbed hold of the towel holder, he found that he was able to turn it, and when he did, the steel door swung open, revealing a gruesome discovery. The first part of the room contained a water heater and other random stuff. However, another door in the room opened to reveal an adjacent room painted completely white. The floors were also white tile and there was an industrial sink against one wall.

"When we pulled the sink out," Chris said, "there was, like . . . blood, a lot of it caked in there." When the sink was removed, Chris remembered smelling a strong odor of bleach. "People died in that room. I know they did," Chris said. He also believes they died in a violent manner.

This was confirmed by God-centered, professional psychic medium Lynne Olson, who wrote in her blog, "I saw horrible things that had taken place in the murder room years past. Among the barely mentionable were men lined up in a row on their knees, hands behind their heads, classic Mob-execution positions. Many were executed in this manner. White tile made cleanup easy."

Olson also claimed to have seen the woman in the sunglasses, solving the mystery of why she had appeared to Chris.

"I saw the ghost of the older woman also sporting huge sunglasses. She was the money counter for all the cash that ran through that house from the Mob's assorted Vegas business activities. I think she was the mother of a major player from that era. She would work up in the attic with 'the boys'—other outfit members who came and went as their assignments dictated. She had absolute loyalty to her son and the outfit. Her ghost showed me that the money was counted and allotted in the attic to avoid notice from the local police, who periodically drove by in the upscale neighborhood. At the time the attic was equipped with blackout curtains so they could work long into the night without drawing attention to themselves.

"This was not a nice little old lady. She was as crude and smoked as many cigars as the men she worked with. I saw a lot of drinking and smoking that went on in the attic as business was conducted. She was also involved with the murder room, sometimes making suggestions about the final disposal of those marked for death."

Olson also claimed to have encountered a ghost who, more than anyone else, knew full well what had occurred in the murder room.

"He was the enforcer for the murder room and general muscle for the compound. When I asked him if he killed people in the murder room, his face went blank and he impassively told me, 'I did whatever needed to be done.' I tried to broach the idea of him moving on, which he flatly rejected with a bitter laugh, then told me, 'There is no heaven for the likes of me.' I asked him why he stayed in the wretched, haunted house. His answer was disturbing. He said, 'We suit each other.'"

Another discovery that seemed to link the house to the Mob was also made by Chris, who found some "old-school, throwaway guns" under the floorboards of the house. The guns, .22 caliber, were often the weapon of choice for the Mob. The caliber appealed to them because it was convenient and more difficult to trace.

While the ghosts may have made a connection with Chris, Heather seemed to be of particular interest to them.

"I would sleep here and I would hear them talking about me in the bed." What Heather heard were male voices making comments about her as she lay, often naked, in bed. The voices were relentless and vulgar, so much so that Heather was convinced people must be living in the attic.

Not only did Heather hear them in bed, she also heard them in the shower. She said that the voices appeared to be telling her they were present and they were watching her. The voices were so persistent that Heather started to feel as if she was going mad.

One time, late at night, she began knocking on the walls of the house, banging to see if she could feel something hollow. On one of the knocks, she got a response. As she knocked on the wall, something behind the wall knocked back, and she heard a growling sound that sent her running back to the bedroom. She sat on the bed, shaking and rocking back and forth, scared to death.

"This house damned near ruined me," Chris said. "Mentally it pulled me away from my family."

"It actually altered his entire emotions—made him do different things," Heather said.

Whatever presence was taking up space in the house had the ability to possess whomever it wanted, and it wanted Chris. The spirit seemed to have a connection with Chris.

"For some reason, we clicked," Chris said. But when that click occurred, Chris became someone he was not. He would become outraged in the blink of an eye. Even the smallest, silliest things, like there being no milk, triggered the rage. Heather even reported his eyeballs turning black at one point. She said he would get mad and then "get crazy."

Nico Santucci, another former owner of the house, knew Chris before and after he owned the house. According to Santucci, the house changed Chris's character significantly.

Enter the Travel Channel's *Ghost Adventures* team, Zak Bagans, Nick Groff, and Aaron Goodwin, three Las Vegas residents. After interviewing Chris, Heather, and Nico, they entered La Palazza at dusk and stayed there until dawn the next day. What they saw and recorded could make a believer out of even the most hardened skeptic.

When Zak and the crew entered the house, it had long ago been sold by Chris and, at some point, the inside had been gutted. Instead of being decorated in any particular style, it had been stripped down to two-by-four studs and plywood sheathing. From the moment they entered the house, crosses and holy water in hand, the team members began experiencing problems with their equipment. The audio died and they discovered that several of their fully charged batteries started to fail. As they walked around the house, they recorded many electronic voice phenomena, called EVP. As they entered the secret room, the recorder picked up an EVP that seemed to say the word *attic*.

Nick almost immediately felt an energy surround and engulf his entire body. When Zak demanded that the ghost appear before them, the camera he was holding stopped working. Shortly after, the detector he was holding—one which records the electromagnetic fields (EMF) that are said to be created by ghosts—made a loud buzzing sound, indicating that it detected an EMF.

When Zak again demanded that the ghost appear, he was told to stop by his fellow team member Nick. When Zak asked him what was going on, Nick told Zak that his face had just changed. According to Nick, Zak's eyebrows had raised and his eyes had shifted, changing his whole face when he spoke.

Aaron then reported that his whole body was tingly, saying that it was the third time he had had that feeling since they entered the house. Right after this, the team heard a loud banging on the plywood floor, followed by a high-pitched, "creepy" singing. The singing sounded as if it was coming from the hidden room, so the team made its way there. It was in this room that the night-vision camera recorded an orb traveling toward Nick, and they heard a woman's voice that appeared to say, "This way."

At a later point in the adventure, around 1:27 a.m., they asked a blonde female volunteer to join them. Their hope was that the woman looked enough like Heather that the ghosts would again make comments. They clad the woman in a towel and placed her in the area where the shower used to be. They left her alone with nothing but a voice recorder strapped to a stud and a night-vision camera recording. As the woman stood there alone in the dark, the voice recorder recorded an EVP that seemed to say, "Kill her." When Zak went back into the room with the girl, they heard a menacing snarl followed by a loud, violent bang.

Zak and his team emerged from the house unscathed, and when it was all over, he showed his findings to Chris and Heather. When he played for them one of the voices that had been captured on tape—the one that seemed to say, "Kill her"—Chris told the team that he knew the voice, explaining that he had often heard it when he walked into the back room of the house.

Chris knew that he wasn't sick, ill, or mentally disturbed. He also knew that he wasn't a bad person, even though the house had started to make him feel as if he was all those things and more. When Zak asked him if he believed in ghosts before he moved into this house, Chris answered, "No."

When Zak asked him if he did now, his answer was quite different. "Oh yeah," Chris said, shaking his head in the affirmative. "You don't ever really truly understand it until it happens to you."

SCHOOL DAYS . . . GOOD OLD GOLDEN GHOUL DAYS

When students go to school, they expect it to be hard. They expect to learn, and they expect to have to study. They even expect their teachers to stay on top of them. What they don't expect is to be haunted.

First days of school were always tough, but it was even more so when you were the new kid—the new kid from another state. Sure, Las Vegas was booming, but Jayme couldn't believe her parents were serious when they told her they were packing up and moving there.

"What is there to do?" Jayme had asked them. "Isn't it a desert? Isn't it hot? Do they have water? Do people even live there?"

"Of course people live there," her mother assured her, "and there's lots to do."

"But my friends are here," Jayme protested. Her mother had promised her she'd make new friends, but her mother had been wrong. Jayme had spent the last two days roaming around the halls, going from room to room, class to class, without anyone even saying hi. And now she was lost. She had made a wrong turn and she had no idea where she was. Jayme was all alone and she hated it. She hated her life, she hated Las Vegas, and she hated Dell H. Robison Middle School.

The halls were abandoned. Kids were already in their classrooms, and Jayme was going to be late. She looked at the room number written on the paper in her hand and then at the numbers on the doors of each room she passed. It was then that she noticed him. He was walking down the hall. Jayme didn't recognize him, but it didn't surprise her because she didn't really know anyone yet. But this man wasn't a student. In fact, he seemed to be dressed more like a janitor. Jayme looked down at the floor as she made her way up the hall toward the man who was approaching her.

She didn't want to look at him. In fact, Jayme preferred not to be noticed at all. But she couldn't help herself. As the man drew closer, something made her look up, and when she did, the sight caused her to freeze. The man was walking down the hall, slowly, deliberately, while staring at his hands—his blood-soaked hands.

Jayme screamed as she ran past him, down the hall, as fast as she could go, until she reached her classroom. She wanted to tell someone—anyone—but who'd believe her?

When the school day ended, Jayme pulled the books from her locker and headed out the double front doors of Dell H. Robison Middle School. She was still a little spooked from what she had seen in the hall, but it was a bright Las Vegas afternoon and the sun felt good on her face. Jayme held her books to her chest and made her way home. She was about two blocks away from the school when she saw something out of the corner of her eye, something that looked familiar— someone that looked familiar.

Jayme turned her head slightly, just enough to see behind her, hoping it wasn't him. But it was. It was the janitor from school, and the blood was still on his hands. Her pace naturally quickened as panic began to set in. She was running before she knew it, the tears flowing down her face. Jayme would've screamed, but she couldn't catch her breath. It didn't matter how fast she went, he was always behind her, walking . . . looking at his hands.

When her house was in sight, Jayme ran even harder—faster than she thought she ever could. She was up the stairs and in the front door, crying hysterically, before she had the courage to look again. Sliding the curtains away from the window, Jayme placed two trembling fingers between the blades of the blinds, prying them open. The janitor was nowhere to be found.

That night the janitor stalked her again as she relived the event over and over in her dreams. The next day Jayme asked her mother to drive her to school. She sat quietly in the backseat, wishing it would take longer to get there than it did.

"Have a nice day, sweetie," her mother said as Jayme got out of the car. She didn't answer. She just closed the car door and stood there, looking at the school. As her mother drove away, Jayme started the slow walk up the path.

"You saw him, didn't you?" The voice came from beside her. It was unexpected and it made her jump.

"Excuse me?"

"Yesterday," the girl said. Jayme had seen the girl before. They had a class together, fourth period—math. "I saw you running home. There was no one following you. You saw him, didn't you?"

"I don't know what you're talking abou . . . "

"It's okay. I saw him too. The first year I came here. Everyone does—everyone who moves from out of state."

"Who is he?"

"No one really knows. Some old janitor, probably."

"But he had . . ."

"Bloody hands? I know. It's real creepy! But don't worry—he'll go away as soon as you go to church."

"Really? Church? All I have to do is go to church? That sounds a little stupid."

"Might be, but it's true. Go to church and he'll leave you alone."

"You sure?"

"Just try it; you'll see," the girl said, walking toward the school. "Oh, and don't worry about running away. He's spooky, but he won't touch you."

Opening in 1973, Dell H. Robison Middle School, also called Dell H. Robison Junior High School, is one of 131 middle schools that serve the Las Vegas area and is home to the "Angels." Each year a little over a thousand students enroll in the school they refer to as simply "Dell H." The school commonly receives high ratings from both students and parents.

Over the years students moving in from out of state have reported seeing a man dressed like a janitor walking the halls of the school. The man, who has blood on his hands, follows the new student home and haunts his or her dreams. He does this until the student goes to church, after which the man leaves the student alone.

But Dell H. Robison Middle School isn't the only school in the Clark County School District that seems to suffer from ghostly apparitions. Elbert Edwards Elementary School also boasts a little school "spirit" of its own. And just like the bloody-handed janitor, this ghost has particular targets of her attention. Teachers and some students have reported seeing a little girl dressed entirely in white. The little girl is most often spotted in room 26 and in the computer room. According to those who have seen her, the young female apparition follows those she has chosen around the school. But the strange thing is, this little spirit is only interested in fourth graders.

Some stories claim the white-clad little girl was once a student at the school, but tragically died in 1990—her first year there. If the stories are true, the little girl would only have made it to the fourth grade. Maybe that's why she only appears to fourth graders. While most stories only have the little ghost harmlessly following her chosen companions around the school, according to other stories, those who are able to see her face find a deformed little girl who screeches when she is looked at. In other versions of the story, the little ghost haunts the dreams of her victims until that child tells another student about seeing her.

Harriet Treem Elementary is yet another school where a ghost appears. In this school the ghost is once again that of a young girl, only this time she is dressed in pioneer clothing. Those who see her say she has a glowing, ghostly face. They also say she cries for help when she is seen. In 2007 a group of college students visited the school with an electronic recording device in hopes of capturing an electronic voice phenomenon, commonly called an EVP. "When we reviewed the tape," according to Sean O'Callaghan and Mike McLoughlin, "we heard our first EVP." It was enough encouragement for the two to form Nevada Student Paranormal Investigation (NSPI). "We have come a long way in terms of knowledge, equipment, and experience, but there is still a lot more to be learned."

And Las Vegas is the perfect place to learn, because elementary schools aren't the only places where child ghosts abound. Las Vegas is a twenty-four-hour town and people don't work normal jobs, nor do they work normal hours. And while it may not seem like it to outsiders, Las Vegas is home to many families, and those families have children—children who need day care.

Little Choo Choo Daycare was one of those centers. Not only did the facility have toys, books, and kids, it also had its namesake—a fully automated toy choo choo train. It was this train that proved to be the source of the day-care center's troubles. According to some reports, a young boy died when he became caught under the wheels of the train and was dragged across the tracks. It was not long afterward that a teacher at the day care supposedly committed suicide.

Whether these events are true or not, the day-care center was eventually closed and now sits vacant. Except, that is, on some nights—and even a few days—when a small boy can be seen digging in the dirt with his shovel. The boy appears out of nowhere and disappears just as quickly. Others walking by the property report seeing a young Black woman appear and then just as quickly disappear into thin air.

BONNIE'S PLACE

Was the Western town at Bonnie Springs too good of a replica? Did it draw the spirits of those who lost their lives on the Old Spanish Trail? Or is Bonnie Springs haunted by the Native American spirits that dwell in the caves nearby?

That couldn't really be happening, he thought to himself. After all, there was no wind . . . at all. It was a calm day; there wasn't even a slight breeze. How could it be moving—by itself—with no one on it? He walked closer to the metal merry-go-round and watched as it turned, slowly at first, then picking up speed.

"It just can't be," he said aloud. But there was no one there to hear him.

The merry-go-round spun faster, and while what he really wanted to do was run away, he couldn't seem to help himself. He walked closer and closer to the spinning toy, slowly stepping over the old wooden fence. The merry-go-round seemed to pick up speed, but just as he approached, it stopped suddenly, without slowing down. It just stopped.

The Wild, Wild West is alive and well just a few miles outside of Las Vegas in a place called Bonnie Springs. Bonnie Levinson, the "Bonnie" of Bonnie Springs, was an ice skater for a Las Vegas casino in the 1950s. In 1952 she bought a patch of land near Red Rock Canyon that already featured a popular bar and riding stables. Bonnie loved animals and the land seemed like a perfect fit.

Since the late 1800s, the area had long served as a watering post for weary travelers along the Old Spanish Trail. Union General John Charles Fremont used the spot as a stopping point before he entered California on an expedition to locate passes for a proposed railway line from the upper Rio Grande to California.

In the late 1960s Bonnie's husband decided to expand the property by building a replica Western town, complete with a saloon, opera house, jailhouse, bank, and a school, as well as a merry-go-round. The construction would be quite a feat since, at the time, the property was all dirt roads and there was no existing source of power. However, being the daughter of a director, Hollywood was in Bonnie's blood. She and her husband hoped that Tinseltown would use their Western town as a backdrop in movies.

By this time, Bonnie already had a rather large collection of animals that she kept on the property. The animals had been given to Bonnie by various individuals, hoping that she would take care of them when they couldn't. Bonnie decided that the addition of the town to the already-existing bar and horse stables would be a great way to build a family-friendly local destination. She hoped that people would come from all over to enjoy themselves at this new venture. What she didn't expect were ghosts.

The Las Vegas Valley is home to the Paiute people. They settled this area long before the white man came to build homes and casinos. In fact, there are caves located in the red rocks of the hills directly behind the ranch that were used by the Paiutes in spiritual ceremonies. These caves, which are protected by the Bureau of Land Management, contain thousand-year-old hieroglyphics.

The Travel Channel's *Ghost Adventures* team, Zak Bagans, Nick Groff, and Aaron Goodwin—three Las Vegas residents—went to Bonnie Springs in search of ghosts. They were joined in their investigation by members of the Las Vegas Paranormal Authority. But before Zak, Nick, and Aaron conducted their investigation, they asked for a blessing from the local Paiute tribe.

"At one time my ancestors roamed throughout these mountains that are here," said Spotted Eagle, the Paiute Spirit Leader. He was dressed in full Native American clothing, complete with headdress, and gestured with the feathers of an American eagle as he spoke. "We came here to gather medicine, to hunt, and to gather food." He instructed the *Ghost Adventures* team to put their hands in the air and receive a blessing. "Whatever you want, now's the time to ask for it," Spotted Eagle told them and pronounced the blessing.

The investigation started in the opera house, which is said to be a hotbed of paranormal activity. "In this area is where there's the most activity," said Cowboy Joe Tasso, supervisor at Bonnie Springs. People in the opera house have reported feeling a cold spot directly in the center of the building, as well as other unexplainable events.

"I have seen a cloud-type deal," said Cowboy Joe, who was also present when, on a separate occasion, the Las Vegas Paranormal Authority did an investigation. While Joe was speaking to one of the crew members, another snapped several photos. In one of the photos, the cloud Joe spoke of seems to have been captured on film.

When the *Ghost Adventures* crew came to set up for the shoot, Cowboy Joe took one of the cameramen into the opera house, which was locked. Right when the key Joe was holding was about an inch away from the lock, according to the cameraman, the lock dropped down and flipped open in his hand.

When they went inside and looked around, Cowboy Joe noticed another strange occurrence as he looked at the wall. "There was four of us in there and there was five shadows on the wall."

The wax museum is another place where ghosts seem to gather. People have reported hearing footsteps there, and one of the figures, depicting a local friar, always seems to be in the wrong place. According to Cowboy Joe, the first year he worked at Bonnie Springs, he would always find the friar down on the ground even though he was actually bolted in place. Cowboy Joe also noted that the wax museum always felt damp or cold, even though there was no air-conditioning in the building.

It was the wax museum where members of the Las Vegas Paranormal Authority reported having an encounter. While in the museum, Christy Silva felt what she described as a "sharp pain" in her head before falling to the ground. Christy reported that as she was coming through the mine, she began to feel a burning sensation on her back. Christy lifted up her shirt, and a large scratch was visible on her back. At the same time her fellow investigator, Diane Giunta, felt a sharp pain in her stomach, "as if someone was stabbing her." When the two called for assistance from Wallie Luna, the group's founder, a "sudden sick feeling" came over him as well.

God-centered, professional psychic medium Lynne Olson also reported a psychic experience with the wax museum.

"I took a psychic look into what had scratched Christy in a prior investigation. Sure enough, there was a common sort of dark entity in the wax museum. I asked my guides what attracted it to that spot. I was shown a lot of hasty, poorly marked graves, and told the wax museum was built on top of the informal wagon-stop graveyard. Men, women, children, and infants lost on the trail or at the wagon stop were quickly buried to avoid illness and keep the bodies from the local coyotes," said Olson. Interestingly enough, as the team was starting its investigation that night, it heard coyotes howling in the background.

At the school where the merry-go-round sits outside, the sounds of children have been heard. "It sounds like kids in the distance," said Cowboy Joe, who stated he has routinely heard the voices and seen the moving merry-go-round. "It happens so much," he said, "I don't even pay attention to it anymore."

Cowboy Joe also related the story of a woman who felt a presence when she was in the school. "A lady said she got feelings and she had spiritual contacts," said Joe. "She said that she heard a little girl saying she wanted to go home."

Psychic medium Olson had a psychic experience with the schoolhouse that may have explained why the girl wanted to go home. "I asked the ghost girl why she wanted to go home. The answer was, she was sick. She told me, 'My tummy hurts' as she cradled her bloated abdomen. She fainted in class and hit the gritty floorboards. As the students and teacher crowded around her, she died."

Psychic medium Olson was also able to see the actual schoolhouse that was present when the property served as a watering point. "What I saw was a much smaller, more modest schoolhouse that belonged to the wagon-stop era. Like many shanty buildings of its time, its scholars could have shot spitballs through the gaps between the wall and floorboards. My guides said the building was used intermittently as different groups of wagon trains passed through. If a group of travelers had a schoolteacher with them, or even an adult with some formal education, school would be held for the children of the families for the few days or weeks they were at the wagon stop."

The Old Spanish Trail was the expressway to California. Thousands of settlers, military personnel, and the like made their way across the dusty, rocky trail. Many of them made the journey in covered wagons. They had to fight off robbers, American Indians, and Mexican nationals who still claimed the area as their own. They traveled without doctors, medicine, or any of the modern conveniences we take for granted. Many were robbed along the way. Others lost their lives to hostiles, influenza, or simply starvation. Perhaps the spirits of those who lost their lives have come to Bonnie Springs Ranch in the hopes of finally finding a home.

It is interesting that during the investigation, both the *Ghost Adventures* team and members of the Las Vegas Paranormal Authority heard a distant chant and the rhythmic *boom boom boom* of drums. Could it be that the spirits of the caves come down to the town to reclaim the area from the settlers who once took it from them?

Bonnie Levinson died on January 29, 2016, at the age of 94. The property was subsequently sold. On Sunday, March 17, 2019, Bonnie Springs closed for good, to make way for the development of Luxury homes. The property put out a statement saying, "Hope your memories are as good as ours and we thank you for your patronage over the years," While Bonnie's dream may be gone, the residents of the place still remain, and it will be interesting to see if they play nice with the new owners.

A HOSTEL FOR THE DAMMED

What if there was a place where all the evil spirits could gather and possibly find a safe haven? What if you could visit that place and commune with those spirits, even if only for a short time? Well, that place exists and the spirits inside are ready and waiting for you to come join them.

The old, abandoned house sat no more than a block away from the iconic Las Vegas Strip. The Tudor-style mansion was said to have once been owned by a prominent Las Vegas family who had long since passed away, but apparently nobody had inherited the home. There were rumors, of course; there always are when a house has sat abandoned that long. Especially this house. Tudor-style homes were not common in the Las Vegas desert, and this home, with its sweeping roofs and stone accents, was a beauty to behold.

It is said a young boy died in the home, his mother joining him in the afterlife though the circumstances surrounding both deaths were not known. There were also rumors of something far more sinister: late night satanic rituals. It all proved too much of an enticement for a teenage Rachel and her best girlfriend, so one afternoon, the pair decided it was time to see what was hiding inside those Tudor walls.

They snuck around to the back of the building, where they found a cover hiding an outside staircase that led to the basement. If the Tudor style wasn't enough of an anomaly, a basement in Las Vegas certainly was. Much of the area is made up of large deposits of caliche that is harder than concrete to break through, making basements a rarity indeed.

This particular basement was tiny, barely large enough for both girls to fit inside comfortably, but fit inside they did, and in so doing they found something that would chill them to the very bone. Rachel went in first and there, in the darkness of the basement, drawn on the floor was a pentagram—a satanic pentagram. It was contained inside a circle, and there were symbols Rachel did not recognize. She stood frozen, just staring at the sight before her, unable to look away. The symbols were all drawn in blood and that blood was fresh. Satanic rituals had indeed been performed in that basement, and as this realization came to Rachel, she began feeling a pressure against her stomach and an overwhelming sense that something was grabbing at her legs.

She wanted to scream, but nothing came out. That was when she heard it, a young boy's voice whispering from the other side, "I need help."

The Wengert Mansion was built in 1938 by Cyril Sebastian Wengert. Designed by architect H. Clifford Nordstrom, the Tudor revival home was among the largest homes in Las Vegas. Wengert and his wife Lottie moved into the home at 1001 South Sixth Street with their children, Marilyn, Ward, Robert, and Shirley. Unfortunately, their son James had already passed away at the tender age of 8 in 1930, before they moved into the home, and they had lost a daughter, Janet Sue, in childbirth a year later. Wengert and his wife were prominent citizens in Las Vegas and were an integral part of the development of many of Vegas' civic organizations and the growth of the local Catholic community. When Cyril died in 1965, the *Las Vegas Sun* noted: "Cyril Wengert is considered one of the leading citizens of Las Vegas." Lottie died three years later, on September 14, 1968, in the bedroom of her beloved mansion.

After the Wengerts' deaths, the 11,000-square foot home sat abandoned until it was eventually purchased by the State of Nevada Bar Association. Almost from the beginning, those who worked there felt an eerie presence—especially in the basement. Most employees didn't feel comfortable going down there, while others reported a feeling of negative energy coming from the small space below the house. Almost nobody felt it was safe to go into the basement. In fact, if it became necessary to go there, for whatever reason, the employees would often head down in groups, so no one would be left alone.

Many employees, after leaving work for the day, would find they were irritable or just didn't feel like themselves. One employee even took to pouring salt on the floor of the back office to keep away whatever negative energy resided in that house. Perhaps the remnants of the rituals and demons conjured in the basement had taken up residency.

The State of Nevada Bar Association eventually sold the mansion to Zak Bagans, paranormal investigator and star of the Travel Channel's *Ghost Adventures*. Zak found the place almost by accident. "I am such a history buff," Zak stated on an episode of his show. "And one of my dreams was always to own a historic home." Zak went on to explain that he found the mansion after simply taking a drive and seeing the home. Something about it "just captured" him and he bought it right away.

Zak immediately began filling the home with paranormal artifacts, some of which he had collected throughout his life and on his ghost adventures, and others which had been sent to him—mostly by people who had experiences with those objects that they didn't want to repeat. His vision was to create a place where the spirits—or whatever they were—that haunted the items could find peace in a place where they could stay, unharmed, almost like a hostel for the dammed. From this vision, the Haunted Museum was born.

The rooms inside the mansion are now, for the most part, themed. In it you can find a creepy closet full of dolls, with one in particular that likes to play tricks on guests and staff alike—it was a vintage doll Zak had to remove from his house because of its negative energy. Another room with a western theme contains a bible once owned by Wyatt Earp and a gun once owned by Jesse James. Still another room is set up to resemble the office of one of the most famous doctors who ever lived: Murad Jacob "Jack" Kevorkian, famous for helping more than 200 people find passage to the other side. In the room next to the office is the VW van Kevorkian used when performing that very task.

Of course, not all the artifacts in the museum are haunted, but those that are often have a horrifying story to tell. In one part of the museum are the remnants of another house, so haunted, so evil, that Zak had the place destroyed almost immediately after he purchased it. He had bought the place, sight unseen, to conduct paranormal investigations based on activities reported there. He had even been warned by a good friend not to enter the house, and, after spending only a short time in there, and feeling the presence of evil, he had the place bulldozed. The only remnants are the staircase to the basement and the ritualistic items found buried in the dirt below, both of which can be found in his museum.

One of the rooms is dedicated to mass murderers the likes of John Wayne Gacy, Charles Manson, Ted Bundy, and Richard Ramirez. The room contains artifacts such as clothing worn by these murderers and paintings made by both Gacy and Manson, as well as the death kit used by Ted Bundy on his victims. And while all of these men have passed on, there is one man who you can actually see in that room—well, his remains anyway. In the back, inside the jail cell, Zak's museum has some of Charles Manson's actual bones.

The museum also includes artifacts such as Bella Lugosi's haunted and cursed mirror, which reportedly saw the death of Frank Saletri who moved into

Lugosi's house after his death. It also houses the cast iron cauldron Ed Gein—famous for wearing the skin of his victims—used to cook those victim's innards. The rear axle from the most haunted car in America, "The Little Bastard," which saw the end of James Dean, rests in one of the rooms, and in a separate room is a chest said to cause death and destruction.

There are, however, two items that are likely the scariest in the entire museum. The first is Peggy, a doll that you must pleasantly greet when you first see her and then bid her adieu to prevent her dark energy from attaching to you and following you home. The other is known as the Dybbuk box. According to Bagans, there are 10 of these boxes and each one aligns with the tree of life. The box in the museum—which is box #1—along with its 9 companions is said to contain all the evil of the twentieth century. Some of that evil was supposedly captured and contained inside a wine box by a Holocaust survivor, whose parents, brothers, sister, husband, two sons, and daughter were all sent to the gas chamber. This box is so dangerous that it was once buried deep in the ground and now sits in a room in the museum where it is surrounded by sage, salt, and a barrier inscribed with a Jewish prayer.

Some believe that little James Wengert followed his parents into the home and was the first to haunt its halls. Perhaps it was he who asked Rachel for help that day. Upon her parent's passing, Shirley—the youngest of the Wengerts—fully believed she would see them inside the home they loved so dearly. "Mother planned this house," she told Bagans. "Every room was hers." It could be that every room still is.

Although the mansion is home to a collection of the most bizarre and demonic artifacts that exist anywhere in the world, Zak has also ensured that part of the home still honors its original occupants. There is a room in the house that is decorated just as it would have been in 1938 and in that room Zak has included the history of the Wengert Family. Zak has even ensured that the home has been included on the City of Las Vegas Historic Preservation List. Las Vegas has honored the Wengerts as well, naming an elementary school Cyril S. Wengert.

The museum is definitely not for the faint of heart. That said, part of the creepiness is due to the decorations, sound effects, and lighting that make the place, well . . . spooky. One of the rooms, the fun house, has a piped-in odor of cotton candy that you will not soon get out of your olfactory system. Still, the tour guides have often reported seeing anomalies. Some have seen dark shadows cross hallways. Others report seeing a little girl standing off to the side when they begin their tour. One female tour guide reported lingering too long near Ed Gein's cauldron. Later that night she dreamt she had been murdered and her body cut up into little pieces—the exact modus operandi of Gein. If you do decide to brave the malevolent spirits that inhabit this abode and want to up the spook factor, you might want to consider one of the late-night flashlight tours the museum offers. Just be careful where you shine that light.

WHAT IS A GHOST ANYWAY?

How do you know when you've seen a ghost? Are they just orbs floating around in photographs, or are real ghosts something more? A hotel in Boulder City has seen its fair share of changes. It has been host to guests, celebrities, and dignitaries. Maybe this historic building is haunted . . . with memories.

It was a warm night in August. Dennis McBride, curator for the Boulder City Museum, and psychic Patsy Welding arrived at the Boulder Dam Hotel to perform a reading. Dennis was writing a nonfiction account of the hotel's history, and he wanted to conclude the work by documenting some of the strange occurrences rumored to have occurred in the historic hotel. McBride himself had reported seeing a ghost in his office in the basement of the hotel, and he wanted to know if the place was indeed haunted.

"Are you ready?" McBride asked as he led Welding and local writer Nancy Ashbaugh into the spacious front lobby. A large fireplace stood against the two-story wall. In front of the fireplace rested a couch and chairs for guests to sit and enjoy the city from the large windows that looked out onto the street in front of the hotel. It was in this lobby that people claimed to have heard singing and piano playing, as well as a smell of cigarette or cigar smoke. From almost the first moment she entered the hotel, Welding seemed to fall into a dreamlike state, moving around the room as if she was hearing and seeing unseen beings. McBride clicked on the tape recorder as Welding began to speak, saying her first impression was that a crime had taken place in the hotel.

"A killing took place and some people knew about it," she said as McBride recorded. She then described a meeting of men in the desert outside of town, indicating that there had been a robbery and that something had been buried in the desert. As a result of that robbery, two men had gotten into a fistfight, and one of them had been killed.

Welding then led the group up the handcrafted wooden stairs that transported guests to the second floor of the hotel and to the rooms. As she passed each room, she placed her hand on the wall, lowering her head and closing her eyes as if the wall was a portal to another time . . . another place. In one of the rooms, she felt that someone must have had an illness because "they had to have ice." She then yelled, "Get the ice!" as if channeling the person who had screamed it originally.

Welding reported that a clandestine meeting had taken place in another room, between a man and a woman. "How thrilling!" Welding exclaimed. After which she described the woman as having good, high color and rosy cheeks, claiming that the woman was "game for almost anything."

Welding went room by room, touching the walls and, in some cases, the doors. She said that some rooms should not be disturbed, while others contained items that were broken, as if from some type of natural event. As she entered one room, she exclaimed, "I really like it!" and stated that the spirit who resided here was a good solid citizen.

The three made their way around the hotel, eventually preparing to enter the basement to get a reading in McBride's office, where he claimed to have seen a ghost. It was in the basement, however, that the reading would take a menacing turn.

"I don't want to go down there," Welding suddenly exclaimed.

Las Vegas of the 1930s was a small town of only five thousand people. Casinos like the El Rancho and the New Frontier were still only pipe dreams. The Union Pacific Railroad had pulled its repair shops out in 1922, leaving a struggling town in the middle of a very hot desert. In order to survive, Las Vegas needed another source of commerce. Enter the United States government.

In 1928, President Calvin Coolidge authorized the building of a dam to contain the Colorado River and produce energy for the inhabitants of Nevada, California, and Arizona. Rumors of a desire to control the Colorado River began as early as 1919. At the time, the mighty Colorado routinely ran its banks, flooding precious farmland and causing thousands of dollars' worth of damage every year. A search was made of over seventy sites in an effort to find the ideal location for the dam. After weighing the pros and cons of each site, the choice was narrowed to two canyons, both located a short distance outside of Las Vegas. In 1928 California Congressmen Philip Swing and Hiram Johnson proposed a bill to build the dam. It was signed into law on December 21, 1928, and when it passed, the tiny town of Las Vegas went wild.

"We got the fire truck out," recalled Leon H. Rockwell, resident of Las Vegas. "Everybody that could hooked on to it! In carts and baby buggies and everything else—just like they was nuts."

In 1929, when city officials heard that Secretary of the Interior Ray Lyman Wilbur was set to visit, they were determined to show Las Vegas in the best light possible. Block 16, the area of town that had become famous for gambling, alcohol, and prostitution, was closed. A banner proclaiming Las Vegas as the gateway to boulder dam was erected across Fremont Street, the main downtown street. When Wilbur arrived, he was given the grand tour and shown a Las Vegas eager for his business and that of his workers.

Unfortunately, Wilbur wasn't fooled by his visit and, unbeknownst to city officials, he had already made the decision to construct a government town, called Boulder City, on land located closer to the construction site. Wilbur viewed Las Vegas as a dirty little town whose residents had only one concern—the pursuit of pleasure. Being a religious man, Wilbur was put off by Las Vegas's flagrant defiance of prohibition laws and its open promotion of prostitution. He would have none of that in his town. Wilbur intended to construct Boulder City with strict rules prohibiting the sale of alcohol, the practice of gambling, and of course, prostitution.

On December 18, 1930, Wilbur revealed his plans for the creation of Boulder City, which he named after the Boulder Dam. The government-built town was to be located six miles from Boulder Canyon, the site of the dam. Wilbur hired S. R. DeBoer, a city planner and landscape architect from Denver, Colorado, to plan the town, which was billed as "a layout which will probably serve as a model in town planning for years to come."

In a press release for the soon-to-be-built town, Boulder City was shown in a very shining light. "The employees of the Government and of the contractors, together with those who wish to engage in business, or to follow their trades or practice their professions, will find in Boulder City all the conveniences and comforts which the Government is able to provide."

The budget for the construction of Boulder City was $2 million, and it was expected to become the new home of approximately three thousand people. The plan was to build a town hall, school, garage, dormitory and guesthouse, auditorium, administration building, swimming pool, playground, and seventy-five "cottages" for employees.

Wilbur was sure that Boulder City would become a "sizable tourist town" with a main transcontinental highway coming in from Arizona. Boulder City seemed poised to fulfill Wilbur's vision. It had everything it needed—everything, that is, except a hotel. If tourists were going to come to the new town, they would need a place to stay. Also, if the government had any plans of showing off its new dam, it would need a place to house dignitaries and government officials.

In 1932, with construction of the dam well under way, plans began for the building of a seventy-four-room hotel in the heart of downtown Boulder City. A permit for the hotel, which was slated to be called the Boulder Inn, was issued to W. F. Grey and his wife, Virginia Lamberson-Grey, on April 2 of that year. Mr. and Mrs. Grey, who were out of Fresno, California, were already successful hotel owners. They hired local architect L. Henry Smith to design a two-story, "fireproof" hotel.

As plans for the hotel were announced, excitement in Boulder City grew. The local newspaper reported: "Sounds too good to be true. A first-class hotel capable of caring for large parties of visitors has been the crying need of the community. The hotel, if built as planned at present, will be larger than the New Apache hotel in Las Vegas. Mr. and Mrs. Grey are to be commended for their initiation of this worthwhile project."

As plans progressed, the town waited with eager anticipation. The local newspaper reported that construction of the hotel would begin in about a month and be finished by September of 1932. According to the paper, the hotel was slated to have "a sumptuous lobby" complete with a "huge fireplace" that will "present a homelike atmosphere."

According to the plans for the hotel, the architecture was Spanish-style and it was to be built of stucco. The rooms were to be decorated by "a master interior decorator," and there were plans for a governor's suite. Steam baths, along with beauty and barber shops, were planned for the basement. There was also to be a patio and "wide driveways." The paper reported that "a large deal of money will be spent by the Greys in exterior and interior decorations."

However, even as the newspaper continued to report that construction of the hotel would "start soon," it never did. By August of 1932, the paper was forced to finally give up hope and report the sad news that the hotel was not to be.

"The lessees have just given us the unwelcome information that it is impossible to raise the required sum and that the enterprise must be abandoned."

It seemed like the hotel would never get off the ground and, in truth, the Boulder Inn never did—at least, not *that* Boulder Inn.

As plans for the original Boulder Inn failed, Paul Stewart Webb, known as "Jim" to his friends, seized the opportunity. In 1933 he applied for, and was granted, a permit from the Bureau of Reclamation to build an elegant hotel. The only problem was that Webb didn't really have the capital needed for a project of that size, so he spent the majority of the spring and summer recruiting investors. The first person he approached was Raymond Spilsbury.

Spilsbury was wealthy—or at least his family was. The money came from the Spilsbury Land and Livestock Company. Webb had met Spilsbury, who was a metallurgical engineer, in Peru when the two worked for the Cerro de Pasco Copper Corporation during World War I.

According to Spilsbury's wife, "When Ray came up to Boulder City in 1933 to visit Jimmy, they got together and decided to form this [hotel] corporation, with Jimmy in charge." She also stated that her husband was "heavily invested in it."

The two men brought in another investor by the name of Austin Clark, a man they had both worked with in Peru, and formed the Hotel Holding Corporation. Webb served as president. The corporation hired Mort Wagner to design the hotel. Wagner designed a Dutch colonial hotel, which was to have thirty-three rooms, each with an adjoining bath. Furniture would be purchased from Baker Brothers, a well-established furniture company in California.

Wagner designed the hotel with six massive columns at the front entrance. The hotel itself was to be constructed of the same stone used for the Arizona state capitol building. The three-story hotel was designed to have a spacious and impressive lobby, as well as a heating and cooling system. It was slated to cost $50,000 to construct.

While the Boulder Dam Hotel didn't open in time for its expected Thanksgiving opening day, it did open only a few weeks later, on December 15, 1933. As reported by the *Las Vegas Review-Journal*, "Boulder City's new and beautiful hotel was opened today to the public for the first time. Howard Doud, manager of the Boulder Dam Hotel, and his staff were busy greeting the interested visitors as they came to inspect the perfection of the building and interior."

From the moment it opened, the hotel was a huge success. Over the years it was visited by the likes of Bette Davis, Will Rogers, James Cagney, Henry Fonda, and Howard Hughes. "America's Sweetheart" Shirley Temple stayed there during a publicity stunt, when she also visited a local school. Newspapers reported that she "went to school for the first time" in Boulder City.

In 1935 the Boulder Dam Hotel was expanded from its original thirty-three to eighty-six rooms. A restaurant was also added in the $60,000 renovation. The hotel and restaurant continued to receive rave reviews. Both were included in the prestigious *Duncan Hines Adventures in Good Eating* and *Duncan Hines Adventures in Good Lodging* national guides. The hotel was also the location where Evelyn Grossman was pampered by the Los Angeles–based *Queen for a Day* radio show.

But while the hotel seemed destined for greatness, its owners weren't always so lucky. On Friday, January 19, 1945, Raymond Spilsbury drove his Pontiac up Emery Way at around 1:30 in the afternoon. He got out of the vehicle, locked it, and made his way southward on Fisherman's Trail, along the Colorado River, where he leapt to his death.

Over the years the hotel continued on, majestically watching all the changes that happened to the small town of Boulder City as it indeed lived up to the vision of Secretary Wilbur. The hotel was updated and remodeled several times as it went from owner to owner, and while the hotel saw both success and failure, its owners were another story entirely. Many of the people who owned the hotel went bankrupt shortly after taking ownership, and several died. One of them was Ted Gursd, who passed away at the age of forty-eight at the dinner table, only a year after he bought the hotel.

In January 1968 the hotel was closed until February of 1969 when it was reopened as a retirement home, which it remained until 1973. The hotel would experience frequent closures, fall victim to vandals, and shelter the homeless before it was once again reborn as a functioning hotel and placed on the National Register of Historic Places.

Although Welding was hesitant to enter the basement, she eventually tried again. As she made her way down the winding stairs, she said she felt as if someone was lying in wait for them.

"I really don't think I'd better go," she said, and then added, "Blood. Lots of blood . . ."

In the book *Ghosts, Gangsters, and Gamblers of Las Vegas,* the authors state: "There are also rumors of a worker who was killed and buried in the basement." Interestingly enough, there are no police or newspaper reports whatsoever about anyone dying or being killed anywhere in the hotel. In fact, there are few police reports of any kind that deal with the hotel at all.

It is also interesting that one of the places where a "presence" is reported as being felt is the kitchen, the same place where Welding said in her reading, "I'd love to eat here, or be here. Even before it was built, this was a good spot."

It is interesting to note that none of the many employees of the hotel, the restaurant, or the Boulder Dam Museum, located inside the hotel, have ever reported seeing ghosts anywhere in the hotel—except, that is, for McBride. This fact then begs the question: Is the Boulder Dam Hotel really haunted?

Maybe it's because the hotel is old, or maybe it's because it has just seen so much transition that people like to think it's haunted. Walking through the halls of the hotel, it is possible to feel a presence, but that presence is history—seventy-eight years of history—not something evil or malicious. It's the presence of guests enjoying a drink and a song by the piano, a child needing ice to fight an outbreak of scarlet fever, or a couple enjoying a midnight rendezvous.

If the hotel is haunted, it's haunted by memories. Poet Solitaire put it best in his poem, "The Boulder Dam Hotel":

> *The famous ones stayed there,*
> *their moments remembered from long ago.*
> *Immortalized by a little brass nameplate*
> *placed on the outside of each door.*
> *You can almost hear them by the pool*
> *or in the café having coffee or tea,*
> *the Presidents, princes, and kings of industry,*
> *names like Roosevelt, Hughes, and even James Cagney.*
> *From elegant ladies lounging in their suites,*
> *to the actors and actresses meeting in the lobby of the hotel,*
> *down the carpeted hallways where Bette Davis might stand,*
> *if only the walls could speak what wondrous*
> *stories they would tell.*
> *So if one goes to Boulder City in search of Ghosts,*
> *go to the Boulder Dam Hotel,*
> *where the famous ones will be your hosts.*

REVENGE IS A DISH BEST SERVED CHILLED

On a ranch just outside of Las Vegas, three killings are committed without witnesses and without satisfactory resolution. Maybe that's why apparitions can be seen on the now-abandoned ranch. Are they looking for their murderers, or for absolution?

"He said *what* about you?" Archibald Stewart asked his wife. The two were standing in the bedroom of their ranch home. Archibald was a large man. He had on tan work pants, a light blue, long-sleeved shirt, and brown pointed-toed boots. He was tying a red silk kerchief around his neck, but had stopped when his wife, Helen, told him about the lies a former ranch hand had been saying about her.

The former hand, a man by the name of Schuyler Henry, had left the Stewarts' ranch, only to be hired by Conrad Kiel, who owned the neighboring ranch. There had been no love lost between Stewart and Henry, nor was it much different with Kiel and Stewart. In fact, Archibald Stewart was not a very likable man in general. He was good at what he did and he knew how to run a ranch; he just didn't care much for people.

"Are you sure it was Henry?" he asked Helen as she started to dress.

"That's what I was told," she said to him. "I didn't actually hear it for myself."

"But you're sure it was him who said it?"

"I'm sure and I don't doubt it."

"That son-of-a . . . ," Stewart said as he finished tying the kerchief. Although he had become very quiet, the anger rising in him was evident. When he finally finished tying the soft material around his neck, he walked out of the bedroom into the front room. His gun belt and pistol were hanging on a coat rack under his hat. He took the hat from the rack and placed it on his head. Then he wrapped the gun belt around his waist. He fastened the buckle and tied the leather straps around his thigh, all the time growing angrier and angrier. When he was done, he walked over to the barn and began to saddle his horse.

"I can do that for you, Mr. Stewart," one of his hands said to him.

"It's all right. I've got it," he answered.

"Where're you going?" the hand asked. Stewart's anger clearly showed on his face. Something wasn't right and it was obvious.

"Over to Kiel Ranch," he said, reaching for the strap from under the belly of the horse. Holding the saddle, he pulled the strap tightly before buckling it and securing the end in its leather holder. "I have business to take care of."

"Well, I'll just get Smokey all saddled up and head on over with you."

"No!" Stewart said. "I'll take care of it myself. You start work on that fence over by the back field."

"You sure, Mr. Stewart?" the hand asked, hoping his boss would change his mind.

"Just do as you're told," he said, placing his foot in the stirrup. He took hold of the saddle horn and hoisted himself up on the horse. With a kick to the horse's hindquarters, he pulled the reins and headed out of the barn.

The ride to the Kiel Ranch was long, but it did nothing to soften Stewart's mood. On the contrary, the more he thought about it, the angrier he became. By the time he reached the ranch, he had built up a full head of steam.

"Where's Henry?" he asked the group of hands as he dismounted. "Henry!" he called out. "Get out here and account for yourself!"

Helen J. Stewart sat on the porch of her ranch home with her children, happy to be off her swollen feet. She was pregnant and showing. It was warm in Las Vegas and she fanned herself as the children played. At first she didn't notice the horse approaching in the distance. It wasn't until it drew closer that she saw the dust and the man riding toward her. The valley was rather flat and it was easy to see people coming at quite a distance. The horse was moving slowly and it seemed to take forever to get there. When the man on the horse finally arrived, he dismounted.

"Mrs. Stewart," he said, sliding from his saddle and looking down at the ground instead of into her eyes. "I come from Kiel Ranch. Mr. Kiel told me to give this to you." He extended his hand slowly. In it was a folded piece of paper. When Mrs. Stewart took the paper, the man looked her quickly in the eye, tipped his hat, and got on his horse as fast as he could without causing insult.

Mrs. Stewart opened the folded paper and screamed, dropping it to the ground. The note simply said: "Mrs. Stewart, your husband is here, dead. Come and take him away."

The seven-acre Kiel Ranch is located in North Las Vegas. It is overgrown with weeds, infested with trash, and a fence around the property seals it off from the public. Besides the land, the only thing that remains is a crumbling adobe building. This building was most likely built before the Kiel clan ever claimed the ranch. When Mormons arrived in Las Vegas, in 1884, they were taught how to make bricks from the Paiutes. They most likely built the home before abandoning it when they left the valley. In fact, there is a chance that the building is over 150 years old. Yet it is not being protected.

"Historically speaking, the city blew it," stated Dr. Michael Green, a local historian and author, in an interview with the *Las Vegas Review-Journal.* "We need to save what we have left of it and replicate what we've lost."

Kiel Ranch was abandoned for decades. As Las Vegas grew around it, the ranch became a makeshift playground for kids and a residence for the homeless. In 1976 the city of North Las Vegas was given the twenty-seven-acre property, which was paid for by generous donors and federal bicentennial funds. City officials promised to create a historic park complete with public trails and campgrounds, but it never came to be.

Perhaps this is why visitors to the ranch report having an eerie feeling while on the property, one that is also felt by anyone who walks by the fenced-in and abandoned ranch. Many also report seeing movement out of the corner of their eye while on the ranch. Others have seen a man running across the grounds in the area where the old ranch house once stood.

Instead of turning the ranch into a park or some other kind of public-use location, the city sold all but seven acres to developers for $1 million. The city used the money to build a parking lot and to put fencing around the property. It also built a canopy over the adobe structure, meant to protect the building, as well as made improvements to Commerce Street, the street adjacent to the parking lot.

At one time North Las Vegas was offered $2.4 million in funds from the US Bureau of Land Management to fix the ranch. However, the city turned the money down. City Manager Gregory Rose indicated that it would take more than that amount to bring the ranch to a place where it could be enjoyed by the public and the city was unable to find partners to contribute to the financial cost. And so, the ranch lay in ruins.

While Las Vegas was rich with grass, in 1884 there wasn't much lumber. When Helen J. Stewart brought her husband home, she was forced to convert doors into a coffin in order to bury him. After she laid her husband in the ground, Stewart called the authorities and pressed charges against Schuyler Henry and Hank Parish. While she suspected Conrad Kiel had something to do with her husband's death as well, there was no evidence that linked him to the murder. An inquiry was made and a grand jury was convened in Pioche. The jury found that Archibald Stewart had showed up to the ranch armed, with the intention of killing Schuyler Henry. The jury came back with a verdict of self-defense, meaning Henry would not have to face murder charges.

Stewart was devastated, but she had children to raise and she wasn't about to let the decision of a jury ruin her life. She would go on to successfully raise her family and become one of the most prominent citizens in Las Vegas. In 1899, fifteen years after the death of her husband, Stewart became the first female postmistress in Nevada. She worked in the "Los Vegas" post office. The name had been intentionally misspelled by the federal government in order to avoid confusing it with the then much larger city of Las Vegas, New Mexico.

Over the years, relations between the Stewarts and the Kiels improved slightly, mainly due to the death of Conrad Kiel. In fact, the two families often did business together. It was on one such occasion, in October of 1900, that Hiram Stewart and his ranch hand Frank Stewart—no relation—rode over to the Kiel Ranch. Upon their arrival, they found the bodies of Edwin and William Kiel, who had been shot dead. Edwin was found in the kitchen, and William was found in the irrigation ditch a short distance from the house. A coroner's inquiry determined that Edwin had killed William in a rage before turning the gun on himself. Stewart and his hired hand were not charged in the incident. However, everyone in the Kiel family, and many in the community, knew the coroner was wrong.

In 1902 Stewart sold William Clark the rights to 1,840 acres of her ranch, for $55,000. In 1905 Clark sold the land in a public auction to start what would eventually become the city of Las Vegas. In 1939 the ranch was purchased by Edwin Losee, who seized an opportunity to cater to those seeking a quickie divorce. At the time, a person needed only to be a resident of Nevada for six weeks before he or she could legally divorce a spouse. Losee saw an opportunity to create a place where stars such as Clark Gable and Marilyn Monroe could spend their time while awaiting the courts. He called the place "Boulderado," and ran it successfully for close to twenty years.

In 1975 forensic anthropologists from the University of Nevada, Las Vegas were granted permission to exhume the bodies of William and Edwin from the ranch. The oft-disputed legend of how the two had met their end had never been resolved, and the anthropologists were determined to do just that. After examining the bodies they were able to determine that their deaths weren't the result of a murder-suicide. Instead, they found that the two had been gunned down and murdered.

Interestingly enough, the Kiel family not only didn't give permission for the bodies to be exhumed, they didn't even know it had happened. Adding insult to injury, after the bodies were removed from their place of rest, they were never returned. Instead, the bones of William and Edwin Kiel lay in a makeshift morgue at UNLV's department of anthropology for more than thirty years.

Murder seems to be the constant theme to a property that history wanted only to forget. The city of North Las Vegas has yet to do anything with the property or the historic building that could, quite possibly, be the oldest in Las Vegas. When Archibald Stewart was shot and killed by Schuyler Henry in cold blood, it started a curse that would last for more than a hundred years. And even though the bones have been removed from what was supposed to be their place of eternal rest, the spirits of the men who once used those bones don't seem to be able to leave.

People who have been to the ranch have seen the ghosts of two men who are apparently trying to get away from something or someone. The two men, who seem to be scared, keep looking behind them as they move. These two men are most likely William and Edwin, trying to get away from Stewart, who seized upon an opportunity for the revenge of his father. Of course, this is Las Vegas, after all, and there is certainly a chance that the two apparitions are simply two unhappily married men who moved to Las Vegas, hoping for a quickie divorce. Maybe the two are running from the commitments they made, terrified that their exes might still be trying to find them.

THE MOST HAUNTED TOWN IN NEVADA

I **N THIS LAST SECTION OF OUR GHOST TOUR,** we'll take a detour and travel 187 miles north of Las Vegas to a little town called Goldfield, Nevada, which is a mecca for ghost hunters, both local and national. It has been visited by teams from Discovery Channel's *Ghost Hunters* and Travel Channel's *Ghost Adventures*, as well as many local chapters of ghost hunters. In fact, Goldfield has been called the most haunted town in Nevada. One of the "haunted" houses—even though it was transplanted to Las Vegas, where it now resides in the Clark County Museum (see chapter 13)—has never lost the spirits it had while in Goldfield.

One of the businesses in this little town, the Goldfield Hotel, houses a ghostly secret—one that involves kidnapping, torture, and murder. But beware: The man responsible doesn't cotton to ghost hunters. So get ready for a uniquely Western experience as we travel to an authentic, Old West, once-booming, rootin'-tootin' ghost town, to see if you dare stay a night in the Goldfield Hotel.

GHOSTS OF GOLDFIELD

In 1902, Goldfield, Nevada, was on its way to becoming the most populated city in Nevada. Ten years later, the town was all but abandoned. In the luxurious hotel that still remains are two ghosts, one who seems to protect and one who wants only to kill.

Elizabeth had been locked in the small room for almost six months. The room was dark, except for the weak beam of light that managed to eke its way through the thick, heavy fabric he had used to cover the window. While the room was originally designed to welcome guests to the luxurious hotel, it had since been stripped of everything, including the bed.

Elizabeth screamed out in pain. "Push, you need to push," the burly woman told her. She was the head madam of the local brothel and was well versed in childbirth, having been a midwife for many a prostitute who found herself with an unwelcomed pregnancy.

Elizabeth screamed again as she pushed, hard, sweat dripping down her forehead and into her eyes. The salt mixed with her tears and it stung, but all she felt was the pain and ecstasy of childbirth. In a moment the pain was over and seconds later Elizabeth heard the baby's cry.

Two men stood outside the door of room 109. The screaming had stopped, and now they too heard the cry of a newborn coming from the room. One man, George Wingfield, was dressed in a fine suit of clothes and was smoking a cigar; the other man was not.

"What do you want to do with the baby?" the stocky man in the dusty clothes asked.

"Take the bastard and throw it down the Hutchins mine. That shaft in the back, the one that went dry last year," Wingfield said as he puffed the cigar, rolling it in his mouth with his fingers.

The man in the dusty clothes shook his head in acknowledgment. Wingfield stopped and stared at the door to the room, taking a long, slow pull on the cigar. "Then tie her back to the radiator," he said before turning to walk away.

"Don't you want to know if it's a boy or a girl?" the man in the dusty clothes asked.

"Why would I care about that? The brat's not mine," Wingfield said, and walked away.

While Nevada is called the Silver State because of its rich deposits of silver, Nevada has also had its fair share of gold deposits, the most famous of which were in a little town called Goldfield. In 1902 the silver mines in Tonopah, Nevada, were in full force, having started up only two years earlier when silver was discovered in the then American Indian campground, by a rancher named Jim Butler. The resulting find sparked a mining boom second only to the famous Comstock Lode that had been discovered decades earlier in Virginia City, Nevada.

Twenty-five miles to the south, in Esmeralda County, the discovery of gold gave birth to the town of Goldfield. Miners and fortune seekers from all over the country swarmed to Goldfield, and by 1907 it had become the largest town in Nevada, with a population of 30,000 people. One of those people was George Wingfield.

Wingfield arrived in Tonopah Springs in 1901. Instead of becoming a miner, Wingfield organized the process of mining—buying mining stocks and claims—by forming a mining company. When he arrived in Goldfield, Wingfield immediately bought the Sandstorm, Kendall, and Columbia mines, to which he eventually added the Red Top and the Jumbo claims. He soon organized the Goldfield Consolidated Mining Company. Besides his holdings in the mines, Wingfield was also into banks and at one time owned more banks in the state of Nevada than anyone else.

In 1904 the growing town was attracting the type of people who had made other boomtowns, such as Tombstone, Arizona, famous. Wyatt Earp arrived in the town and, seeing it as a perfect place to make money, wrote to his brother Virgil, encouraging him to come to the town where "money was flowing like wine." Virgil came to Goldfield, and while Wyatt worked as a pit boss in Tex Rickard's Northern Saloon and Gambling Hall, Virgil was hired on as deputy sheriff. Virgil would eventually die there in 1905 after contracting pneumonia.

By 1908 Goldfield had three newspapers, five banks, a mining stock exchange, three railroads, and four schools. It also had a hotel that was considered one of the most luxurious west of the Mississippi. Called the Goldfield Hotel, it was designed by architect George E. Holesworth, and built on the site of the Nevada Hotel, which had burned down in the fire of 1905. The four-story hotel, which cost $300,000 to build, had 154 rooms, each with telephones, electric lights, and heated steam.

The lobby was gorgeous. A gold-leaf ceiling rested atop mahogany-paneled walls. Crystal chandeliers adorned the room, which was decorated with furniture covered in black leather upholstery. The hotel was originally owned by J. Franklin Douglas, along with other investors, who brought in chefs from Europe to cook in the hotel's opulent restaurant. It even had an Otis elevator, one of the first in the West. The hotel appealed to Goldfield's high society and was an immediate success. It also appealed to Wingfield, who, along with hotel entrepreneur Casey McDannell, purchased the hotel from Douglas shortly after it opened, and it is from there that the stories abound.

When he was only thirty years old, Wingfield was the most powerful man in Nevada. He already owned the majority of the buildings in Goldfield and was a multimillionaire. Wingfield was married to Maud Murdock and was reported to be as cruel as he was unfaithful. One of his mistresses was a prostitute named Elizabeth. According to legend, Elizabeth had managed to get herself pregnant by another man. This was very displeasing to Wingfield who, when he found out, kidnapped Elizabeth and chained her to the radiator in room 109 of the hotel, never allowing her to leave. When Elizabeth finally gave birth, the baby, according to legend, was thrown down an abandoned shaft of one of the mines. Elizabeth met her death in room 109 under ghastly circumstances. While some say she was strangled, others claim she was simply starved to death.

As they entered the Goldfield Hotel in Goldfield, Nevada, Zak Bagans and Nick Groff couldn't help but be a little apprehensive. As part of Travel Channel's *Ghost Adventures,* they had experienced many strange occurrences and seen many unexplainable events, but they all paled in comparison to what had happened at the Goldfield Hotel. It was here in this very hotel, early in their career, that the two fledgling ghost investigators had led an investigation by a group of public ghost hunters. While in the basement they recorded, on video, bricks being thrown around the room and two-by-four studs levitating. Several members of the team also had rocks thrown at them in the hallway on the fourth floor.

As it turned out, they had good reason to be apprehensive.

When the *Ghost Adventures* crew entered the Goldfield Hotel for the second time, they were not alone. After Zak and Nick's initial trip to the hotel, six years earlier, electronic voice phenomena (EVP) specialists Mark and Debby Constantino, along with a news crew from Reno, Nevada, entered the hotel and captured a "class A" EVP. The Constantinos went into the exact room in the basement where Zak and crew had captured video recordings of bricks being thrown and boards being levitated during their first visit.

While in that room Debby asked the ghosts if they were the ones who had thrown the bricks and boards. "If you guys did it," Debby said holding a voice recorder, "could you all just tell me in the recorder if you did it?"

When the recorder was later listened to, a voice could be heard clearly saying, "Thank you, but we've done it," right after Debby asked her question.

Mark and Debby joined the *Ghost Adventures* crew on its second investigation. Upon entering the hotel, the crew made its way up to the fourth floor. It was on this floor, back in the 1900s, that an ex-con by the name of Curley Joe had been killed in a gunfight. Curley had been found fatally wounded by his wife. His killer was never identified. It was also on this floor that the *Ghost Adventures* crew members had rocks thrown at them in 2004. At that time, Zak had asked the ghosts to give the members of the team a sign that they existed. In fact, he specifically asked the ghosts to throw something at them. After he asked, many members of the team had been hit with rocks. Now, in 2010 as Zak recalled what had happened to them on the fourth floor, Nick Groff was struck by a rock, much like the ones that had been thrown in 2004.

"Something just got thrown at me," Nick said. "It bounced off me. It came from the stairs and hit me in the back." The rock could be heard hitting the floor on the voice recording device.

Two years earlier, in 2008, on the hundredth anniversary of the hotel, the current owner of the Goldfield Hotel, Red Roberts, contacted The Atlantic Paranormal Society (TAPS) and invited it to investigate the hotel. "I really don't believe in ghosts," said Roberts. "But I hope the TAPS team will show me proof that will make me change my mind."

On the fourth floor, the floor where Curley Joe had been killed, TAPS lead investigators Jason Hawes and Grant Wilson reported seeing shadows moving at the end of the hallway. The TAPS team also felt something in the area around the elevator on the second floor. "I get the craziest feeling around this elevator," said Steve Gonsalves, tech manager for the TAPS team. It was into that elevator that a man had supposedly been thrown to his death from the second floor in the 1900s. It was also on the second floor that the TAPS team heard footsteps from the end of the hall and saw a shadow.

The shadow, according to Steve, "looked like something solid, something rigid, something that had substance to it." Steve also acknowledged that the mind can play tricks on you in the dark and that it was hard to say if the shadow was real.

Like the TAPS team, Zak and his crew also had experience with footsteps. It was on that same level that Mark and Debby Constantino, along with Aaron, heard and recorded footsteps. The footsteps seemed to be coming from above the three of them, heading toward Zak and Nick, who were standing still on the floor above them.

But it was probably in room 109, the room where Elizabeth was said to have met her demise, that most of the activity was detected by both teams of paranormal investigators. When the *Ghost Adventures* crew first investigated the hotel in 2004, it captured an orb of light running down Zak's arm. Zak had been sitting in the room, near the radiator, while trying to make contact with Elizabeth. The orb, which was captured on a video recorder, seemed to follow Zak's bent arm, as if stroking him.

At that time Zak and his crew described the room as "welcoming and loving." However, on this trip the atmosphere seemed somehow darker and foreboding. As Zak and Nick entered the room, Nick immediately felt sick. They both also heard what sounded like a female crying. The TAPS team had recorded a voice in room 109 that seemed to be saying, "Get the bitch out." The room was occupied by a female member of the TAPS team at the time.

While on the first floor outside of room 109, Debby asked Elizabeth which member of the team she wanted to communicate with. When they later listened to the recording, they heard a voice that seemed to say, "I want to talk to Zak."

The *Ghost Adventures* crew then set up a PX device in the room. According to Zak, a PX device "detects changes in its surrounding environment by the manifestation of spiritual energy, which, in turn, triggers a built-in phonetic vocabulary programmed into the device, allowing spirits to string together actual words."

The device sat in the room for thirty-nine minutes without making a sound. However, when the crew came back to the room, it suddenly went off, saying "Hi" as Nick approached. It then gave the crew what seemed to be a chilling warning—"Will kill"—but then added the words "enter," and "sit."

Zak asked the spirit, "Are you a man or a woman?" To which the device answered "female." Zak then asked the ghost if it was Elizabeth and got the response "hide." While Zak pleaded with Elizabeth to keep talking, the voice recorder picked up a voice that seemed to be from someone other than Elizabeth. The voice said, "You're $@#n' in my house."

As the team was standing in the hallway outside of room 109, the PX device started making a horrific sound and then said the word "video." The voice recorder next to the PX device recorded the word "Elizabeth" at the same time and Nick immediately felt sick. A recorder being held by Mark picked up a voice that seemed to say, "Now let's get Zak."

Previously, on the third floor of the hotel, the spirits of the Goldfield Hotel seemed to recognize Zak and his crew. Mark and Debby were using a voice recording device when they picked up a voice saying, "They're back. What do you want?"

Could one of the two voices recorded have been Elizabeth, warning the team about another, darker presence that intended to hurt the ghost hunters? Could that presence possibly be Wingfield, still protecting the dark secrets contained inside the Goldfield Hotel? After seeing all the evidence collected by the TAPS team, Red Roberts said, "I can tell you something right now, you are converting me."

GHOST HUNTING 101

So you want to be a ghost hunter? Well, before you set out, you'd better have the right tools and equipment, and there will be some terms that you'll want to become familiar with. So, with that in mind, welcome to Ghost Hunting 101. Please take your seats; it's gonna be a bumpy ride!

GHOST TERMS DEFINED

Cryptid: A creature or a plant whose actual existence has not yet been proved.

Electromagnetic energy: The energy ghosts are said to be made of.

EMF: Electromagnetic field.

EVP: Electronic voice phenomena.

Ghost hunt: Going to a place where there have been no reported sightings of ghosts in order to collect data (film, photos, sounds, eyewitness accounts, and other evidence).

Ghost investigation: Going to a known haunted place to collect data and other evidence to prove or disprove the haunting.

Orb: A ball of transparent light being transferred from a source.

Paradise: What is given to you at the crap table.

Paranormal phenomena: Events that cannot be explained.

Phonetic generator: Piece of equipment that spirits can manipulate to choose specific words by using their energy.

Place memory: A haunting incident, usually traumatic, that loops itself over and over again (also called "residual haunting").

REM-Pod: A round container with light-emitting diode (LED) lights on top that illuminate when the presence of electromagnetic energy is detected.

Residual haunting: A playback of a past event (also called "place memory").

Sensitive: A person with heightened sensitivity to his or her environment.

Scrying: The practice of looking into a suitable medium, such as a crystal ball or mirror, in the hopes of detecting messages from spirits or to see visions of the past or future.

GHOST-HUNTING KIT: WHAT YOU'LL NEED TO GO HUNTING YOURSELF

- REM-Pods
- Digital recorder
- Static night-vision camera
- Infrared camera with DV recorder
- External infrared (IR) illuminator
- Electromagnetic field (EMF) detector
- Thermal camera
- Ion generator (to provide spirits with that little bit of extra energy they need to come forward)
- Digital video camera
- White-noise generator
- Digital thermometer / thermal scanner, to find cold spots
- Wireless microphone
- Flashlight with spare batteries
- Motion detectors
- First-aid kit
- Notebook with pens and pencils
- Appropriate clothing for the weather

BEFORE YOU GO:

Become familiar with the area:
- Check it out in daylight.
- Look for obstacles and possible dangers that may be hard to see in the dark.

Make sure you are not trespassing:
- If you are on private property, get permission first.
- Let police know of your presence.
- If you are asked to leave, do so immediately.

A few other important reminders:
- Bring ID (in case you are stopped by the police).
- *NEVER* go alone.
- Psychic hours are considered to be from 9:00 p.m. to 6:00 a.m.
- Find out all you can about the history of the place before you begin.

WEBSITES

Here are some extra sources and reading material just in case you want to join an actual ghost-hunting team or do a little more research on ghostly happenings in Las Vegas:

bigfootspad.com
elitevegasparanormalsociety.com
ghostanomalyresearchproject.com
ghostvillage.com
hauntedhoneymoon.com
hauntedhovel.com
lvparanormalresearch.webs.com
mightbehaunted.com
nspisite.webs.com
paranormalsocieties.com
redrockcanyonparanormal.com
thehauntedmuseum.com
theshadowlands.net

BOOKS

Austin-Peters, Tracie. *Welcome to Haunted Las Vegas, Nevada.* Atglen, PA: Schiffer Publishing, 2009.

Cavanaugh, Liz, Michelle Broussard Honick, and Vernell Hackett. *Ghosts, Gangsters, and Gamblers of Las Vegas.* Atglen, PA: Schiffer Publishing, 2009.

Oberding, Janice. *The Haunting of Las Vegas.* Gretna, LA: Pelican Publishing Company, 2008.

Oesterle, Joe, and Tim Cridland. *Weird Las Vegas and Nevada.* New York: Sterling Publishing, 2007.

Thorn, Adam. *Las Vegas Guide to Haunted Places.* CreateSpace Independent Publishing, 2018.

HAUNTED HOTELS AND CASINOS

Aladdin Hotel (now Planet Hollywood): Visitors to the seventh floor of the hotel report hearing a key in the door of the Panorama Suite. They also report hearing whispering in the foyer. Those staying in the suite claim to have heard the buzzer ring with no one there and items appearing from nowhere.

Bally's Las Vegas Hotel & Casino: Guests claim to see the ghosts of people lying in their beds who died in the 1980 MGM fire.

Caesars Palace Las Vegas Hotel & Casino: A water faucet in a restroom, located at the bottom of the escalator in the Forum Casino, turns on and off by itself. While the faucets have an automatic sensor, if a hand is placed under this particular running faucet, it will shut off.

Circus Circus Hotel & Casino: Loud cries for help are heard in the poker room, as well as in some of the rooms in the hotel. A lady who stayed in room 123 is supposed to have killed her little boy, and then herself. The two are said to haunt the room, looking for the woman's husband and the boy's father.

Dunes Hotel and Casino (now Bellagio Las Vegas): Guests used to claim they could feel cold spots throughout the main tower. A lounge was located on the top floor of the hotel. At night, after the lounge closed, a blue glow could be seen and voices heard when no one was there.

Excalibur Hotel Casino: Guests who walk down the hallway of the tenth floor report feeling like someone is walking directly behind them. Guests claim that as they walk down the hallway, whoever is following them whispers in their ear as if the person's lips were only an inch away.

Flamingo Hotel & Casino: Benjamin "Bugsy" Siegel is said to haunt the area close to the garden where the plaque honoring his contribution to Las Vegas is placed.

Hotel Apache: Much of the paranormal activity in this hotel centers around room 400—a room that is not connected to the rest of the hotel. It may have once been used as a skim room for the mob. The second floor is also a source, where a paranormal spirit has been seen walking out of walls and across hallways.

Luxor Las Vegas: The casino is said to be under a curse from the initial build. Many ghosts are said to haunt the resort, including a middle-aged man in a striped brown suit who wanders the hallways of the upper floors; a young woman dressed in red who walks around the area where the buffet once stood; and a young man who walks the casino floor.

MGM Grand Hotel & Casino: Employees who work the appropriately named graveyard shift claim to see the figure of a person lying on the beds in many of the rooms.

The Mirage Resort & Casino: The Danny Gans Theater is supposed to be haunted. Employees have reported hearing the automatic-sensor faucets go on by themselves.

The Moulin Rouge: Although the casino no longer exists, people have reported hearing music coming from the property where the casino once stood.

Railroad Pass (Boulder City): Employees report seeing dark figures in the steakhouse and in the warehouse, after which they experience a cold chill.

Suncoast Hotel & Casino: The faucet in one of the bathrooms is reported to go on by itself, and footsteps have been heard in one of the stalls.

Tropicana Las Vegas Hotel & Casino: Guests who have taken photos of the hotel exterior report a strange purple or blue haze in their developed photos.

Whiskey Pete's Hotel & Casino: Supposedly "Whiskey Pete," whom the casino was named after, was a real person who sold moonshine during Prohibition. Many guests claim to have seen an old man who seems to be watching over them.

MAP TO VEGAS HAUNTS

Want to visit all the spooky places mentioned in *Haunted Las Vegas* for yourself? This is where you'll find all the addresses, telephone numbers, visiting hours, and other important information. Some of the sites are located on private property and permission must be granted to visit them. Others, such as the Clark County Museum, Madame Tussauds Wax Museum, and Zak Bagans' The Haunted Museum require an entrance fee, although that fee is sometimes nominal.

Before heading out to see the places mentioned in this book, you may want to check directly with the locations to see if any special arrangements are required. Also, remember that Las Vegas is a bigger town than it first appears and walking from place to place is harder than it looks—especially in the summer months.

An option is to take a guided tour hosted by your very own personal mortician. Haunted Vegas Tour & Ghost Hunt will take you on an air-conditioned bus ride to many of the spots mentioned in this book. You'll even be able to get out of the bus at two of the parks. Group rates are available.

Haunted Vegas Tour & Ghost Hunt
(866) 218-4935
www.hauntedvegastours.com
The Haunted Vegas Tour & Ghost Hunt begins with a pizza party in the Tuscany Casino at 8:00 p.m. Running time is approximately 2.5 hours.
General admission tickets are $119.95 per person.

CHAPTER 1: "I'LL BE SEEING YOU"
Carluccio's Tivoli Gardens
1775 E. Tropicana Ave.
Las Vegas, NV 89119
Unfortunately this wonderful piece of Las Vegas history is no longer open. The Liberace Museum closed on October 17, 2010, and the restaurant closed shortly after. The building is still there, but you won't be able to enter it.

CHAPTER 2: ELVIS HAS NOT LEFT THE BUILDING

Las Vegas Hilton (now Las Vegas Hotel & Casino)
3000 Paradise Rd.
Las Vegas, NV 89109
(888) 732-7117
thelvh.com
The only way you are going to see the Elvis Suite is to rent it—and that is expensive. Do yourself a favor and don't try to sneak up in the elevator to take a peek at the door of the suite—that's all you'll be able to see—as security frowns upon it!

CHAPTER 3: THE MAN WHO INVENTED LAS VEGAS

Flamingo Las Vegas
3555 Las Vegas Blvd. South
Las Vegas, NV 89109
(888) 902-9929
flamingolasvegas.com
Benjamin "Bugsy" Siegel's memorial is easy to find. Just go into the Flamingo and head to the back of the hotel, into the outdoor garden. If you get lost, any employee will be happy to help you find it.

CHAPTER 4: SEEING REDD

Shannon Day Realty
5460 S. Eastern Ave.
Las Vegas, NV 89109
This home has been converted into a business and is not open to the public. However, you can drive by and see the sign in front of the house, complete with two red foxes.

CHAPTER 5: AT THE CORNER OF FLAMINGO AND FOREVER

Site of the shooting: Flamingo and Koval Lane
This is a busy intersection, especially at Koval, so be careful if you plan to visit this site.

Suge Knight's old Las Vegas home: Corner of Tomiyasu Lane and Loma Vista Avenue

This privately owned mansion is in a gated community around the 7010 block of Tomiyasu Lane. It is nestled in between Loma Vista, Monte Rosa, and Tomiyasu.

CHAPTER 6: IN THE PRIME OF HIS LIFE

Oasis Motel

1731 Las Vegas Blvd. South
Las Vegas, NV 89104
(702) 735-6494

If you've read this story, you know this motel is not in the best area of town. If you choose to take the trip down the Strip to the motel, be careful! When you walk into the arch, room 20 is easy to find. Just remember that this is a business and they may not want you hanging around staring at a room. Of course, if you really want the full experience, you can always rent the room for the night.

CHAPTER 7: THE LAST TIME AROUND

The Orleans Hotel and Casino

4500 West Tropicana Ave.
Las Vegas, NV 89103
(800) 675-3267
orleanscasino.com

While the casino itself is open to the public, the only way you can get into the showroom is to buy a ticket and see a show . . . maybe Bill Medley.

CHAPTER 8: THE BEST ROOM IN THE HOUSE

Hotel Apache

128 E. Fremont Street
Las Vegas, NV 89101
(800) 937-6537
binions.com/hotel/hotel_apache.php

Don't forget to rent one of the hotel's ghost hunting kits!

CHAPTER 9: A CASINO'S CURSE

Luxor Las Vegas
3900 Las Vegas Blvd. South
Las Vegas, NV 89119
(877) 386-4658
luxor.com
While the casino has been remodeled, you can still see many of the places in the casino where hauntings have been reported. You won't be able to go up to where the rooms are, but you won't have to; all you have to do is look up.

CHAPTER 10: ONE LAST SOLO

900 West Bonanza Rd.
Las Vegas, NV 89106
The Moulin Rouge no longer exists.

CHAPTER 11: A TRAGEDY THAT STILL HAUNTS VEGAS

Bally's Las Vegas
3645 Las Vegas Blvd. South
Las Vegas, NV 89109
(877) 603-4390
ballyslasvegas.com
When the fire struck the hotel, it was the MGM Grand. It is now Bally's Las Vegas. The building was sold by the MGM, who opened another, much larger casino at the corner of Tropicana and Las Vegas Boulevard. Although the building has been remodeled, the tower where the fire occurred still remains.

CHAPTER 12: WE'LL LEAVE THE LIGHT ON . . . THE GHOST LIGHT, THAT IS

The Venetian Las Vegas
Madame Tussauds Wax Museum
3355 Las Vegas Blvd. South
Las Vegas, NV 89109

(866) 841-3739
venetian.com
Tickets $36.99
Hours: 10:00 a.m. to 8:00 p.m, 365 days a year Happy to promote its ghosts, the museum sometimes offers an after-dark tour of the museum (usually around Halloween).

CHAPTER 13: SO VEGAS HAS A GHOST TOWN?

Clark County Museum
1830 S. Boulder Hwy.
Henderson, NV 89002-8502
(702) 455-7955
clarkcountynv.gov/Depts/parks/Pages/clark-county-museum.aspx
Tickets $2 (No, that isn't a typo!)
Hours: Daily 9:00 a.m. to 4:30 p.m. (closed Thanksgiving, Christmas, and New Year's Day)
This museum is worth the trip! Even if you don't find a ghost, you'll see a snapshot of Las Vegas that few get to see. It's a fun place, and the staff is very knowledgable.

CHAPTER 14: THE TIKI BAR BE OPEN

The Golden Tiki
3939 Spring Mountain Rd.
Las Vegas, NV 89102
(866) 222-3196
thegoldentiki.com
A Tiki bar extravaganza, this place is a can't miss spot for anyone visiting Las Vegas. It's so fun even the local poltergeists can't resist. Reservations are not needed, but are recommended if you want a booth.

CHAPTER 15: THE LITTLE CASINO THAT COULDN'T

Planet Hollywood Resort and Casino

3667 Las Vegas Blvd. South

Las Vegas, NV 89109

(866) 919-7472

planethollywoodresort.com

Sadly, the Aladdin no longer exists, but the Panorama Suite is still there. You can see it online, but the only way you're going to see it for real is to rent it—or gamble heavily, in which case the casino will comp it for you. Do yourself a favor and don't try to sneak up in the elevator to take a peek at the suite. Security frowns upon it!

CHAPTER 16: MR. PETRIE

Las Vegas Academy

315 S. Seventh St.

Las Vegas, NV 89101

(702) 799-7800

schools.ccsd.net/lva

This is a functioning school in downtown Las Vegas. While you can't go inside, you can still take a look at the exterior of the beautiful building. If you want to see inside the theater, you can support the school by attending one of its many performances. Who knows, maybe Mr. Petrie will be there as well.

CHAPTER 17: DEMON SWING

Fox Ridge Park

420 Valle Verde Dr.

Henderson, NV 89014

This is a tricky one, because the boy ghost supposedly doesn't come out to play until after 12:00 a.m. and the park closes at, you guessed it, 12:00 a.m. If the Henderson Police catch you in the park after hours, they will make you leave.

CHAPTER 18: STONEY'S STORY

Craig Road Pet Cemetery

7450 West Craig Rd.

Las Vegas, NV 89129-6030

(702) 645-1112

craigroadpetcemetery.org

Hours: Monday through Friday, 8:00 a.m. to 4:00 p.m. and Saturday and Sunday by appointment only. This graveyard is open to the public, and employees will be happy to show you where Stoney's headstone is, if you'd like to see it.

Boulder City Pet Cemetery

As the saying goes, "It can only be found by those who know where it is." This cemetery is just outside Boulder City. Take the road to Laughlin and when you get a couple of miles down the road start looking to the left side. If you look closely, you'll see headstones. It's easier to find the graveyard in the daylight, but spookier to go there at night.

CHAPTER 19: HELL HOUSE

Bannie Avenue, Las Vegas

The house, which at times is occupied and at others is not, is located at the end of Bannie Avenue in the section of town called the Scotch 80s. Take the West Charleston exit off of I-15 and go west till you reach the appropriately named Shadow Lane. Turn south on Shadow Lane and go to Waldman Avenue. Turn west on Waldman and go to Westwood Drive. Turn south on Westwood and go to Bannie Avenue. Turn east on Bannie and go to the end of the street.

CHAPTER 20: SCHOOL DAYS . . . GOOD OLD GOLDEN GHOUL DAYS

Dell H. Robison Middle School

825 Marion Dr.

Las Vegas, NV 89110

(702) 799-7300

Elbert Edwards Elementary
4551 Diamond Head Dr.
Las Vegas, NV 89110
(702) 799-7320

Harriet Treem Elementary
1698 Patrick La.
Henderson, NV 89014
(702) 799-8760
Please remember that these ghostly locales are actual, functioning schools and are not open to the public. Please do not go there and frighten the children.

CHAPTER 21: BONNIE'S PLACE

Bonnie Springs has closed to make way for developer Joel Laub's luxury homes and is not open to the public.

CHAPTER 22: A HOSTEL FOR THE DAMMED

Zak Bagans' The Haunted Museum
600 E. Charleston Blvd
Las Vegas, NV 89104
(702) 444-0744
thehauntedmuseum.com
Hours: Wednesday through Monday, 10:00 a.m. to 8:00 p.m.
Tour rate are $48; $79 for the RIP all access tour (local, senior, and military discounts available).
The RIP grants you access to several rooms not included on the regular tour, plus you get a free t-shirt if you survive to the end. For an extra spooky experience, opt for the late night flashlight tour.

CHAPTER 23: WHAT IS A GHOST ANYWAY?

The Historic Boulder Dam Hotel

1305 Arizona St.

Boulder City, NV 89005

(702) 293-3510

boulderdamhotel.com

Room rates start at $64 per night.

The Boulder Dam Hotel is a functioning hotel with a restaurant, art gallery, and museum. The three-story structure is open to the public, and if you don't cause too much trouble, the staff will generally let you walk around the hallways on the upper floors.

CHAPTER 24: REVENGE IS A DISH BEST SERVED CHILLED

The remains of Kiel Ranch are located on the corner of North Commerce Street and West Carey Avenue (near Losee Road). It is the property of North Las Vegas and is not open to the public.

CHAPTER 25: GHOSTS OF GOLDFIELD

Goldfield, Nevada, is 186 miles northwest of Las Vegas on US Highway 95. Its current population is around 268. The Goldfield Hotel is not open to the public.

REFERENCES

"I'LL BE SEEING YOU"

Carluccio's Italian Restaurant (carlucciosvegas.com).

Carluccio's Tivoli Gardens, personal visits and observations by the author.

Cavanaugh, Liz, Michelle Broussard Honick, and Vernell Hackett. *Ghosts, Gangsters, & Gamblers of Las Vegas*. Atglen, PA: Schiffer Publishing, 2009.

Fox 5 News report, "Haunted Carluccio's" (ccoli.com/videos/yt-slThZx6lddU).

Haunted Vegas Tour, personal visit and observations by the author, September 19, 2010.

Interview with Alfredo Rangel, employee at Carluccio's Tivoli Gardens, June 3, 2010.

Interview with Michael Carrico, EVP researcher/cryptozoologist, July 30, 2010.

Liberace Foundation and Museum (www.liberace.org/About-Liberace.htm).

Liberace Museum, personal visit and observations by the author, June 7, 2010.

The Museum of Broadcast Communication (museum.tv; museum.tv/eotvsection .php?entrycode=liberaceshow).

Oberding, Janice. *The Haunting of Las Vegas*. Gretna, LA: Pelican Publishing Company, 2008.

Oesterle, Joe, and Tim Cridland. *Weird Las Vegas and Nevada*. New York: Sterling Publishing, 2007.

West, Adam, and Jeff Roving. *Back to the Batcave*. New York: Berkley Trade, 2004.

ELVIS HAS NOT LEFT THE BUILDING

Cavanaugh, Liz, et al. *Ghosts, Gangsters, & Gamblers of Las Vegas*.

Interview with Michael Carrico, July 30, 2010.

Kanigher, Steve, "Elvis Presley: A love affair," *Las Vegas Sun*, February 14, 2010.

The Master Returns . . . Dixie Dooley (houdiniexperience.com).

Newton, Wayne, and Dick Maurice. *Once Before I Go*. New York: William Morrow & Co., 1989.

Oberding, Janice. *The Haunting of Las Vegas.*

Oesterle and Cridland. *Weird Las Vegas and Nevada.*

The Official Vegas Travel Site (vegas.com/elvis/).

Papa, Paul. *It Happened in Las Vegas.* Guilford, CT: Globe Pequot Press, 2009.

Viva Las Vegas, The Internet Movie Database (IMDB) (imdb.com/title/ tt0058725/).

Wayne Newton.com, the official site of Mr. Las Vegas (waynenewton.com).

THE MAN WHO INVENTED LAS VEGAS

The Benjamin "Bugsy" Siegel monument and rose garden, personal visits and observations by the author.

Cavanaugh, Liz, et al. *Ghosts, Gangsters, & Gamblers of Las Vegas.*

Haunted Vegas Tour, September 19, 2010.

Interview with Michael Carrico, July 30, 2010.

Oberding, Janice. *The Haunting of Las Vegas.*

Papa, Paul. *It Happened in Las Vegas.*

SEEING REDD

"America's Most Haunted," The Travel Channel (travelchannel.com/travel/ americas-most-hauntedplaces/page-1.html).

Associated Press, "Redd Foxx dies in L.A. Hospital of heart attack," October 12, 1991.

Bates, Warren, "Foxx wins suit against talent agent asking for $50,000," *Las Vegas Review-Journal*, February 26, 1991.

Cavanaugh, Liz, et al. *Ghosts, Gangsters, & Gamblers of Las Vegas.*

Cotton Comes to Harlem, IMDB (imdb.com/title/tt0065579/).

Find a Grave (findagrave.com/cgi-bin/fg.cgi?page=gr&GRid=2704).

Harlem Nights, IMDB (imdb.com/title/tt0097481/).Haunted Vegas Tour, September 19, 2010.

Interview with Michael Carrico, July 30, 2010.

The Official Site of Redd Foxx (cmgww.com/stars/foxx/foxx.html).

Oberding, Janice. *The Haunting of Las Vegas.*

Papa, Paul. *It Happened in Las Vegas.*

Paskevich, Michael, "Redd Foxx fans feel sense of loss at comedian's death," *Las Vegas Review-Journal*, October 13, 1991.

Redd Foxx (reddfoxx.com).

The Royal Family, IMDB (imdb.com/title/tt0101187/).

Sanford and Son, IMDB (imdb.com/title/tt0068128/).

Steptoe and Son, IMDB (imdb.com/title/tt0057785/).

Various visits to the home of Redd Foxx, 2010–11.

White, Ken, "Music, laughter comfort Foxx fans," *Las Vegas Review-Journal*, October 16, 1991.

AT THE CORNER OF FLAMINGO AND FOREVER

2Pac, The Official website (2pac.com).

Bates, Warren, "Shakur dies of wounds," *Las Vegas Review-Journal*, September 14, 1996.

Black Panthers (blackpanther.org/Legacy1.html).

Browne, David, "A Death 4Told?," *Entertainment Weekly*, October 4, 1996.

Cavanaugh, Liz, et al. *Ghosts, Gangsters, & Gamblers of Las Vegas.*

McQuillar, Tayannah Lee, and Fred L. Johnson III. *Tupac Shakur: The Life and Times of an American Icon.* Cambridge, MA: Da Capo Press, 2010.

Oberding, Janice. *The Haunting of Las Vegas.*

Philips, Chuck, "Who Killed Tupac Shakur?," *Los Angeles Times*, September 6, 2002.

———, "How Vegas police probe floundered in Tupac Shakur case," *Los Angeles Times*, September 7, 2002.

Poetic Justice, IMDB (imdb.com/title/tt0107840/).

Puit, Glenn, "Rapper in fight for life," *Las Vegas Review-Journal*, September 9, 1996.

———, "Shooting witnesses won't talk," *Las Vegas Review-Journal*, September 10, 1996.

———, "Sources: Quarrel on tape," *Las Vegas Review-Journal*, September 10, 1996.

———, "Vigil held for slain rap star," *Las Vegas Review-Journal*, September 15, 1996.

———, "Shakur videotape scrutinized," *Las Vegas Review-Journal*, October 4, 1996.

Scott, Cathy, "Tupac seen in fight on video," *Las Vegas Sun*, September 11, 1996.

———. *The Killing of Tupac Shakur*, Las Vegas, NV: Huntington Press, 2002.

———, "Lack of a witness aids Tupac's killer," *Las Vegas Sun*, January 20, 1997.

Weatherford, Mike, "Troubles didn't stop Shakur's rise to fame," *Las Vegas Review-Journal*, September 14, 1996.

IN THE PRIME OF HIS LIFE

Associated Press, "Show's cast plans tribute to dead actor," *Las Vegas Review-Journal*, March 30, 1999.

Biography for David Strickland, IMDB (imdb.com/name/nm0834362/bio).

"Famed gambler Ungar dies at 45," *Las Vegas Sun*, November 23, 1998 (lasvegassun.com/news/1998/nov/23/famed-gambler-ungar-dies-at-45/?history).

Ghost Adventures, Travel Channel, (travelchannel.com/TV_Shows/Ghost_Adventures).

"Haunted Vegas: A few questions with Zak Bagans of *Ghost Adventures*," *Las Vegas Weekly* (lasvegasweekly.com/news/2010/oct/27/hauntedvegas-zak-bagans-ghost-adventures/).

Joe Oesterle, Artist, Writer, Bon Vivant (joeartistwriter.wordpress.com).

Koch, Ed, and Jace Radke, "Questions linger in death of actor," *Las Vegas Sun*, March 23, 1999.

Lowry, Ben, "Actor finds stardom in death," *Las Vegas Review-Journal*, March 31, 1999.

Macy, Robert, "Strickland spent his last hours in part of Las Vegas known as the 'naked city,'" *Las Vegas Sun*, March 25, 1999.

Mad About You, IMDB (imdb.com/title/tt0103484/fullcredits#cast).

The Mayo Clinic (www.mayoclinic.com/health/bipolardisorder/DS00356).

Oasis Motel, personal visit and observations by the author on October 15, 2010.

"Professional poker player Stu Ungar found dead in hotel room," *Las Vegas Sun*, November 23, 1998 (lasvegassun.com/news/1998/nov/23/professionalpoker-player-stu-ungar-found-dead-in-/).

Schoenmann, Joe, "Actor's last night retraced," *Las Vegas Review-Journal*, March 26, 1999.

———, "Actor who killed self faced charges," *Las Vegas Review-Journal*, March 24, 1999.

———, "Actor found dead in LV motel room," *Las Vegas Review-Journal*, March 23, 1999.

Suddenly Susan, IMDB (imdb.com/title/tt0115376/).

Wagner, Angie, "Actor found dead in Las Vegas motel," *Las Vegas Sun*, March 22, 1999.

THE LAST TIME AROUND

Anton, Mike, "Remembering a blue-eyed soul brother," *Los Angeles Times*, November 12, 2003.

Cavanaugh, Liz, et al. *Ghosts, Gangsters, & Gamblers of Las Vegas.*

Classic Bands (classicbands.com/BobbyHatfieldInterview.html).

Delaney, Joe, "Righteous Brothers sparked 'blue-eyed soul,'" *Las Vegas Sun*, May 4, 2001.

Dirty Dancing, IMDB (imdb.com/title/tt0092890/).

Ghost, IMDB (imdb.com/title/tt0099653/).

The Righteous Brothers Official Website (righteousbrothers.com).

Rock & Roll Hall of Fame (rockhall.com/inductees/righteous-brothers/bio/).

Spectro Pop (spectropop.com/remembers/BHobit.htm).

Top Gun, IMDB (imdb.com/title/tt0092099/).

THE BEST ROOM IN THE HOUSE

"Apache Hotel at Binion's is a 'portal for paranormal," Fox Five New, Las Vegas, June 20, 2020.

"Binion's Hotel and Casino," *Ghost Adventures,* Season 16, Episode 3, Travel Channel.

Horwath, Brian, "Refurbished Hotel Apache opens today in downtown Las Vegas," *Las Vegas Sun*, July 29, 2019.

Hotel Apache (http:// binions.com/hotel/hotel_apache.php).

Hotel Apache, multiple personal visits and observations by the author.

"I Survived the Haunted Apache Hotel Tour inside BINION'S Hotel & Casino Las Vegas," Las Vegas and Beyond, August 7, 2020.

Kostek, Jackie, "Haunted Las Vegas: Paranormal activity at historic Hotel Apache," KNTV, October 28, 2020.

Khalyleh, Hana, "We hunted ghosts in famous haunted Las Vegas locations. Here's what we found," *Reno Gazette-Journal*, October 17, 2019.

Schulz, Bailey, "Celebrities flock to Las Vegas. It started with this downtown hotel," *Las Vegas Review-Journal*, October 5, 2020.

A CASINO'S CURSE

Ask Mr. Sun, "What happened to the theme in Vegas' theme resorts?," *Las Vegas Sun*, September 30, 2009.

Benston, Liz, "Luxor files lawsuit over lighting system," *Las Vegas Sun*, August 8, 2003.

Cavanaugh, Liz, et al., *Ghosts, Gangsters, & Gamblers of Las Vegas*.

Gibson, Tiffany, "MMA fighter accused in death of ex-UNLV football player at Luxor," *Las Vegas Sun*, June 21, 2010.

Green, Steve, "Luxor in legal battle over name of Liquidity bar," *Las Vegas Sun*, April 5, 2010.

Hansen, Kyle, "Ex-boyfriend pleads not guilty in Luxor dancer's death," *Las Vegas Sun*, February 16, 2011.

Interview with Michael Carrico, July 30, 2010.

Luxor Las Vegas (luxor.com).

The Luxor, multiple personal visits and observations by the author.

McCoy, Cara, "Man sentenced to life in Luxor pipe bomb case," *Las Vegas Sun*, January 7, 2010.

Oberding, Janice. *The Haunting of Las Vegas*.

Scott, Cathy, "Arrest in Luxor slaying," *Las Vegas Sun*, October 17, 1997.

Smith, Rod, "MGM Mirage offers to buy Mandalay Resort Group for $7.65 billion," *Las Vegas Review-Journal*, June 5, 2004.

"Valli leaving Luxor early," *Las Vegas Sun*, November 26, 2005 (lasvegassun.com/news/2005/nov/26/valli-leaving-luxor-early/).

Waddell, Lynn, "Resort opens a new era in LV," *Las Vegas Sun*, October 15, 1993.

"Woman commits suicide inside Luxor," *Las Vegas Sun*, September 26, 1996. (lasvegassun.com/news/1996/sep/26/woman-commits-suicide-insideluxor/).

Valley, Jackie, "Dancer in Luxor's 'Fantasy' show missing since Sunday," *Las Vegas Sun*, December 16, 2010.

ONE LAST SOLO

Ainlay Jr., Thomas, and Judy Dixon Gabaldon. *Las Vegas: The Fabulous First Century*. Charleston, SC: Arcadia Publishing, 2003.

Basten, Fred E., and Charles Phoenix. *Fabulous Las Vegas in the '50s: Glitz, Glamour & Games*. Santa Monica, CA: Angel City Press, 1999.

Cavanaugh, Liz, et al. *Ghosts, Gangsters, & Gamblers of Las Vegas*.

James, Ronald Michael, and Elizabeth Safford Harvey, Ann Harvey, and Thomas Perkins. *Nevada's Historic Buildings: A Cultural Legacy*. Reno, NV: University of Nevada Press. 2009.

Land, Barbara, and Myrick Land. *A Short History of Las Vegas,* 2nd Edition. Reno, NV: University of Nevada Press, 2004.

Las Vegas Now (lasvegasnow.com; lasvegasnow.com/Global/story.asp?S =1299079).

Moehring, Eugene P. *Resort City in the Sunbelt: Las Vegas, 1930–2000,* 2nd Edition. Reno, NV: University of Nevada Press, 2000.

———, and Michael S. Green. *Las Vegas: A Centennial History*. Reno, NV: University of Nevada Press, 2005.

Oberding, Janice. *The Haunting of Las Vegas*.

The site of Moulin Rouge, personal visits and observations by the author.

Weatherford, Mike, "Casino's short life belies storied history," *Las Vegas Review-Journal,* May 30, 2003.

We Shall Overcome (nps.gov/nr/travel/civilrights/nv1.htm).

A TRAGEDY THAT STILL HAUNTS VEGAS

Arnett, Peter, "How it happened: Fire got lots of help from people," *Las Vegas Review-Journal*, November 23, 1980.

Broderick, Chris, Untitled, *Las Vegas Review-Journal,* November 23, 1980.

Cavanaugh, Liz, et al. *Ghosts, Gangsters, & Gamblers of Las Vegas*.

Clark County Fire Department, MGM Fire Investigation.

"Makeshift morgue pressed into service," *Las Vegas Review-Journal*, November 22, 1980.

Manning, Mary, "MGM fire changed safety standards," *Las Vegas Sun*, January 25, 2008.

———, "Past tragedies at Las Vegas resorts led to safer visits for today's guests," *Las Vegas Sun*, January 26, 2008.

Oberding, Janice. *The Haunting of Las Vegas.*

Papa, Paul. *It Happened in Las Vegas.*

Scripps, Cynthia, "MGM hotel rescuer unidentified," *Las Vegas Review-Journal*, November 22, 1980.

WE'LL LEAVE THE LIGHT ON . . . THE GHOST LIGHT, THAT IS

Madame Tussauds Las Vegas Wax Museum (madametussauds.com).

"Madame Tussauds Wax Museum," *Ghost Adventures,* Season 4, Episode 4, Travel Channel.

Madame Tussauds Wax Museum, personal visit and observations by the author, September 10, 2011.

Observations made by the author while working as a security officer in the Copa Room of the Sands Hotel and Casino, August 1990–June 1996.

Papa, Paul. *It Happened in Las Vegas.*

Pilbeam, Pamela. *Madame Tussaud and the History of Waxworks.* New York: Hambledon and London, 2003.

SO VEGAS HAS A GHOST TOWN?

Chambers Walker, Patricia, and Thomas Graham. *Directory of Historic House Museums in the United States.* Walnut Creek, CA: AltaMira Press, 2000.

Clark County Museum, personal visits and observations by the author, July 2011.

Clark County Parks and Recreation (clarkcountynv.gov/Depts/parks/Pages/clark -countymuseum.aspx).

Crosby, Gregory, "Tales of Vegas past: The silent houses of Heritage Street," *The Mercury*, September 4, 2003.

Interview with Mark Hall-Patton, Clark County Museum administrator, July 29, 2011.

James, Ronald, et al. *Nevada's Historic Buildings: A Cultural Legacy.*

Nevada Commission on Tourism (goldfield.travelnevada.com/).

Oberding, Janice. *The Haunting of Las Vegas.*

Papa, Paul. *It Happened in Las Vegas.*

Peterson, Kristen, "Here today, there tomorrow," *Las Vegas Sun*, October 2, 2008.

———, "The past is always present at Clark County Museum's Heritage Street," *Las Vegas Sun*, August 23, 2010.

Vegas.com, The Official VEGAS Travel Site (vegas.com/attractions/outside_lasvegas/floydlamb.html).

Vanderploeg, Frances, "Ghost hunters to dish on local haunts," *Las Vegas Sun*, October 30, 2008.

THE TIKI BAR BE OPEN

"Chinese Poltergeist," Ghost Adventures, Season 23, Episode 7, Travel Channel.

Frequent visits by the author (very frequent visits).

Interview with Branden Powers, Golden Tiki owner, June 14, 2022.

Ogulnik, Jason, "Animatronic pirate skeleton Captain William Tobias Faulkner is shown at The Golden Tiki in Las Vegas," *Las Vegas Review-Journal*, September 16, 2015.

THE LITTLE CASINO THAT COULDN'T

Cavanaugh, Liz, et al. *Ghosts, Gangsters, & Gamblers of Las Vegas.*

Koch, Ed, "Wayne Newton recalls resort's troubled past," *Las Vegas Sun*, August 18, 2000.

———, "Wayne Newton owned the Strip," *Las Vegas Sun*, May 15, 2008.

Moehring, Eugene P. *Resort City in the Sunbelt: Las Vegas, 1930–2000*, 2nd Edition.

Paranormal Knowledge (paranormalknowledge.com).

Wayne Newton.com, The official site of Mr. Las Vegas (waynenewton.com).

MR. PETRIE

Austin-Peters, Tracie. *Welcome to Haunted Las Vegas, Nevada*. Atglen, PA: Schiffer Publishing, 2009.

Bond, Tiffannie, "Ghost Story: 'Mr. Petrie' spooks school," *The View Neighborhood Newspapers,* October 25, 2000.

Cavanaugh, Liz, et al. *Ghosts, Gangsters, & Gamblers of Las Vegas.*

Interview with Michael Carrico, July 30, 2010.

The Las Vegas Academy Theater (lvacademytheatre.org).

Oberding, Janice. *The Haunting of Las Vegas.*

Papa, Paul. *It Happened in Las Vegas.*

The Shadowlands (theshadowlands.net).

DEMON SWING

Austin-Peters, Tracie. *Welcome to Haunted Las Vegas, Nevada.*

Cavanaugh, Liz, et al. *Ghosts, Gangsters, & Gamblers of Las Vegas.*

Fox Ridge Park, personal visit and observations by the author, October 24, 2011.

The Haunted Honeymoon (hauntedhoneymoon.com).

Haunted Vegas Tour, September 19, 2010.

Haunted Vegas Tours (hauntedvegastours.com).

Oberding, Janice. *The Haunting of Las Vegas.*

Oesterle, Joe, and Tim Cridland. *Weird Las Vegas and Nevada.*

Przybys, John, "Be very afraid . . . or not: Haunted Vegas Tour takes guests on a ghost hunt," *Las Vegas Review-Journal*, March 13, 2005.

Red Rock Canyon Paranormal Society (redrockcanyonparanormal.com).

Vanderploeg, "Ghost Hunters to Dish on Local Haunts."

STONEY'S STORY

Boulder City Pet Cemetery, various personal visits and observations by the author, 1990–2011.

Craig Road Pet Cemetery, personal visit and observations by the author, August 11, 2011.

Ferguson, Lisa, "Goodbye, dear friend," *Las Vegas Sun*, April 2, 1998.

Hagen, Phil, "Valley hosts fairy shrimp, pet cemetery," *Las Vegas Sun*, August 2, 1997.

Jaynes, Mike, "The Ethical Disconnect of the Circus: Humanity's Acceptance of Performing Animals," *Between the Species*, Issue VIII, CalPoly.edu, August 2008.

———, "The death of Stoney the elephant: The abuse, neglect and death of a performing elephant in Las Vegas" (animalrights.about.com/od/saddest-show/a/StoneyDeath.htm).

Keele, Mike, Karen Lewis, and Terrah Owens, "Asian Elephant: North American Regional Studbook Update," Association of Zoos and Aquariums, May 1, 2005–July 16, 2007 (labanimals.awionline.org/legal_affairs/ringling_bros/exhibits/Exhibit_36.pdf).

Koch, Ed, and Jace Radke, " 'King Arthur's Tournament' producer Jackson dies," *Las Vegas Sun*, December 31, 1998.

Find a Grave (findagrave.com/cgi-bin/fg.cgi?page=gr&GRid=25221866).

National Geographic (animals.nationalgeographic.com/animals/mammals/asianelephant/).

Oberding, Janice. *The Haunting of Las Vegas*.

Oesterle, Joe, and Tim Cridland. *Weird Las Vegas and Nevada*.

Oregon Zoo (oregonzoo.org).

Performing Animal Welfare Society (pawsweb.org/save_the_bulls.html).

Reid Norman, Jean, "Proposal for pet cemetery near animal shelter quashed; Boulder City moves to locate cemetery near wastewater treatment plant," *Las Vegas Sun*, October 19, 2009.

Schoenmann, Joe, "Legislation would allow pets, humans at same crematory," *Las Vegas Sun*, May 26, 2011.

Smithsonian National Zoological Park (nationalzoo.si.edu/).

"Stoney, Asian Bull Elephant," YouTube (youtube.com/watch?v=f1e_jhFeCxY).

Stoney the Elephant page (myspace.com/stoneytheelephant).

"Surplus Animals: The Cycle of Hell, A Study of Captive Wildlife in the United States," Performing Animal Welfare Society.

HELL HOUSE

Green, Michael, "Las Vegas Mob," *The Online Nevada Encyclopedia*, May 19, 2011.

Griffin, Dennis N. *The Battle for Las Vegas: The Law vs. the Mob*. Las Vegas, NV: Huntington Press, 2006.

Interview with Michael Carrico, July 30, 2010.

La Palazza house, personal visit and observations by the author, July 11, 2011.

"La Palazza (Las Vegas)," *Ghost Adventures,* Season 4, Episode 9, Travel Channel.

Lawrence, Christopher, "Paranormal encounters spook 'Ghost Adventures' trio," *Las Vegas Review-Journal*, October 10, 2010.

Olson, Lynne, Lynne Olson's Paranormal TV Blog, *Ghost Adventures: "La Palazza,"* November 13, 2010.

Rilling, Deanna, "Haunted Vegas: A few questions with Zak Bagans of 'Ghost Adventures,'" *Las Vegas Weekly*, October 27, 2010.

SCHOOL DAYS . . . GOOD OLD GOLDEN GHOUL DAYS

Austin-Peters, Tracie. *Welcome to Haunted Las Vegas, Nevada.*

Cavanaugh, Liz, et al. *Ghosts, Gangsters, & Gamblers of Las Vegas.*

Nevada Student Paranormal Investigation (nspisite.webs.com).

Oberding, Janice. *The Haunting of Las Vegas.*

Rhodes, Julian, "Ghost hunting: UNR students take a scientific approach to real haunted houses," The Nevada Sagebrush, October 28, 2008.

The Shadowlands (theshadowlands.net).

BONNIE'S PLACE

Bonnie Springs (bonniesprings.com).

"Bonnie Springs Ranch," *Ghost Adventures,* Season 4, Episode 18, Travel Channel.

Bonnie Springs Ranch, personal visit and observations by the author, October 30, 2011.

Green, Marion, "Bonnie Springs Ranch namesake dies at age 94," *Las Vegas Review-Journal*, February 7, 2016.

Interview with "Cowboy Joe" Tasso, supervisor of Bonnie Springs Ranch, October 30, 2011.

Las Vegas Paranormal Authority (lvparanormalauthority.com).

Lynne Olson's Paranormal TV Blog (mediumlynneolson.wordpress.com).

Moapa Paiutes (moapapaiutes.com).

National Park Service (nps.gov).

Newburg, Katelyn, "Bonnie Springs Ranch near Las Vegas to permanently close Sunday," *Las Vegas Review-Journal*, March 13, 2019.

Przybys, John, "If spirit moves you, visit spookiest spots in Southern Nevada," *Las Vegas Review-Journal*, October 23, 2011.

A HOSTEL FOR THE DAMMED

Biddle, Kenny, "A Closer Look at the Bela Lugosi "Haunted" Mirror," *Skeptical Inquirer*, January 10, 2019.

Find a Grave, findagrave.com/memorial/13078656/cyril-sebastian-wengert

Harnick, Chris, "Get to Know the Lore Before Zak Bagans Opens the Dybbuk Box on Ghost Adventures: Quarantine," ENews, July 1, 2020.

Hutchinson, Sean, "Mirror, Mirror: Zak Bagans Shares the True Story Behind The Haunted Museum's Most Cursed Object," *Mental Floss*, October 8, 2021.

Lawrence, Christopher, "Zak Bagans conquered the Dybbuk Box during his quarantine," *Las Vegas Review-Journal*, June 5, 2020.

Moss, Charles, "Finally, the truth behind the 'haunted' Dybbuk Box can be revealed," INPUT, July 8, 2021.

"Museum of Madness," Ghost Adventures, Season 19, Episode 7, Travel Channel.

"The Haunted Museum," Ghost Adventures, Season 15, Episode 13, Travel Channel.

"The Wengert Mansion," The Historical Marker Database, hmdb.org/m.asp?m=114796

Visit by the author, June 13, 2022.

WHAT IS A GHOST ANYWAY?

Austin-Peters, Tracie. *Welcome to Haunted Las Vegas, Nevada*.

Boulder City/Hoover Dam Museum (bcmha.org).

Boulder City Museum and Historical Association archives.

Boulder Dam Hotel, personal visit and observations by the author, October 27, 2011.

Cavanaugh, Liz, et al. *Ghosts, Gangsters, & Gamblers of Las Vegas.*

Ferrence, Cheryl. *Images of America around Boulder City.* Charleston, SC, Chicago, IL, Portsmouth, NH, San Francisco, CA: Arcadia Publishing, 2008.

The Historic Boulder Dam Hotel (boulderdamhotel.com).

Hogan, Jan, "Boulder Dam Hotel: From celebrities to spirits," The View Neighborhood Newspapers (viewnews.com/2003/VIEW-Jun-11-Wed-2003/anthem/21465494.html).

McBride, Dennis. *Midnight on Arizona Street: The Secret Life of the Boulder Dam Hotel.* Boulder City, NV: Boulder City / Hoover Dam Museum, 1993.

Oberding, Janice. *The Haunting of Las Vegas.*

Papa, Paul. *It Happened in Las Vegas.*

Rouff, Brian, "Giving up the ghost in Boulder City," Living Las Vegas Blog, April 3, 2009.

REVENGE IS A DISH BEST SERVED CHILLED

"A century turns," *Las Vegas Sun,* December 30, 1999.

City of North Las Vegas (cityofnorthlasvegas.com).

Curtis, Lynnette, "Kiel Ranch history fading: Former hangout for gunslingers becomes campsite for homeless," Las Vegas Review-Journal.com, June 26, 2006.

Knapp, George, "Historic Kiel Ranch in shambles," 8newsnow.com.

———, "Kiel Ranch: A historic disgrace in North Las Vegas," 8newsnow.com.

Manning, Mary, and Andy Samuelson, "A gamble in the sand: How Las Vegas transformed itself from a railroad watering hole to the 'Entertainment Capital of the World,'" *Las Vegas Sun,* May 15, 2008.

McGee, Kimberley, "Hauntings and spirits and spooks—oh my," *Las Vegas Sun,* October 30, 1998.

Nevada Division of State Parks (parks.nv.gov).

Oberding, Janice. *The Haunting of Las Vegas.*

Papa, Paul. *It Happened in Las Vegas.*

GHOSTS OF GOLDFIELD

The Atlantic Paranormal Society (TAPS) (theatlantic-paranormal-society.com).
The Goldfield Historical Society (goldfieldhistoricalsociety.com).
"Goldfield NV," *Ghost Adventures,* Season 4, Episode 17, Travel Channel.
"Spirits of the Old West," *Ghost Hunters,* Season 4, Episode 408, Syfy Channel.
Spirits-Speak, the official site of Mark and Debby Constantino (www.spirits-
    speak.com).
Travel Nevada (travelnevada.com).

ABOUT THE AUTHOR

Paul W. Papa is an award-winning writer of both fiction and nonfiction, winning the prestigious Will Rogers Medallion Award for his book *Desert Dust*. Paul has lived in Las Vegas for more than thirty years (making him practically a native). During that time, he developed a fascination with the town, and all its wonders, while working for more than fifteen years at several Las Vegas casinos. In his role as a security officer, Paul was the person who actually shut and locked the doors of the Sands Hotel and Casino for the final time. He eventually became a hotel investigator for a major Strip casino, during which time he developed a love for writing stories about uncommon events. In addition to his nonfiction work, Paul has a paranormal noir series, called *Night Meyer*, that is set in the Las Vegas of the 1950s. When not at his keyboard, Paul can be found investigating some old building, talking to tourists on Fremont Street, or sitting in a local diner hunting down his next story. You can stay in touch with Paul by signing up for his newsletter at paulwpapa.com or on his Facebook page at facebook.com/PaulWPapa/